THE KINGDOM OF ASSASSINS

Political perception is not political reality.
Your perception is your enemy's deception.

ERIK MACKENZIE

Cover designed by 1106Design.com
Interior Formatting by "http://erikastokes.com/" Erika Q. Stokes
and "http://1106design.com/" 1106Design.com for paperback print version

Copyright © 2014/2015 by Erik Mackenzie

Published in the United States

Library of Congress Cataloging-in-Publication Data
Mackenzie, Erik
The Kingdom of Assassins/Erik Mackenzie
  I. Title
    1. Counter-terrorism-Fiction 2. New York City, Saudi Arabia-International thriller 3. Espionage thriller (Intelligence) 4. Political Thriller I. Mackenzie, Erik, 1972

The Kingdom of Assassins (novel)
ISBN: 978-0-9837615-6-3

Kingdom of Assassins (Manga: Japanese comic book) coming soon! Written, Designed and Printed in the United States of America

Thank you.

FOR MY PARENTS

CONTENTS

CHAPTER 1

SANDS OF THE PROPHET

I am the scourge of God chosen
To Chastise you, since no one knows the remedy of your sin
Iniquity except me. You are wicked but I am more wicked
Than you, so be silent.

—TAMBURLAINE THE GREAT, 1398

Saudi Arabia—Ten Years from Now . . .

ŠAHRĀZĀD TRAVERSED THE burning sands of the Prophet on a black Arabian stallion. Muscles working like pistons, the horse carried its royal owner up and down the shifting dunes of the land the Saudis called The Kingdom. With each step, the stallion's hooves sank into the dunes, and wind erased the tracks behind.

Golden sand whispered over the landscape, stinging the princess's skin. The grains themselves were like sugar or salt, dry and perfect. Here in the desert, it was not acts of man that shaped the world, but wind and sand alone. Both spoke to Šahrāzād now: *You have no choice. You cannot go back.* In addition to being the daughter of Saudi Arabia's king, Šahrāzād was also the chief financial officer of Amarco—The Kingdom's state-owned oil company and the wealthiest corporation in the world. Despite her Harvard education, she was poorly prepared for what lay ahead.

It had been more than ten years since the Arab Spring, yet no spring had come to The Kingdom. That would soon change, she knew. Whether the change would lead to Renaissance or Dark Age, none could say. She endeavored to be a spark for political change. Having no desire to be trapped by fate like everyone else, she longed for something more. She wished to be molded not by culture, but by the force of her own will.

The wind dusted sand across the veil covering Šahrāzād's face and hair. Looking up, she could see her falcon circling in the clear blue sky above. Aside from horse and falcon, she was alone in the desert. She looked at her watch, a gift from her father. Micro-inscribed on the back was a reminder: "Time is all we have, the past is a memory and the future is ours to dream, yet the present slips past us."

She thought about her father's voice, and how it always tasted like liquid gold and honey. For as long as she could remember, she'd been able to taste sounds. *Synesthesia,* they called it. The peculiar gift, considered a useless curiosity by science, conveyed things to her that others could not perceive: whether a person who spoke was truthful or lying, arrogant or humble. The ability colored her perceptions and her memories.

She gazed up as the saker falcon glided to her, flaring its wings and wrapping its black razor talons around her leather gauntlet. The bird looked at her and blinked, then let out a screeching call that tasted metallic. After a moment, the falcon left her arm and returned to the sky.

Seeing movement in the distance, Šahrāzād lifted her veil. She fished out the grain of sand which immediately lodged in one eye, and squinted through the shimmering blur of a heat-mirage. After a moment, a shape emerged: a man on horseback, descending a large sand dune. He vanished behind a second dune. Šahrāzād was beginning to think she'd imagined him when he reappeared a moment later. He was her CIA contact, and the reason for her presence here. She pulled her veil back into place and tapped the pocket holding the encrypted memory card. The card held evidence on the missing money from Amarco: hundreds of millions in U.S. dollars.

As the man drew nearer, she saw his face: eyes of stone set in iron cheeks. He rode a strong black stallion. "*As-salaamu aleikum,*" he said. Peace be upon you. He spoke perfect Saudi Arabic, but his voice tasted like poison.

"*Wa aleikum salaam,*" Šahrāzād replied. Unto you be peace.

The stranger pulled his horse alongside hers. "You have the item," he said with a too-wide smile. The muscle below his left eyelid vibrated.

Šahrāzād's skin turned cold. "What item?" she asked.

"The disk."

"I'm hunting with my falcon."

A muscle on the stranger's face twitched, and his jaw tightened. "And I am the sword of the Redeemer," he said.

Šahrāzād felt fear ripple through her, but contained it. The man drew a curved knife and lurched at her. She tried to back up, but her horse spooked and threw her. She landed on her face, momentarily stunned. She felt her teeth dig into her lips, tasting blood mixed with sand.

Her attacker leaped from his horse and came at her, slashing with the blade. Šahrāzād rolled onto her back, the white heat of adrenaline pulsing through her like electricity. She drew her legs up to her chest, as if curling up in defeat—then snapped both feet into her assailant's face, doing her best to break his neck. The man staggered back a step, spitting teeth, then surged forward.

Šahrāzād drew a small Glock pistol from her waistband and fired twice. The first bullet hit him in the left eye, the second in the forehead. She rolled aside as he fell, his life leaking into the sand. She gazed at the stranger. She hated killing, but he'd left her little choice. She felt guilt in the act, but not in his death. She pushed those thoughts aside and continued with the task at hand. She took a moment to soothe the horses after the gunshots, then knelt to search the man's body. *"uTlubuu al-'ilm min al-mahd 'ilaa allaHd,"* she said to herself. Seek knowledge from the cradle to the grave. She found a cell phone, some matches, and a small camouflage-pattern Wenger Swiss Army knife.

She removed the phone's battery so she couldn't be tracked, and pocketed her finds. The man carried no ID, and no tattoos were evident. She snapped photos of his face with her camera. It was then that she noticed the blood on her hands, already drying in the desert heat. She poured water from a small bottle and rubbed her hands together. The blood turned rust-brown. She tried rubbing her hands harder, but the blood worked its way into the swirls of her fingerprints and the fresh crack in her watch crystal. The dead man's open eye was drying out in the merciless 120-degree heat.

Šahrāzād calmed herself, feeling a strange unity with the desert. She gazed up at the falcon as it circled above, a natural hunter. Someone knew. It could only be the Americans, or someone in The Kingdom. Either way, that meant they had to kill her. Despite the situation, she smiled. What was it the Americans said? *Strike one.*

In the distance, a tsunami of sand filled half the sky: a sandstorm, coming her way like an angry *djinn.* Such events could be beautiful—the way the airborne sand filtered the light—and Šahrāzād had always admired them. From a distance—which was where she intended to keep this one.

It was an eight-hour ride back to camp. In a world that tore time apart and shrank the space between all people, there was something refreshing about the solitude. Tethering the second horse to her own, she mounted up and headed back. The falcon followed, screeching to the heavens.

CHAPTER 2

HARBINGER

If history were taught in the form of stories,
it would never be forgotten.

—RUDYARD KIPLING

THE MOUNTAINOUS TERRAIN of Afghanistan was like a Martian landscape, pocked with craters from artillery shells. Mike "Mac" Maclaymore's ears rang with a pain that shouted into his bones as heavy machinegun fire sounded close by.

More shots rang out, and a phone rang—Mike woke up on the floor beside the bed in his New York apartment. He got up carefully, a habit he'd developed while sleeping in the deserts of the Middle East and Afghanistan where scorpions sometimes crawled into sleeping bags. He'd remember that hot sting forever.

He groped in the darkness, missing the phone. He squinted at the clock, which glowed against a negative-image skyline:

dark buildings specked with lighted windows, set against a black sky. The clock's green diodes read 2:30 a.m., and the phone's third ring told him he wasn't going back to sleep without answering. He picked up.

"Mac?" said the voice on the phone.

Mike recognized the rugged voice of the man who'd raised him, Aleister Maclaymore, his uncle and the department's counterterrorism chief. "Yeah," Mike answered, still barely awake.

"The intel is good. The raid's a go for five a.m."

"We got the warrants?"

"No-knock night warrants," Chief Maclaymore replied.

Mike supposed that was good news. "We need them alive," he said, still groggy. "Have to find out why they're here."

"From the intel, an attack by Tamerlaine is going to happen soon," Chief Maclaymore told him.

"We need details," Mike said. "Where. When. What. In case they have a backup cell."

"Agreed."

"I'm being transferred to Intel tomorrow," Mike said. He looked at the clock again.

"Today, actually."

"This is your case, you should see it through. You almost caught Tamerlaine many years ago, that makes you the best man for this. I can hold up the transfer, but not for long. And you or Eva will have to leave the unit in a week, regs say no married couples working together."

"We're getting divorced."

"Until that day, you're married. Them's the rules. Take it up with the brass."

"You're the brass."

"I know you're bitter about the Internal Affairs investigation," Aleister told him, "but it's over. I'll see you in a few hours."

"Ten-four." Mike hung up. He paused for a moment, thinking of the anonymous tipster's voice telling him an attack was going to happen soon. He thought back over the hours of gumshoe work, the wiretaps, the warrants and stakeouts. The tip had led to something so big, it was like a lottery ticket—one that could save lives.

Mike thought about his future. He had a few choices ahead of him. He'd made a million mistakes in his life, lived wrongly in many different ways and made too many unnecessary sacrifices. A gold cross hung from his neck, a Christmas gift from his son Chris. He gazed at it for a moment, then tucked it back under his shirt. In the living room there was an old photograph of Chris at eight, pressing his young face against a cold glass window as he finished drawing *I love you* on the frost-covered glass. He took a photograph of it with his cell phone. Other memories rippled through him, triggering a cascade of images in his mind's eye. He pressed the image on his cell screen, and a video played: his son on a bicycle, Mike letting go as Chris rode without training wheels for the first time. "Daddy, look at me!"

He played another video, of Chris doing push-ups. "Put your hands in front of you, feet back, legs back, butt up, and go up and down," Mike said on the screen.

"Like this?" Chris did a pushup.

"Great!"

Another video showed Chris doing somersaults and martial arts hip throws and counting in Japanese. Yet another showed the two of them in Colorado, atop a hill surrounded by mountains. A black-and-red bat kite rode the air above them, set loose when a sudden gust of wind snapped the kite-string. "Daddy, Batty escaped." The video clip ended with Chris watching the kite fly off on its own. The image of his son looking up at the bright blue sky was seared into his memory, like a message chiseled in stone. His memories were like stars fading as the sun rises in the morning. He didn't want the sun to rise, he just wanted to see the stars in the sky.

Mike pushed the thoughts of his son from his mind; the memories were just too painful. He stared at the ceiling for a while and thought about not getting up. He didn't want to live like this anymore. Then he forced himself out of bed. His joints cracked and his body ached, making him feel older than his years. Short nights didn't used to feel so hard.

He looked at the half-completed, thousand-piece jigsaw puzzle on his kitchen table. When finished, it would depict *Alice in Wonderland*'s Red Queen and the Queen of Hearts facing each other. Beside the puzzle were two photographs of his mother: one taken in Red Square, the other at Checkpoint Charlie. Near the table was his painter's easel, with an unfinished scene of a city park, half-sketched and half-painted, as if he'd been exploring without being quite sure of his destination.

He made his way to the refrigerator, which was covered with various news clippings: Former soldier now NYC Cop stops $100 million dollar heroin trafficking deal; Cop's son missing; Cop's mother killed by Russian Military Intelligence

Officer and Mobster "Vronsky"; Cop's son killed by assassin, from Kish Iran, others still at large. He reminded himself of the past every day. He didn't want to lose himself in the present, like everyone else; it kept him grounded but in a distorted way. How one's past caught up with them. His time in Afghanistan as a Special Forces soldier seared into his soul and recently, his undercover investigation to stop a massive heroin deal, that brought him the deaths of his own mother and son. The sacrifices were too great to be worth doing good anymore.

He glanced at the dirty dishes in the sink and opened the freezer, which was stacked high with breakfast burritos. He popped one in the microwave and gazed at the wedding band in Eva's ashtray—his father's wedding band, given to Mike by his mother. Eva had his mother's ring; it was only natural for both rings to stay together. He remembered the rings meant a lot to him. His father had died while his mother escaped East Berlin during the Cold War, so that Mike could be born in freedom. He had an old photo of his parents, taken in East Berlin, and a more recent photo taken before she died.

He looked at a picture of Eva and himself together, taken atop Mount Everest. "We're just two snowflakes on a mountain-top, yet we are both on top of the world," she told him when they reached the summit. Taking in the remains of the past, his mind roamed. Should I have faith? Should I have doubt? What I desire, my grail, is the past, but it's only a memory. I want my future to be like the past, even if only a sliver of what once was. "Ten years," he said aloud, gazing at the ring.

His apartment was too big for one person now, too empty. People would kill for an apartment like this in the city, but he didn't care anymore. He just wanted Eva back. He toyed with the ring while the burrito cooked, eventually slipping it on his finger. When the microwave dinged, he slid the ring back off and put it in his wallet.

Moving to the bathroom, he splashed cold water on his face, toweled off and regarded the soon-to-be-divorced man in the mirror. Arctic gray eyes stared back at him, rimmed by little red veins. Small white strands had somehow appeared in his dark hair, and when he stretched, his joints made popping sounds. His youth had slipped away. And while a large part of him didn't want to do this anymore, another part of him wanted to see it through—and he wouldn't go back on his word. He was half realist and half idealist. The things that made him go forward were the things he cared about: his honor, his word. And yet he hated both. The world was a dungeon, and he needed to escape it. He trudged back to the kitchen, taking his toothbrush with him so he wouldn't have to repeat the trip.

Colorful fish darted through a tank in the living room, just below a shelf filled with football, wrestling, and martial arts trophies. A few hundred painted tin figurines of soldiers from different historical periods lined the other shelves, and his father's two 16th-Century Samurai swords—the daishō: two swords, katana and wakizashi—hung on the wall.

A couch faced the TV. On the wall above it was a replica of the Shield of Achilles; according to Greek mythology, the original was forged by Hephaestus, god of fire. The gold and silver shield was decorated with highly detailed etchings of two Greek cities: one at peace, the other ruined by war. Mike looked at it every day. On the opposite wall was an American flag, given to him by the U.S. State Department on the death of his father. Below it was a silver Gurkha knife, a gift from Aleister, celebrating Mike and Eva's climb to the top of Mount Everest.

Scooping up a prescription bottle, he popped a few blood pressure pills before retrieving his burrito. If he could find his pants, inhaler, keys with Cheshire Cat thumb drive and a clean shirt, he'd be good to go.

Two hours later, in the pitch black of early morning, stars scudded across a cloudless sky. The temperature was brisk enough for a fleece pullover. Mike shared the back of the counter-terrorism van with three other cops, the hum of surveillance equipment, and the smell of old coffee and burnt, stubbed-out cigarettes. For the past half hour, they'd been parked on a side street in the East Village, staring at live video of an apartment building a block away.

Mike's wife, Captain Eva Maclaymore, sat in one of the oversized van's two swivel chairs, listening to a headset. She wore slick yet feminine business attire. Mike found himself staring at the band of light-colored skin where her wedding ring used to be. He hadn't seen her in weeks. She was still gorgeous; her bronze Venezuelan skin, thick chestnut hair and emerald-green Irish eyes made for the perfect mix of all-American girl and exotic Latina.

They'd met on the job, which was odd because both of them normally avoided relationships with co-workers. The job itself was hard enough; no one wanted to bring it home. Beyond the initial physical attraction, Mike had felt an instant connection to someone fiercely independent, yet intellectually and emotionally flexible. Their different tours of duty had made things difficult at first. They got together whenever they could, for four hours or thirty minutes or even five, treasuring each shared moment. Looking at her now, sorting through more than a decade of memories, he had to remind himself they were about to get divorced.

Eva's grandfather had been FBI. Her great grandfather had come off the boat from Scotland, while her mother's ancestors had migrated from Spain to Venezuela, and eventually to the U.S. Some of Eva's relatives had been killed by the flamboyant dictator Hugo Chavez, for the crime of speaking out against "*El Presidente.*" Distrust of authority was in her genes.

Eva rose from the chair and came to Mike, nodding toward the door. They stepped outside. "Do you miss me?" she asked in a smoker's voice tinged by hard liquor.

Mike didn't answer.

"Been a long time," she added.

"For you or me?" Mike asked.

"I think you. You look like shit. How's your therapy?"

"Finished." Mike was relaxed but tired; nothing could rattle him.

"What are you, some type of Buddhist?" Eva asked.

"That's a compliment."

"I love your comebacks."

"Everyone's an asshole on this job," Mike told her. "It's a defense mechanism."

Eva nodded her agreement. "What do you want?"

"I want to move forward."

"But you haven't, have you?" She looked at him, first with anger, then a smile. She saw another supervisor waving her over. "I'll be right back," she said, and walked away.

Mike reviewed the interaction like rewinding a video, thinking how he felt and what he could have said, and fearing that the chasm between them was too great—that no combination of words could paint an accurate picture of the emotions swirling through the vast ocean of his soul. And yet the words he'd said in the past were like gold coins thrown into the sea—little pieces of treasure.

Mike waved as he spotted Chief Maclaymore, walking toward the van in a suit. He moved with a subtle trademark limp, remnant of a heroic gun battle waged decades before, in the first Iraq war. The older man carried himself like the last of the hard line of men who'd defended America in the blackest hours of World War Two. It was the little things about the job that had kept the older man at it for so many years. Aleister was the opposite of everything the department had largely become, and was rarely involved in the petty internecine politics of One Police Plaza. In a world of paper tigers, he was among the last remaining lions.

"Hello," Mike said. The two of them man-hugged and entered the van.

"I knew you'd stay, Mac," Aleister told him, taking one of the chairs and lighting up a Don Pepin Garcia cigar. Once in place, it seemed to grow from the space between his steel-gray beard and moustache, as if it had always been there. The tip glowed orange for a moment, fading when Aleister exhaled. At least he didn't smoke the cheap ones.

Mike unclipped the tarnished, battered detective's shield from his belt. He'd been meaning to have it re-dipped to make it gold again, but kept putting it off. Clipping the badge to a shield holder, he hung it from his neck. There would soon be a large number of heavily armed cops running around, and he had no desire to be shot by accident.

Eva walked back into the van. "ESU is ready," she said into the radio.

Mike had seen the department's Emergency Services Unit, or SWAT team, in action before. Every time, he'd remember when he did operations in the Middle East and Afghanistan.

"Stand by," Eva said into the radio.

Mike gripped the door handle. "I'll be back," he said. He pushed the van door open and jumped to the ground. The block was a small cluster of brownstones and squat old condos, surrounded by towering skyscrapers. A nearly full moon cast a ghostly light over the scene. He turned the corner to get a good look at the building about to be invaded.

Seconds later, he heard Eva's voice on the radio, "Go! Go! Go!" Five ESU vans converged from both sides of the block, spilling dozens of black-clad tactical officers in body armor, balaclava masks and Kevlar helmets. Armed with M4 assault rifles, they stormed the steps of the target building and smashed in the door, flooding inside.

Outside, the street seemed deserted. Mike crouched between parked cars; they had a better chance of stopping stray bullets than he did. After a moment's delay, flash-bangs and tear-gas grenades went off inside the building. Car alarms howled in protest as shattered window glass rained down like a hailstorm. The sound of pistols and submachine gun fire followed.

Something caught Mike's eye in the building across the street: a muzzle flash in a dark window. Someone on an upper floor was shooting into the raid site.

A voice yelled over Mike's radio. "10-13! Cop shot!"

"Sniper across the street!" Mike answered. "Third floor! I'm going in the front!" Memories of war flooded into his mind, but he pushed them back out just as fast. He put a bullet through the sniper's window and ran toward the building, wondering why it hadn't been cleared and secured before the raid. Or perhaps it had been, and someone had slipped in anyway.

Rushing inside, Mike found himself in a vestibule area, with three hallways leading off in different directions. It was eerie-quiet. He looked up the stairs, but saw nothing. Adrenaline welled up inside him, and his stomach twisted in pain.

He punched his weapon out before him and circled the base of the stairs. He saw the answer to his earlier question: two cops lay unconscious at the base of the stairwell, alive but cuffed and gagged.

At the end of a long hallway leading to one side of the building, an exit door was cracked open. Mike hurried down the hall and peered outside. Twenty yards off, a dark form fled down the garbage-strewn alley. But was he the sniper, or a bystander fleeing the gunfight?

Sudden footsteps sounded on the stairs behind him. Mike spun around and got a quick glance at a man with a rifle, jumping off the stairs and running down another hall, one that led to the back of the building. Mike rushed to follow, radio at his lips. "Perp in sight! Male, six feet! Foot pursuit behind the building!"

Reaching the end of the hall, Mike looked outside. "Running southbound!" he said into the radio. Judging by the distance the suspect had already covered, Mike doubted he could catch him. He broke into a sprint anyway.

The world narrowed around him as his eyes focused on the sprinting figure ahead. It was not reality, but a sort of hyper-reality, almost drug-induced, or pornographic reality. He pushed himself to move faster, using his mind to overcome the lactic acid burn while trying not to trip. His quarry made a quick right. Mike stopped at the corner and peered around it at the same time the sniper looked back. The rifle started to swing his way. Mike ducked back as bullets shrieked past him, tearing chunks from the brickwork corner.

Mike looked again, just in time to see the sniper hang a left. Mike ran to the next corner, lungs and thighs on fire. When he peered around this time, the sniper was waiting for him. He felt the bullet rip his ear and tear through his hair.

Mike ducked back, peeled off his jacket and threw it past the corner at head-height. While the sniper wasted a second shooting at the jacket, Mike leaned out near the ground and fired empty.

The sniper dropped. Mike reloaded and stepped into the alley, keeping his weapon aimed at the now-still figure as he moved toward it. He couldn't help thinking that violence seemed to follow him, a flood waiting to happen, held back by the crumbling dam of civilization. Fate and choice brought different men to the same destination.

Reaching the sniper, he stepped on the man's H&K rifle and slid it away. Blood pooled around the dead man's head, rendered black by moonlight.

"Perp down," Mike said into the radio, and holstered his gun. He closed his eyes and took a deep breath. The smell of fired shots assailed him. His eyes snapped open and he stared at his hands, squeezing them into fists. The deep breaths weren't helping, so he took a hit from his inhaler.

Police helicopters roared overhead, jolting him back to the moment as their searchlights swept the alley. Remembering his jacket, he picked it up and put it back on. Cold air seeped through the bullet holes. Gazing down, he saw that his gold cross necklace had become tangled with his badge. He tucked it back under his shirt. Looking around, he saw two plastic recycling bins, an old shopping cart with its wheels torn off, and dozens of old coffee cans filled with rusted bolts and nails. What a place to die. And it had almost been him tonight.

He played the scene over in his mind: the chase, the shooting. He hadn't even seen the man's face, just a shadow in the alley. He wondered how many would grieve his own passing, when it came. Friends and family, of course. Fellow cops, in their own way. And that was it. To everyone else—to society—he was just another uniform, another number. He felt his asthma acting up, and took a hit from his inhaler. War is a lottery of death, not survival of the fittest, but survival of the lucky.

Suddenly ESS cops and fellow detectives were hustling his way and gathering around, saying things he didn't quite hear until Eva pushed through them, and her voice seemed the only thing in the world—a beacon he could focus on. She was backlit like an angel, by the halogen flashlights of the cops behind her. "Are you all right?" she asked, hand brushing his arm. He could see her holding back; she wanted to say and do more, but didn't. Part of it was her job; another part, perhaps something more.

He wanted to pull her close, kiss her, taste her and run his hands through her hair. He wasn't sure that was still appropriate. In fact, he knew it wasn't, so he just stood there feeling awkward. He managed a nod instead.

She leaned in and touched him on the shoulder and gave him a quick peck on his cheek. She still smelled and tasted like sin. "Should have been a fireman," he said, finding his voice. "Any cops dead?"

"Two look critical," she answered. "Would have been more without you." Her face suddenly went pale. "Oh my God," she said, and raised a hand to his head. It came away bloody.

"It's just my ear." He'd actually forgotten about it. He felt the ripped flesh with his fingers.

Eva took him by the arm. "Come on, let's get you checked out."

"I can live without an ear, can't I? Worked for Van Gogh."

"And look how he wound up," Eva replied.

They made their way back to the van. As they approached, Mike's boss and sometime partner Sergeant Jack Arnold—who always showed up late to everything—approached and shook hands. "You did great today. We live in a dog-eat-dog world, and you had your day."

"Thanks," Mike said. Somehow Jack had managed to find a sharp gray suit to wear, and one of his many gold watches. Mike suspected he kept a suit in his trunk.

Jack adjusted the Rolex on his wrist. "No—thank you," Jack said. "Fuck the PC crowd and fuck this fucking cesspool scumbag city. You're what this country needs." Mike felt a quick pat on the back, and Jack was gone as swiftly as he'd come.

"What did we get in the raid?" he asked Eva.

"Very little."

CHAPTER 3

OASIS

Faith is an oasis in the heart which can never
be reached by the caravan of thinking.
—KAHLIL GIBRAN

SAYF SAT ALONE AT A large conference table on the top floor
of the Burj Khalifa, a stalagmite-shaped skyscraper in the
gleaming desert city of Dubai. The panoramic view seemed
to go on for hundreds of miles. The buildings below looked
like little bricks in the sand. In the back of the ornate room,
hundreds of leather-bound books lined wooden shelves, gold
accents picking up the light. Bleached human skulls served
as bookends.

At Sayf's desk was a collection of photos depicting his
world travels. On the table, was a silver coin from Tamburlaine,
the infamous 14th century conqueror. One of the photos
showed Sayf ringing the bell at the NYSE for one of the many
oil and gas companies he owned. Another was of him shaking

hands with oil and gas commodities traders at the NYMEX in Battery Park City. Other photographs showed Sayf as a Special Forces soldier of The Kingdom of Saudi Arabia, posing with an AK assault rifle while on a secret mission in the Hindu Kush mountains.

He admired these images of himself. It was something he'd always been obsessed with; becoming his own personal ideal, his own hero, a man of action. His arms were tanned and sinewy from the hardships of war. His face was like carved stone, so unlike the many Saudi princes who chose to live an easy and hedonistic life devoid of meaning. He was proud of his thirty-seven confirmed kills, and wished he'd killed more.

How many kills could the other princes claim? He often asked them as they spoke at various parties and functions. He was disgusted that they were so unaware of reality and yet benefitted from the actions of men like himself. Had he not been a prince, he would still be a self-made man—by any means necessary. He twisted in his chair and cracked his back from both sides. The world wore on his bones, and he was going to wear on the world back.

Sayf loved the taste of history, and saw it as it was made—in blood. Above him on the wall was Woodville's 1911 *Retreat from Moscow by Napoleon*. On another wall, Stanislaw Chlebowski's 1878 *Amir Tamerlaine, the 14th century conqueror, and distant relative of Genghis Khan, visiting the defeated Ottoman Sultan Yildirim Bayezid the 14th*. Both paintings were originals. One had red and white contrasts, the other green and gold. They reminded Sayf of the transient nature of history, of victory and defeat and—most importantly—of his hero and the man he strove to emulate: Timur the Great. *kul yawm min Hayaatuk SafHa min taariikhuk,* he thought. Every day of your life is a page of your own history.

His hand ached as he signed check after check, one of many old injuries from too much Judo, Kurash and fencing. He set the gold-plated pen aside, next to a large, deep blue piece of uncut Tanzanite gemstone. He cracked his knuckles over the thirty-foot mahogany table, taking in the room around him. He took a few pills and a sip of water, and gazed at the paintings. They were a true reflection of who he was, his love of history and the men who changed it, and of his desire to be one of those men, wielding the absolute power to alter the course of human events.

He took a moment to admire his new, custom-made gold-and-ivory cufflinks and tailored Italian suit. The latter was sharp yet conservative, and perfectly Saudi. He plucked a large red apple from a bowl on the table, feeling its firmness and noting the way its redness faded around the bottom and top of the fruit. He tried squeezing it, and it seemed that abstract ideas and designs had overtaken his own senses of sight and touch—as if reality has been replaced not by the real, but by the machinations of his own plots. His whole existence was now based on what would soon transpire, the plots that must be executed with precision if he was to reap the rewards of complete success and live forever in history. He knew that total destruction was the risk of naked ambition, and he accepted that.

Picking up the pen, he wrote check after check to charities around the world, to help with buying food, medicine and other essentials for the poor. Having spent a large portion of his life in the oil and gas business, where his profits reached into the hundreds of millions, he felt the need to give something back.

Among the charities Sayf supported was the Children's Fund of Afghanistan and Central Asia. He dedicated the charity fund he owned to his older brother, whom he'd killed when he himself was a boy. They'd been racing cars, reckless in the way that youth is, and Sayf had wanted to win at any cost, even if his older brother died. He'd also known that his brother's death would give him his father's throne. He'd both adored and felt resentful of his older brother, who had been so composed, so handsome—a perfect prince from an Arabian fairy tale. He would have been a great king. Sayf was secretly glad he'd killed him.

He looked up at his older brother's photo on the wall, his teenage youth frozen for eternity. He paused for just a moment while writing the check to Afghanistan, recalling the time he'd spent there. The landscape was sparse, with few trees. Dirty children with dead or missing fathers had fought in a junkyard, victims of a drone attack. He'd seen what the drones had done. At first he'd hated them, but then his eyes had opened and he'd seen that he too could make and use them. He now had thousands of drones, though few people knew of this.

He looked at another photo from that day, of children fighting over scraps of metal they'd sell to traders. One boy with a missing arm had found some copper wire. A larger boy struck him in an attempt to take it. Sayf had pulled out his H&K .45 pistol and fired into the air.

Everyone froze. He made sure the first boy kept the copper wire, gave them both two silver coins and told them to leave in different directions. Afterward, Sayf pulled a few chocolate bars from his pack and handed them out to the rest of the kids. Pushing the memory aside, he signed the check and moved on to the next. A knock at the door interrupted his progress.

"My prince, are you there?" said a voice from the hall.

"Enter."

A fierce-looking man stepped inside. Khalid was strong, poised and focused, as were all good paramilitary soldiers. He closed the door behind him. He was in his late twenties, with a goatee and black hair, with a few strands of white. He wore a conservative blue suit. Khalid stopped at a respectful distance. Sayf handed him three different passports. The top one was Iranian.

"We will succeed," Khalid said.

"Yes. You've healed quickly," he said, referring to the necessary plastic surgery." The pain in Sayf's hand returned as he signed another check.

"When this is over, I'll need surgery again," Khalid said.

"Understood."

"Some things didn't go as planned," Khalid told him, his tone strong but anxious.

"From now on, they will have to," Sayf said. "Do we at least know the identity of the person with the memory card?

"No," Khalid told him. "The one we sent to meet him was found dead in the desert. His phone and horse are missing."

Sayf sat back for a second, thinking. He touched his face, and did not blink. "Know this," he said then. "I want success as much as one desires to breathe when drowning to death." Sayf seethed at the failure but held his tongue; showing too much emotion was a sign of weakness. Still, he was human and couldn't always be restrained. He let his stone face show just enough anger, holding the rest in check. "*yad waaHida maa tusaffiq,*" he said. A hand cannot clap itself. His voice was sharp as a knife, with a calculated detachment, as if all of his thoughts were based on terrifying logic.

"That is why you are a great leader." Khalid smiled, and Sayf nodded in return.

"Good," Sayf told him. "Can anything be traced back to us?"

"No."

"Can we track the dead man's phone?"

"Not at present," Khalid informed him. "Someone must have destroyed it or removed the battery."

"What about our terror cells in America?"

"No others have been compromised. Everything is in place. We shall succeed."

"Good," Sayf replied. "There is joy only in doing, not in waiting and not in planning. Soon we must step from the shadows . . . Are you ready for your vacation to New York?"

"The plane leaves soon," Khalid told him. "Have the trade agreements gone through yet?"

Sayf nodded. "There is one holdout. The others have all signed." The agreements concerned the founding of a new international gold bank to serve as a regional alternative to the World Bank and the International Monetary Fund, both of which were controlled by the West. He planned to rig the system in the same way the Dutch East India Company had before America, and just as America now did with the IMF, World Bank, WTO and the dollar reserve currency.

"History will remember you," Khalid told him.

"God gives to those who are strong," Sayf replied. "I will be traveling to Strasbourg in France for a few days to renew contracts at the European Union Headquarters. Is there anything else?"

"What else do you wish, my prince?"

Sayf held up the apple. "To take a bite out of the Big Apple," he said—and did.

CHAPTER 4

INTERMEZZO

Tones sound, and roar and storm about me
until I have set them down in notes.
—LUDWIG VAN BEETHOVEN

T HE RAYS OF THE RISING SUN sliced through the spaces
between New York City's buildings like sharp shards
of glass, finding Mike on the street next to the raid site. The
adrenaline of the chase had long since burned off. He felt
almost like a junkie coming down from a high. The morning
light only added to the punishment. Fatigue seeped deeper
into his pores as the minutes ticked by.

The place had harbored a terrorist cell, and no one had
been taken alive. When offered a chance to surrender, the last
survivor had started shooting instead: suicide by cop. The
dead men had been planning something big. None of them
had been identified yet, through fingerprints or DNA processing. It seemed the terrorists had been cautious in their affairs,

leaving little useful evidence behind. Mike had wanted them alive to answer questions—but had no doubt the world was a better place without them.

For the hundredth time he found himself wondering where the anonymous tip had come from. Without that, they would never have found this place. How did the tipster know where the cell was, and why had he called the police? Was his life in danger? What else did he know? Mike had to assume that whatever the dead men had been planning was still moving forward. How many more terrorists were out there, committed to the same mission? To others? Mike knew this was just the beginning, one cell of many—and that the newly dead were a part of something larger. He just had to figure out what.

He'd wanted to put the cell under surveillance, but that had been deemed too risky; if a terrorist attack took place while the cell was being watched, people would die. If the media found out about it, the mayor's career would be over and the feds would move in and take over the case. So the raid had been ordered. It would never be said that more lives might have been saved if the police hadn't just watched and waited.

Now came the hard work: tending wounded cops, hauling off the dead and sifting what they'd left behind, hoping a lead would come out of it. He'd put too much time into this case already, and his best information had come from a well-informed but nameless caller.

Part of him wanted to leave the case and the unit and just bide his time until retirement, when he could leave the chaos of the job behind. But another part of him couldn't do that because he wanted to know what he didn't know. The terrorist cell was proof that an attack was coming, and that those involved were pros.

He slugged back an iced black coffee, ducked under the crime scene tape and walked down the alley to the scene of his shooting. The body had been taken to the morgue, but the blood was still there, dry and brown on the asphalt.

He wandered back to the building where the raid had taken place, but didn't go inside. Instead, he walked the alleys around it. He came across a garbage bin covered with unreadable graffiti in silver and black. He put on purple nitrile gloves and opened the lid to look inside, jumping back as a rat darted out and hit the ground running.

Catching his breath, he leaned forward and peered into the rusting dumpster. It seemed to be half beer cans and half dead cockroaches. Finding a bag of burned papers, he emptied it on the ground and poked through it, but didn't find much. The largest remaining piece was a partial photograph, in which he could just make out a coffee-cup-and-bean logo. No name was visible. He took a picture with his cell phone, and pocketed the burned photo. Odds were it would turn out to be meaningless, but it would be vouchered just in case, along with thousands of other pieces of evidence collected over the next few days.

"Curious way to pass the time, Michelle." Mike turned to see Sergeant Jack Arnold, immaculate in his gray suit. Jack was lean and muscular and, at the moment, chewing a piece of gum. The veins on the sides of his head rippled as he chewed.

"Its Mike or Mac, asshole. The frenemy of my frenemy is my frenemy."

"Hmm . . . So you keep your friends close but your frenemies closer?"

"Nothing like lies to bring people together," Mike said.

"So what are you doing?"

"I was hungry."

"Good you got gloves on. This city is a fucking cesspool, I hate it."

"You have a bad reputation, Jack," Mike said, wiping the dumpster's rust stains from his shirt. "But I like people with bad reputations. In fact, I haven't heard enough bad things about you."

"I guess that's a compliment," Jack said." He looked around. "Your soon-to-be ex-wife, she's so hot. What would you think if I dated her?"

"You, me, Octagon, no ref," Mike said.

"Why is everything so competitive?" Jack replied.

"That's the way the world spins. No offense but you're so smug you look like you're being pleasured by a politician."

"Thanks." Jack paused for a second.

"Just for the record, Jack, I hate working with you."

"I'm fine with hate. I can deal with it if you can."

"You're not a bad guy," Mike told him, "no matter what the world thinks of you."

"This could have been worse."

Mike nodded. "I'm hoping we just stopped it from getting much worse. Care to join the evidence search?"

"And soil my $2,000 Brooks Brothers suit? Pass. You think we stopped it?"

"Slowed it down at least."

"How did you know they'd be here?" Jack asked.

"Little bird told me." Might as well have, Mike thought. "Can't give up my source," he said. "The secret to success is not telling anyone all of your secrets."

"Where did you learn that?"

"Afghanistan."

"Tell me more."

Mike tensed with the memory, images and emotions flooding his mind. "I was in a battle with my company in Panjshir Valley, over fifteen years ago. It happened in a poppy field allegedly protected by warlords paid by the CIA. Tamerlaine was rumored to be one of them. He killed my best friend, and almost got me, too."

Mike closed his eyes and remembered his best friend Eddie beside him, unmoving. When he turned him over, Eddie's eyes were dead. Mike looked around but didn't see or hear anyone coming. He felt for a pulse: nothing. He took Eddie's vest off and started compressions: one, two, three, four, five . . .

A gun was pointed at Mike, and he stopped the compressions. Another gun appeared. He put his hands up and carefully got to his feet, then grabbed the barrel of the first AK, twisting the rifle away and firing at the second man while shoving the first to the ground. The tribesman drew a pistol as he fell, but Mike was faster and shot him dead before he could fire.

Mike dropped on his belly, lying next to the two men he'd just killed, their bodies ugly as the blood pooled out of them and turned brown. Their skin shaded bluish from the cold. He scoped the terrain in all directions, but the rest of the attackers—probably fearing an airstrike—were already gone.

The cold, dry air bothered Mike's lungs. He was already recovering from a cold, and having asthma didn't help matters. He opened a med pack and gave himself a shot of adrenaline. He could feel his blood warming as the hormone rippled through his system.

"Tamerlaine?" Jack asked when Mike had finished his story.

"Yeah. No one really knows who he is, whether he's Iranian or something else, whether he's really a billionaire or not."

"Why does he call himself Tamerlaine?" Jack asked.

"We were told Tarmashirin Khan, Tamburlaine, Tamerlaine—also known as Timur the Lame of the Middle Ages—used human skulls to build towers. He was a distant relative of Genghis Khan, the most ruthless conqueror in the world, who built an Empire from Turkey to the Borders of China. Tamburlaine is buried in Samarkland in a Jade sarcophagus. It's said that whoever disturbs the tomb will be cursed. The Russians did, and the Nazis invaded the Soviet Union. The Emir Tamerlaine of today uses skulls for decorations."

"Scary shit," Jack said.

"My unit was told a secret. It turned out to be a test. Then they showed us the tunnels, lined with tens of thousands of skulls. The caves are far bigger than the Paris Catacombs. We spent a lot of time down there looking for Tamerlaine, the Iranian backed drug lord, but never found anything. He was a ghost. He could be in multiple locations at once; all confirmed signings. Most of the worst things that happened in Afghanistan and Pakistan, he was involved with. But we could never draw a bead on him. We got into a firefight and good men died. I was almost captured. Some say he was behind that. Other things happened that I can't talk about. Rumor was, even the CIA had never actually seen him. Some doubt he even exists, but for a while it was my job to look for him."

"You think this Tamburlaine guy is part of this?" Jack asked.

"I don't know," Mike said. "But the Iranians might be."

"Why?"

"Because his operations tend be successful."

"All this shit keeps coming home," Jack said. "People like us, we're just pawns in a larger game."

"If we're pawns," Mike said, "then what are the Tamerlaines of the world?"

"Players. Making the real moves while we scramble around trying to figure out what they're up to." Jack sighed. "Any news on who killed your son?"

"Some guy named Rahman, the Prince of Kish," Mike said.

"It's still early," Jack announced. "We need to knock on some doors, find out about the raid site."

Ten minutes later, they stood before the old brownstone next door, tapping on the building superintendent's door. Jack shifted a toothpick in his mouth and cracked his knuckles. "Boxing arthritis," he said.

"Getting old sucks."

"No argument there."

Jack rang the buzzer beside the door.

An older man's voice finally answered. "Hello?" The sound was low and far away.

"It's the police," Mike said to the door. "We need to speak to you about the neighbors." If the guy thought he was in some kind of trouble, they might be waiting all day.

"Okay, give me a second," the voice said. A moment later, the door swung open to reveal an elderly bald man in a dirty white tank top. "What do you want to know?" His voice was suddenly high-pitched with anxiety. Mike could see the man was fearful and holding it all back, like a dam about to burst.

"What can you tell us about the men who lived next door?" Jack said. He never peppered anyone with questions, but asked one question at a time, letting them talk. People liked to talk, people wanted to tell their secrets or someone else's—but they had to be relaxed, coaxed into it.

"Lots of people coming and going," the super told them. "Almost always dropped off or picked up, like maybe they didn't have cars or didn't want to drive much or hang around here." The man turned fidgety, and stuck his hands in his pockets.

"How many people?" Jack said.

Mike pulled out his cell phone, using it as a notepad. The super stopped and looked at it for a moment. Mike showed him the screen. "Notes," he assured him.

The old man nodded. "A few here and there, usually one to three men together. They seemed well-dressed and always on their cell phones. That's all I know. I heard about what happened. It's all over the news, every damn channel."

"What's your name? We need it for our follow-up report," Mike said.

"Bob Trillfinis, I've lived and worked here going on thirty years now."

"Thanks for your help," Jack told him.

The super nodded and was about to close the door when Mike asked, "You wouldn't happen to have any video?"

"Come on, then, let's get it over with."

They followed him inside. The apartment was crammed with newspapers and books. Mike saw dictionaries, volumes on philosophy, art and history, alongside popular bestsellers and leather-bound classics.

The super led them to a side room with flat-screen monitors showing real-time views of the lobby and exterior. The outside camera was mounted on a corner of the building, looking sideways—so it also showed the view in front of the building next door. "Tell me they record," Mike said, looking at the monitors.

"Of course they record. What time did you want to look at?"

They sped through video of the last twenty hours. At first they saw hundreds of cops in the area, but before the raid it was virtually a ghost town. No one entered or left the building next door. Going back, they saw two men arrive on foot.

"Can you go further back?" Mike said. "I want to see where they came from."

The super continued rewinding. They watched the men walk backward across an empty block and get into a small gray car at the curb. One of them pocketed a cell phone as he slipped backward into the car. Jack saved his notes and called Detective Wellerin on his cell. "Gray Toyota parked a block and a half north. Is it still there?"

"Just a sec," Wellerin answered. "Still there. What about it?"

"Belongs to our perps," Jack said. "Get a warrant."

"I'm on it." Wellerin appeared on one of the video monitors, checking out the car and photographing the plate with his cell.

Mike looked to the recorded video, now frozen on a monitor. A suspect stood by the car with a cell phone to one ear. "We're going to need a warrant for phone calls, too," Mike said. "All calls going to and from any phone around the raid building."

"Got it," Wellerin said.

"And someone has to go through all the video recordings, looking for license plates." He turned to the super. "How far back do you keep these?"

"Seventy-two hours. Then they overwrite. Cheaper that way."

"So much for that lead," Jack said.

"We still have the car," Mike told him. After copying the video, they went down to look at the vehicle. Detective Wellerin met them halfway, a plastic evidence bag in one hand.

"Captain Maclaymore called her uncle and got a warrant right away, so I broke into the car."

"That was fucking fast," Jack said.

"Helps to have family on the bench," Mike said.

"I called for a tow, prints and DNA," Wellerin told them. "So far it looks like the car was wiped clean. Plate says it's a rental under a false identity. Only thing in the car was this." Wellerin held up the evidence bag, which held a brochure for an import/export business called BRS Trading and Holdings.

"Is the address legit?" Mike said.

"Google says yes."

"Worth a look," Mike decided.

Jack nodded. "I'll run any names connected to the business or the building."

"Right." Mike looked to Wellerin. "Do a stakeout and see if anything comes of it. If you see anyone coming or going, give me a call ASAP."

"Ten-four," Wellerin said. "I'll do a full investigation, see what credit cards were used in the area, Internet activity, the works."

Mike spotted Eva coming out of the mobile command center trailer and heading his way. The other cops watched as she walked by. They'd have to be dead not to look; every insecure man would want to be seen with her as his own Helen of Troy. Mike stopped to look himself when she paused to take a long sip of coffee and light a cigarette. Its tip glowed red and faded. She exhaled a gray wisp of smoke that disappeared in the cool fall air.

Their relationship was like a puzzle with pieces from different boxes; some fit, others never would—an intoxicating brew of love, lust and companionship. The memories were all too real, but the puzzle pieces had become scattered until nothing seemed to fit at all anymore. The trouble was, the only future he could see for himself was one with her in it. Ignoring the arriving shift and the news crews three blocks away, he walked over to meet her.

"I had butterflies today," she told him, exhaling more smoke as they made their way back to the trailer. "Just like my first arrest."

Mike nodded toward the cigarettes. "Those things will kill you."

"At least I know what I'll die of." She put her cigarette on the ground and stepped on it, twisting her foot to extinguish its fire. "Would you believe Internal Affairs towed my car?"

"You're on duty and responding to an emergency. And it's a government vehicle. Doesn't make sense."

"I'm also getting written up."

Mike shook his head. The whole department had become Kafkaesque. "This department is destroying itself," he said. "Gandhi and Mother Theresa would get in trouble here." He leaned against the trailer beside them. "What's the city going to say about the raid?"

"Political perception is not political reality," Eva said. "They sometimes downplay terrorism in the name of political correctness and sometimes don't. The government does whatever seems to be in their own best interest at the moment. Things like this are why I won't drink the fucking Jim Jones Kool-Aid or kiss Don Vito Corleone's ring." She said the words with a certain weariness, as if she'd said them a hundred times in her head, and had finally become so tired of all of the bullshit she had to say them out loud.

"You should tell all of them what you really think," Mike said. "Make use of that black belt in verbal karate."

Eva almost laughed. "That'd get me far. I'm a captain, and that's as far as I'm going to go with my mouth. I'm not going to give the mayor any sugarcoated hand jobs."

Mike pulled a water bottle from his pocket, offered her some and took a sip as they watched the sun rise higher in the sky, making the world light again.

Eva looked at him. "Will things get worse?"

"Things will get better," Mike said.

"I always loved your bullshit," Eva told him. "And thanks for trying to make me feel better." She sighed, massaging her forehead. "Do you have faith?"

He thought for a moment about what she was asking. The truth was, he did have doubts, and he hated that.

"In what we do," Eva clarified. "*Quo vadis?* Where are we going?"

Mike was silent for a moment, then said, "We're a society of false gratitude, of Pontius Pilates. Politicians wash their hands with our blood."

"Agreed," she said.

"So, no. I'm not a believer anymore," Mike announced. "Do you have faith?"

Eva turned away instead of answering. "How much is enough?" She sipped her coffee.

"I guess we're in the same boat," Mike said. "And I'm dying for an ice-cold beer."

Eva smiled. "Without caffeine and alcohol, the whole department would collapse."

"You're such a downer," Mike teased.

Eva smiled. "Yes sir! So how was your computer security training, by the way?"

"I learned how to hack a cell phone and use it as a tracking device." He pulled out his sleek, custom-built "candy bar" cell phone.

"Show me," Eva said.

Mike tapped the phone screen. "The last number you called was One Police Plaza, and yesterday you went food shopping."

"You're a real white hat hacker," she told him. She paused, thinking. Mike noticed a slight change in her but continued. He activated a program on his phone, that linked it up with her phone. "So where do we go from here?" he asked, and watched for her reaction.

"I need a break."

Mike paused. He didn't like the news. Her answer knocked the wind out of him, like he'd been punched in the stomach. He didn't want to answer, and saw that she didn't either.

"We'll talk about this another time," she said.

Mike checked an incoming text message. "Day tour evidence collection team and crime scene unit coming in," it said. He watched the detectives arrive. He could always spot plainclothes or off-duty cops by that certain weathered look of disillusionment etched in the crevices on their faces. Their eyes were no longer filled with hope, because they saw only unfiltered reality.

"Let's go inside." They stepped into the mobile command center and sat in the back. There was a single small coffee machine, no bathroom and droning fluorescent lights. Typical department logic: a place to drink and no place to pee.

He saw a second mobile command center pull up by a group of counter-terror cops setting up equipment. Another group was busy assembling a tent. Eva poured two coffees to cure their grogginess while Mike fired up a touchscreen tablet PC.

"I had to pay for that fucking coffee machine out of my own pocket," Eva told him.

"I'm not surprised," Mike said. "Thank you." She handed him a cup. He took a sip and set it down. "Something just doesn't jibe here," he said.

"I know, but you'll put the pieces together."

"Thanks. Anyway, the tip I got said they were planning something, but didn't say what. We did a lot of legwork to make sure there were no loose ends. Then it turns into a bloodbath."

"But doesn't it make sense that anyone who knew about them would also know what they were planning?" Eva asked.

"Maybe," Mike said. "Doesn't mean they want to share. They might have figured we'd get answers from the perps."

"Best-laid plans," Eva said.

"Even dead, we usually learn something. But these guys, it's like they have no past."

Eva nodded. "Scary. A person's identity is their past. You have to find out who called in that tip."

"Wish me luck. Oh . . ." He fished around in his pocket and found the photo he'd taken with his cell. "I found this in a trash bin out back. Probably nothing, but still."

Eva looked at the photo on his cell phone. "Coffee beans? Garbage."

Mike shrugged. "I sent a tech to look through the rest of the trash."

"Anything else?" she asked.

"Jack got hold of the perps' Internet provider, but they can't find any browsing history."

"That's a first. Why not?"

"Jack thinks maybe some anonymizing software that prevents monitoring."

"Just fabulous."

"The march of progress," Mike said without enthusiasm.

Forty-five minutes later, Aleister arrived with ESS Lieutenant Lynam in tow. Mike shook hands with both.

"You're a dying breed, Mac," Aleister told him. "Your father would be proud."

"Thanks."

"Good to see ya, Mike," Lynam said with the firm handshake of a former All-American Football player, then quickly departed. Mike was glad that Aleister was his uncle; he'd been a father to Mike, helping his mother to raise him after Mike's father passed away. Despite his position in the department, he didn't put on airs, and never engaged in the Machiavellian power politics of City Hall or One Police Plaza. The latter was known in the ranks as the Death Star or, occasionally, the Tower of Mordor. Aleister pulled out a Don Pepin Garcia cigar, held it to his nose and inhaled. "Would you like one?"

"No thanks," Mike said, watching as Aleister snipped the cigar's tip with a steel cutter and lit up inside the trailer. Technically, that was against the rules, but the chief wasn't likely to be called on it. The flame burned indigo blue. Thick gray smoke rings drifted upward with each puff.

Aleister checked his vibrating cell and answered. He listened for a moment, saying only "yes" and "okay" before hanging up.

"What?" Mike said.

"The Ring of Steel is being upgraded," he said, referring to the city-wide network of radiation and chemical detectors. "Need to get that done ASAP."

"Is this because of the raid?" Mike asked.

"Partly. We have to make sure it's damned near perfect. The upgrade was already scheduled. The commish thought we should speed it up. The mayor and the president are going to ask about this, and he wants to have the right answers. I texted Jack to go to the Ring center.

"You should come," Aleister said.

"How well does it work?" Mike asked cutting him off.

Mike and Aleister looked at each other. "If anything radioactive comes in, we'll know it," Aleister said. "If we're lucky, we might even stop it." He held up a radiation-detecting pager, a small monitoring device with a tiny screen.

Thirty minutes later, Mike walked into the newly-built Ring of Steel computer room, located beneath the MetroTech center in Brooklyn. He wore a sharply conservative Kenneth Cole suit with Versace tie.

"Nice tie," Jack said, by way of greeting. He seemed just a tad territorial, and uncharacteristically awkward.

"You too, you closeted metrosexual. I hear this is going to be your new gig soon?"

"Yep," Jack confirmed. "I'm the main guy overseeing the upgrade. You should come on, too. It's a lot less paperwork and political bullshit."

"Can you be less dickish?" Mike said.

"Nope."

"I think that's why the chief wants me to come here."

"He trusts you, and this is perfect for you. If you decide to transfer NO more investigations, and you're needed here. Right now it's being upgraded, and there's a rush on it."

"I'll think about it." Mike looked around. The place was another secret den. There were dozens of monitor screens, and dozens of cops to look at them. Each screen showed video, along with radiation or chemical readings. "So this is the fabled Ring of Steel," Mike said to himself.

"Most of it," Jack told him. "Some buildings have cement barriers as well as the radiological and chemical detectors. We get all the feeds in here. It's based on a system in London."

"If this is the future," Mike said, "I don't like it."

"Some of the civil engineers call this Fortress Urbanism," Jack told him. "But nothing's failsafe."

"I just wanted to pop in and check the place out." Mike shook Jack's hand. "See where you and Aleister have been disappearing to."

"Still pretty secret so far," Jack said. "Not like the one by South Street Seaport."

"Aleister coming by later?" Mike asked.

"He's at some bullshit meeting about the Ring. Maybe later. It's ironic, since they want this thing to never break down or be down. Yet it's like they have meetings just to see how other meetings went. One big government blowjob."

"You're the engineer," Mike said.

Jack smirked. "I'll tell you how this stuff works another time, since you're a virgin at this."

Mike eyed the dozens of flat screen computer monitors on the wall. "How far do you trust it?" he asked.

"It's pretty solid, considering the government built it."

"I would have thought something like this would be at One Police Plaza," Mike said.

"Brooklyn's better. Out of sight, out of mind."

"Can the bad guys get around all this?"

"The Ring? If I were a bad guy, I'd go for a conventional attack. Nothing fancy for the monitors to sniff out."

"I think you might be right," Mike said. "But our perceptions shouldn't guide our investigations."

Jack's cell buzzed. He checked the text. "Wouldn't you know it. Another meeting."

"I don't know when this will be the right time but I just wanted to say I'm sorry about your father," Mike said in regards to his father's suicide. Jack turned and nodded as if he was thankful of the comment and walked away.

C H A P T E R   5

DANCING IN THE LABYRINTH OF THE ROYAL HOUSE OF SAUD

All warfare is based on deception.

—SUN TZU

Š AHRĀZĀD AND HER YOUNGER COUSIN Aaliyah approached
the glimmering Al Faisaliah Center Hotel and Business
Center in Riyadh, Saudi Arabia. It was late morning, and
thousands of demonstrators swarmed the streets around a
massive, horseshoe-shaped building nearby. The people were
frustrated, poor, and disillusioned with the government.

Šahrāzād squeezed her cousin's hand tightly, so they
wouldn't become separated as they made their way through

the angry crowd. It helped that Šahrāzād was dressed as a man, with beard, white robe, head scarf and prosthetics to make her feminine features masculine. The day was already scorching hot, and being on the street felt like suffering the whim of some giant child with a magnifying glass, trying to incinerate humans instead of insects.

Šahrāzād's emotions seethed and burned at all of this. *I must change my homeland, no matter what the cost, for myself or anyone else.* Freedom of speech and thought, and tolerance of ideas were needed for progress, but that wasn't where The Kingdom was headed. Ignorance was a prison, and her people were in a prison of their own making, as was so much of that part of the world. What could she do? To remake the fading Kingdom into something that lifted all on a rising tide. Were people meant to be captives of their own history, their narrative and identity? Was determinism stamped into their souls at birth—could they break the chains? Am I the Hercules, the chain-breaker? The past might have to be smashed, but destruction was the origin of all creation . . . I will be the spark . . .

Šahrāzād read some of the protestors' signs as they passed: "The government is not us!" . . . "The Government lies!" . . . "You've stolen billions as we struggle to eat!"

She thought for a moment that if these people only knew how hard it was for the king to prove transgressions and correct every prince who abused his position, and every government official who misused funds . . . If they could only comprehend the magnitude and unwieldiness of the bureaucracy that accompanied the administration of justice.

But perhaps it was time for a clean slate. The Kingdom was at a turning point, facing reform, implosion, revolution, dictatorship or some combination thereof. The next few weeks would determine The Kingdom's fate, and perhaps that of the entire Muslim world.

She saw a cleric standing in the center of the town square, with a long beard and eyes like black coals. Stepping onto a wooden platform, he raised a bullhorn to his lips and began to chant. "Down with the government! Down, down, down!"

Across the square, an army tank squatted between buildings, a metal beast. To her it looked to be awaiting orders to crush the voices—and bodies—of the protestors. Government flyers rained from the sky as a plane passed overhead. She snatched one from the air and glanced at the words: "All demonstrations are banned and curfews are in effect. Anyone on the street is subject to immediate arrest." The warning served only to enrage the crowd. Someone threw a Molotov cocktail at a car, setting it ablaze.

Šahrāzād and Aaliyah moved on. Passing the hotel, they entered a nondescript building a few blocks away. Once inside, they made their way to a small and plainly furnished condo. Aaliyah removed her veil and embraced her cousin.

Šahrāzād could feel Aaliyah's body shaking, and indicated the security monitors. "It's okay. No one followed us." She removed her disguise carefully, as if disassembling a puzzle she wished to rebuild later.

Aaliyah nodded, grabbed two bottled waters from the fridge and led the way to the basement "clean room," where they knew they would not be overheard or electronically surveilled.

The room was simple, with a small desk and three chairs. Aaliyah scanned the space with an electronic bug sniffer. "It's safe," she announced after a moment. Šahrāzād took a seat, slipped off her shoes and massaged her fatigued feet. "I was almost killed today," she said. Šahrāzād felt relaxed and warm—*dafi*—around Aaliyah. Her cousin's voice tasted like *Basbousa saudi*, a sweet dessert.

"What happened?" Aaliyah asked.

"The CIA handler never showed. It was someone else. He's dead. I still have the flash drive."

"Something like this was bound to happen," Aaliyah said. "We're moving forward, so close to the edge."

"I have to assume my real contact is dead or turned, or that the CIA wants me dead. Or maybe someone in The Kingdom. My brother Sayf says the Iranians are up to something, a plot against The Kingdom. People are watching."

"How do you know?"

"Someone gave me false info to see if I'd pass it on."

"Saudi Intel is looking for leaks and moles," Aaliyah said. Šahrāzād nodded. "I need to know who's behind this."

"Did the real contact know your name?"

"No. I need to know how much they know, whoever they are. And I'm not sure I can trust the intelligence on either side."

Aaliyah was thoughtful for a moment. She remembered Umar al-Husayni, the Saudi diplomat in New York. "I got a call from Umar," she said. "He wants you there. Something big."

Šahrāzād considered for a moment. She'd built up so much here, and had so much to do, she didn't want to just get up and leave. But he wouldn't have called unless the news was important. Her father was going to be in New York soon anyway, and he'd also asked her to come. "Umar has given us so much," she said. "I have something to show you." Šahrāzād took out her camera and showed Aaliyah a photo of the man who'd tried to kill her.

Aaliyah gasped at the image of a face with two bullet holes in it, then leaned in for a closer look. "I recognize him, I think. But I'm not sure from where. He reminds me of a police officer I saw in Riyadh a few times, but I never knew his name."

"I've never seen him before," Šahrāzād said. "Perhaps I will go to New York. Do the killers know about Umar and his father, the general?" Šahrāzād asked.

"No. But the general says he's close to finding out who Tamerlaine really is since there is an Iranian plot against The Kingdom. Tamerlaine was the world's most wanted and dangerous man, but no one had a clue as to his identity. "Umar says there are both Iranian cells and Tamerlaine cells in the U.S. and in The Kingdom."

"Whatever Tamerlaine is doing," said Šahrāzād, "it's connected to the plot against The Kingdom."

"Confirmed?" Aaliyah asked.

"Evidence, photos and insider stuff from Umar," Šahrāzād told her.

"Right after the Pakistani coup, there were some very large financial transactions reported in the news in Afghanistan."

"Is the truth ever on the news anymore?" asked Šahrāzād. "What have you heard?"

"Hundreds of millions in gold and silver bullion, U.S. dollars and Chinese Renminbi, all sent to Pakistan, by someone in Kish, Iran." Aaliyah handed her a small silver foil packet with a mini SD memory card.

"This is an encrypted nano GPS transmitter. It's a type of spydust. You put it on someone and load the app on your device."

"What are the drawbacks?"

"It lasts an hour and takes ten to fifteen minutes to start working."

Šahrāzād slipped it in a pocket.

"I think everything is connected to what's happening here," Aaliyah said, "—the rumors and arrests in The Kingdom."

"I'll have to go to New York," Šahrāzād decided. "Umar must have something. He wouldn't have asked me to come unless it could change everything." She paused for a full minute.

"*'a'mal khayr wa 'ilqahu fii al-baHr,*" Aaliyah said. Do good and cast it into the sea.

She didn't want to leave, there were too many things going on—but this could be the break she needed to learn more about those plotting against The Kingdom.

THE ASSASSIN

هیچ چیز واقعیت مطلق، همه مجاز است

Nothing is an absolute reality, all is permitted.
—VLADIMIR BARTOL

A MAN SAT TIED TO A CHAIR, wide awake. The veins in his eyes were deep red. Blood caked around his swollen face, and a red bandana had been stuffed in his mouth. His eyes bulged like a fish that had been caught by a fisherman. Another man stood in front of him with his back turned, gazing at himself in a mirror. He turned to face the man in the chair. He was about the same height and weight as the captive, but leaner and more muscular. He took a long silver needle to extract fluid from a small bottle, then looked at the tied man's ears.

"The ears, they are not quite right," he said in perfect English. "Do you know what I want? I'm Khalid, by the way.

It's nice to meet you, Reza. I want you to tell me everything."
The captive nodded quickly, gaze moving from captor to needle
and back again.

"I need to know everything, since I'm going to take over
your life." He plunged the needle into the prisoner's arm
and pressed the plunger all the way down, injecting him. He
watched as the man's eyes closed for a moment, and his muscles
lost their tension. "So what's it like, Reza? Being a mole for
the Iranian government? A sleeper in Amarco?" He pulled the
bandana from Reza's mouth. Reza gasped a few gulps of air
and, after a few moments, entered a state of artificial relaxation.
"It took me years," he answered at last.

"Did you know I was watching you? That we were watching you?" Khalid asked.

"No."

"Did you know I was mirroring you?" Khalid looked him
directly in the eye.

"Mirror?" Reza said.

"Being you as you lived, ghosting you as you lived," Khalid
explained.

"No," Reza answered.

"You are going to tell me everything, yes?" Khalid stared
into his eyes as he asked.

"Yes." Reza nodded.

"You are being honest with me?"

"Yes."

"Good. So what's it like, Reza? You can call me Khalid,
it's okay."

"What is, what is what like? I don't understand."

"What's it like meeting your ghost? The new you? Me?" Khalid stared at him without blinking. Reza nodded and took a deep breath. Sweat ran down his face, and he bit his lip. "You and your government are going to attack the U.S.," Khalid told him. "Or so it will seem. You will be famous. You see we figured something out with the first Iraq War. The U.S. will not let any Arab nation annex another Middle Eastern nation. And so we must have a plan. You're part of that plan, a big part."

An hour later, Khalid wrapped Reza's body up in a colorful red and gold carpet. He then tied a few silver chains around the carpet and put it in a chest. The chest he placed in a car trunk. He took off his latex gloves, which were covered with crimson red. He put the gloves in a small metal coffee can, and set them on fire. Thick black smoke filled the air. He threw some salt water on the fire and buried the metal can in the sand near the beach. He opened Reza's wallet, looked at the driver's license and credit cards. He then studied his own face in the car mirror. The plastic surgeon had done an excellent job. He looked just enough like Reza for the plan to work.

CHAPTER 7

KNEE-DEEP IN THE DEAD

Politics have no relation to morals.
—NICCOLO MACHIAVELLI

M IKE SAT AT HIS DESK in the squad room, nursing his fifth cup of coffee, feeling burnt out and wired at the same time. His eyelids twitched from lack of sleep and too much caffeine. He set the coffee down and massaged his eyes. He then twisted and cracked his neck. Looking around, he felt a mild case of vertigo and nausea, doubtless from lack of sleep and job fatigue. He stared at the picture of Eva on his cell phone, which then rang in his hand, jolting him back to the moment. "Yes?" he said, picking up.

"I'm texting you an address to go to," Wellerin told him. "And we got a warrant for cell phones used in the raid area."

"Gotcha, thanks." Mike hung up. The text came through a moment later. He made his way across the room to Eva. "Cell phone warrant from the raid came through. We got an address on a cell phone used at the raid site. The address goes back to the cell's owner. This is a huge lead."

"Anything on the other cell?" she asked.

"The guy on the video with his cell? We got nothing, it was a burner."

"I'm listening," Eva said.

"Wellerin texted me the cell phone warrant: any phone linked to the raid. One phone came up; it goes to Umar al-Husayni, a Saudi diplomat who lives here in New York City. He's got diplomatic immunity, so we can only talk to him."

"So a Saudi diplomat used a phone or is linked to a phone possibly used by terrorists. I guess if we crack this case we'll be paying higher gas prices." Eva slipped into her jacket. "I'm coming with you." This was good, Mike thought. The more they were together, the better.

It was late morning when they arrived at the Upper East Side apartment on York Avenue. The structure was over 25 stories high and cold winter white, with tinted windows to keep the sunlight out. He remembered seeing a jumper there, many years ago. Half the body had hit a car; the other half had landed on the sidewalk. At first he'd thought someone had cut the victim in half and tossed the pieces out a window. But it had turned out to be a suicide; the falling body had hit someone's balcony rail on the way down. It was one of the job's downsides: no matter where he went in the city, some gruesome memory was always waiting, like a ghost from the past. He didn't want all of his memories to be violent, sad or tragic, but that was the path his past had set him on.

He sneaked a look at Eva, and all of that fell away. He could picture himself walking away from it all and retiring—but not without her. He just wanted to hold her hand and go for long walks on the beach, or hike the Rocky Mountains and cuddle during a cold night—leaving this forsaken city forever.

"It's strange to see you again after so much time," Eva said.

"Was it stranger for me to be gone?" he asked.

"You need a break."

"Hello," the doorman said. It was the same guy Mike had spoken with on the day the jumper died. The man displayed no hint of recognition, and Mike didn't enlighten him. Instead he showed his shield. Moments later, Mike and Eva paused outside apartment 1716. The door was not quite latched. Mike put his ear to the door, but heard nothing. An odor seeped from the room. "Something dead in there," he whispered. "Police!"

He and Eva drew their guns, and he kicked the door open. The smell was stronger now; it smelled like day-old vomit and burned, rotten, red meat. Not a new death. If it was murder, the killer was likely long gone.

Mike went in first, leaving the lights off just in case. He used his cell as a flashlight, raising it above his head to see in the darkness, and moving it around so he wouldn't be a target. Eva did the same. Mike held his gun close to his stomach, to make it harder for someone to grab. They worked as a team to clear the living room, kitchen, hall and closets. He noticed a safe behind a desk in the living room. It was open and mostly empty, except for a few gold coins and some colorful foreign currency notes.

They entered the bedroom last. Heavy curtains made the room almost dark—but not so dark that Mike couldn't see the dried blood on the white shag carpet. He eyed the shape of a dead body on the bed while Eva opened the curtains.

A man—presumably the one they'd come to question—was tied up on the bed, nude and headless. His hands were bound behind his back with duct tape. Judging from the marks on the body, he'd been tortured for some time. Mike tried not to gag at the putrid smell.

"I think we need to call this shit in." Eva shook her head and covered her nose, hating the pungent smell of death. She sometimes acted like she was made of ice, but she was more like glass. Her face showed what she was feeling, even when she was in "Captain Mode." She holstered her gun, clenched her jaw and gagged from the rancid smell . . .

"You all right?" Mike asked.

"I'm okay. You?" She asked.

"Fine. Why would anyone kill a Saudi diplomat?"

"Robbery, blackmail, terrorism, state-sponsored assassination, spying—take your pick."

"The diplomat was in the area of the raid," Mike said.

An hour later, Aleister and the medical examiner had come and gone, along with Homicide, Crime Scene and the morgue.

"Umar al-Husayni," Eva told Mike. "His father is Saudi Arabia's top general."

"Field Marshal of the Army," Mike added, checking his notes. "Heads the whole thing. U.S. State Department has someone coming over from the Saudi Embassy."

"Has anyone told the general yet?" Jack asked has he walked in.

Always late to the important places, Mike thought, but at least he showed up.

"Intel told the Saudi mission," Eva replied.

"Any ID yet on the guy you nailed in the alley?" Jack asked Mike, typing something on his cell.

"Not that I know of, but that's a really PC way of putting it," Mike said. "I have to go to the morgue on that; I was told a cousin is coming so we can get a confirmed identity on a dead body." Having family members ID bodies was a precaution designed to prevent bodies from being switched to prevent the ultimate form of identity theft, the body switch: killing one person and getting rid of the body and then having a cohort ID the body of an unknown person as someone else who'd died of natural causes.

A well-dressed man in a sharp black suit knocked on the door and showed himself into the apartment. He was tall, lean and well-groomed. Mike didn't recognize him, but he'd been cleared by the cop posted in the hall. Jack excused himself to take a phone call as the newcomer approached. "I'm Mr. Abdul from the Saudi Embassy," he said.

"I'm Detective Maclaymore," Mike replied, shaking hands.

"I'm Captain Maclaymore," Eva said, offering her own hand and shaking.

"We need to do our own report whenever there's a crime involving a diplomat," Mr. Abdul said.

"I hear ya," Mike told him.

Abdul stood near the safe, taking dozens of pictures with this cell phone.

Mike paused in thought, then started searching, having waited until the dusting of prints and photographs were done by Crime Scene as to not disturb the evidence. He started on top of the refrigerator, inside dresser drawers and cabinets. He walked into the bedroom and looked under the bed, behind the table next to the bed and—there. He saw a cell phone. He picked it up and saw it had been turned off. He switched it on; it was password protected.

He pulled out his own cell and turned on the UV light from an app on his phone, using it to illuminate the diplomat's cell. He saw that the numbers 5187 had been pressed more often than the others. Not knowing the correct order, he pressed 5871, 7851 and 8715. The phone unlocked. He then pressed 1 for voicemail. A robotic voice asked for a code to access the voice mail. He used the same number backward, and it worked.

"I'm not here right now, leave a message," said the diplomat's recorded voice on the cell's messaging voice mail. It was the same voice that had phoned in the anonymous tip. Mike played that tip over in his memory, like a recorder in his own mind's ear: "An attack is going to happen, the man they call Tamerlaine may be behind it," the tipster had begun. Mike put the phone in his pocket and walked back into the living room.

Eva was watching Mike. He saw her face change when she looked at him, as if she sensed something amiss.

Eva answered her cell and walked into one of the other rooms. She returned a few moments later into the living room. "So the Saudis wanted you here?" she said to Mr. Abdul.

"It's complicated, but yes," Abdul said.

"I'm sorry for your loss," Eva said.

"Thank you. What do you have so far?"

Eva turned to Mike and he got the not-so-subtle hint. "Not enough to draw any clear conclusions," he answered.

"So what is clear?" Jack asked.

"Time of death 24 hours ago, maybe a few hours more. Torture, beheading and a motive that may include a simple push-in robbery and murder. Looking at how little is left in the safe."

"They hit the jackpot." Jack said, studying a gold coin on the edge of the safe.

"Ah," said Mr. Abdul. "I am here, since he is one of our citizens."

"Some of the material here is likely sensitive," Mike said. "But it seems most of the contents of the safe are gone. If he had any flash drives or mini-CD-RWs, they were taken."

Mr. Abdul looked closely at the safe. It was mostly empty, except for a few gold Krugerrands and Chinese Gold Panda coins, and a few paper currencies in the form of Renminbi, Yuan, euros, dollars and Swiss francs. From all appearances, it seemed like the robbers had been in a rush and had pulled the contents of the safe into a backpack, bag or suitcase, leaving a few items behind when they bolted.

Abdul's cell rang. "Pardon me." He strode into the next room for privacy. He was back in less than a moment. "A cousin will make the formal identification," he said.

"We were informed that a family member of the deceased would make a formal ID soon," Mike said. "Makes the paperwork simpler."

Abdul excused himself as his phone vibrated with another call.

"I recognize the voice on the phone message," Mike whispered to Eva. He leaned close. "It's the same voice that gave me the tip on the building we raided."

"Interesting stuff," Jack chimed.

Eva said nothing at first, but looked surprised "Maybe he was more than a diplomat," she suggested. He didn't like the word "spy," which was what she meant. He'd left that world years ago, but his past had recently started catching up to him. It was as if his own history had a mind of its own, wanting to alter his present and his future, stripping him of what little free will he had left.

"Spy?" Mike replied. "The warrant showed this guy called one of the men at the raid on the safe house from the raid a few days before, and then phoned the tip to me anonymously. And now he's dead in his apartment. Coincidence?"

"Wouldn't be the first diplomat-slash-spy," Jack said.

"It doesn't make sense yet," Eva said.

Abdul returned to the living room and hung up his phone.

"I guess Umar was planning for retirement," he said, looking at the empty safe.

"Or using the money for—" Jack stopped his sentence. Mike cringed, but was glad Jack had caught himself. Mike looked to Abdul, who kept his composure.

"Has anyone checked for video at the security office downstairs?" Eva said.

"Wellerin's downstairs in the manager's office," Jack said. "He's got something for us."

Mike headed out.

He reached the first floor moments later, finding the manager's office in a converted back room. Detective Wellerin sat hunched over a computer monitor, scratching his thin Serpicoesque beard. "What's up, Mac?" Wellerin said, still staring at the video on the computer screen.

"You tell me. What have you got?"

"Yesterday at 11:17 p.m.," Wellerin announced, "this man is seen entering the building. He leaves at 12:19 a.m. It must have been a short torture."

"That's the guy I killed in the raid," Mike said.

"The doorman says he was visiting apartment 1716, and Umar told him to let the visitor in."

"What was his name?" Mike asked.

"He signed in as Babar."

"I always seem to get the megillahs," Mike said. "Never mulligans." He looked up at one of the video monitors, which showed footage from the day before the raid. He watched the murderers come in through the building's front door. "They'll start an autopsy on the diplomat," Mike said.

"We're going to have to test any DNA from this crime scene, and see if we get matches from the men killed in the raid."

"Should get a hit," Wellerin said to Mike.

"What are you thinking?" Eva asked.

Mike looked around the apartment, paused for a second, and walked over to the safe again. He looked over the foreign currency notes and gold coins, then moved to the wall and took down a painting. There was nothing behind it. He looked up at the ceiling, then went into the bedroom. He checked under the bed again, and inside the closet.

"What are you looking for?" Eva asked.

Mike didn't respond. Something caught his eye; on top of one of the dressers he saw small, red, Russian matryoshka dolls. He picked one of them up. It had large black eyes and was very detailed, with drawings of Russian fairytale characters. One was an older lady—a witch which he recognized as Baba Yaga—while another was the beautiful blonde girl Vasilisa. That had been his mother's name as well. It referred to a Russian Cinderella, a character in a group of Russian fairytales his mother had told him as a child. He opened up the doll, finding a small electronic circuit board and a micro-SD card. "Got it!" he called out.

"Mini video camera?" Eva said.

"Yep."

Mike took the card out and popped it into his cell. There were dozens of videos on the card. He scrolled through them, picked one from the day before and fast-forwarded. Both Jack and Eva walked over to look. On the video, they saw the man that Mike had killed. He was with another man, who was a bit taller and more muscular about 5'11" and a solid 180 lbs. He looked very ex-military.

The two of them dragged Umar into the bedroom, tied him up, put him in a chair and put duct tape on his mouth.

The larger of the two men took out a needle and injected him. The other man produced what looked like a set of medieval knives. A few moments later, they removed the duct tape from their captive's mouth. He slouched in the chair, and his captors began speaking in Persian. Mike turned up the volume to listen.

"I'm a tad rusty from not being in the Middle East for so long," Mike said.

"*Leih kholt Lel police?*" said the man with the needle.

"Why did you tell the police?" Mike translated aloud.

"*Yahjeb alayh,*" Umar replied.

"I had to," Mike said.

The captor continued: "*Betaaref aan El moukhaberee?*"

"Do you know about the leaker in Arabia and their identity?" Mike said.

Umar again: "*La.*"

"No," Mike translated.

"*Betaaref eindana nookhbeaeem CIA FBI?*" said the man with the needle.

"Did you know we have moles in the CIA and FBI?" Mike repeated in English.

"*La,*" Umar stated.

"No," Mike said.

"*Ma be'der akabeeek el ma,*" Umar added.

"I can't tell you what I don't know," said Mike.

"*Rah oulak el baarefo.*"

"But I will tell you everything I know."

"*alfarsy alkhas bk hw jyd lal'erby. t'erfwn lmada aym athdth elykm fy hq alfarsy?*" asked Needle-Man.

"Your Persian is good for an Arabian," Mike translated. "You know why I'm talking to you in Persian, right?"

Mike stopped the video to answer his cell; it was a detective at the morgue calling him. "We just got a call," the man told him. "Someone's on their way to ID the body."

"Ten-four," Mike told him. "I'll be there ASAP."

CHAPTER 8

SWORDS AND SCIMITARS

*Ultimately, what separates a winner from a loser
at the grandmaster level is the willingness to do the
unthinkable. A brilliant strategy is, certainly, a matter
of intelligence, but intelligence without audaciousness is
not enough. Given the opportunity, I must have the guts
to explode the game, to upend my opponent's thinking
and, in so doing, unnerve him. So it is in business: One
does not succeed by sticking to convention. When your
opponent can easily anticipate every move you make,
your strategy deteriorates and becomes commoditized.*

—GARRY KASPAROV, CHESS GRANDMASTER

IN A LARGE GYMNASIUM beside the Royal Palace in Jeddah,
Saudi Arabia, two men dueled with sabers. Flexible steel
swords clashed as the combatants lunged and retreated, gliding

back and forth with red lights and green lights on the tables. Both men wore white Kevlar uniforms and metal mesh masks. The swordplay was furious: cuts and thrusts, parries and counter-parries, all at lightning speed. A green light went to the man on the right: one point. The man on the left lunged forward. The man on the right parried the sword, countered and touched him on the chest—making Prince Sayf the winner. He was swift on his feet, filled with energy and a lust for victory. Sayf always dueled like a cobra; he was calm and relaxed, yet exploded with enormous power when he saw weakness—always going for the kill. He removed the dueling mask and wiped the sweat off his face with a bright white cotton towel. The other man took of his mask.

"You fought well today, my prince."

"You are quite the competitor," Sayf told him. "Olympics a decade ago?"

"Trials only."

"Still very impressive."

Twenty minutes later, Sayf was on a large table, nude and lying on his stomach while an attractive, nude, Asian woman placed hundreds of acupuncture needles into his back. Someone knocked at the door. "Enter!" Sayf called out.

The same man from the gym came in. "My prince," he said in a low voice.

Sayf twisted his head to get a good look at him.

"Yes?" Sayf's tone was firm and cold.

"Your father would like to see you."

Sayf held his tongue. "He will have to wait."

"I must ask you this."

"What?"

"Why do you train?"

Sayf paused and exhaled. He was still cooling down from the workout. "We now live in an age of guns and bombs, computer viruses and multimedia propaganda. But the reason I train in ancient martial arts is to get back into the old ways. They give discipline, and make men taste blood in their own mouths. It trains one to see violence up close, and to know it for what it really is. If you want to succeed in life, do things yourself and get your hands bloody." He smiled as he toweled off.

"So that's why you joined the military?"

"Yes," Sayf told him.

"I see." He smiled, seeing that Sayf became more relaxed when speaking of himself.

"Give me half an hour. I need to wash up."

Forty-five minutes later, Sayf was on his way. Outside, the sun blazed in the early afternoon, its burning yellow glow turning the Arabian sands a golden brown. Sayf admired the 3,281-foot-tall Burj al Mamlakah—The Kingdom Tower—in the distance.

Putting on his sunglasses, he walked along the edge of the massive stadium courtyard. With its palm trees, bodyguards and swimming pools, the palace was an oasis, almost a man-made Eden. Sayf hated it; the place seemed so fake it was closer to Disneyland than Arabia. But the sky was a perfect blue, the palm trees green, and the sand of the desert like tanned sugar; these alone were perfect.

Sayf entered the main building. Guards were everywhere, and there were scores of security cameras, manned by unseen police. Sayf strode down a long, white, stone hallway. At the end was a massive door that some said dated from the Middle Ages. It was kept as a work of useful art, old blackened wood with iron straps and hinges that creaked when the door moved.

Passing through this, Sayf entered a boardroom dominated by an ebony table over sixty feet long. Half a dozen Islamic Museum Knights stood along the walls; medieval suits of armor, each one dating from a different period of historical Islam. One was from the Ottoman Empire; it had a pointed helm, scale mail covering the neck, and a bar of metal as a nose guard, damascened with gold. The suit had a fifteenth-century Turkish saber with an ivory white handle at its waist, and a long spear held upright in one hand. It had belonged to a Janissary slave soldier.

Another suit was from the Mamluk period. The helmet was of gold, and chain mail covered the face. The suit held a round shield that was pointed in the middle and colored with geometric patterns of blue and green. A curved scimitar hung at the waist. A third warrior from the past was a grand Mughal. The helmet was silver, with beautiful etched poetry and a pointed nose guard. The suit's hands held a bow and a beautiful curved sword encrusted with rubies on its hilt.

At the far end of the room was Sayf's father, the king, an impressive man in his mid-sixties. He wore a conservative Western business suit, custom-tailored in Italy. The King putted golf balls into small holes in the artificial turf that covered the floor beside the windows. Sayf's escort nodded to Sayf and left the room.

The king and Sayf hugged and kissed on both cheeks in the traditional way. *"Shukran jazillan,"* Sayf said.

"Ahlan Wa Sahlan," his father answered. "How was your training?"

"I get better with each session," Sayf told him.

"As we all should." The king putted a ball into a hole. "And how is it going with Amarco?"

"Excellent."

The King nodded in reply.

"But, I would rather return to Afghanistan and Pakistan, to help with the children's charities we have there."

"You have obligations to The Kingdom first. Your sister knows this more than you." The king picked up the ball and positioned it for another putt.

"I take after you, my king . . . What do you think of Iran?"

"I do not wish for war, but the nation of Persia has sharp swords and might do us harm." The king putted with his golf club, and missed.

"I see," Sayf said. "It seems they will draw and strike at any moment."

The king paused and exhaled "We do have reports . . ."

"Of?" Sayf prompted.

"Breaches."

"If this is true, we shall root them out."

"I wish for peace," the king said calmly. "We depend too much on men, on kings, and not on institutions and sound policy. This must change."

"Our nation, our lands are stained in blood and bound by the blood of the tribes," Sayf said. He loved his father, but hated his politics and the direction he had chosen for the nation and culture; all of it was against what the lessons of history had taught them. His father was cutting covert funding to those Sayf agreed with, people whose efforts were undermining the West and others who stood in the way of The Kingdom's greatness. But he knew his father would never listen.

"I am aware that peace is a contract," said the king.

"As is war," Sayf added. "So it's swords into plowshares?"

"Yes, war is not always with swords or blood; it is against man's nature . . . To be true to nature is to be a dune in the sand."

"Life is more like fighting than dancing," Sayf observed.

"Fighting is a dance, my son."

"That it is. I shall dance and fight as you wish, father," Sayf said.

"These past soldiers in this room, from Akbar the Mughal, Saladin, and Suleiman the Magnificent, they were mountains, creating a political economy out of toil and charisma but not dunes. Time ends all kingdoms and all things," The king smiled. "As Ibn Khaldun would have said it."

"What is your counsel?" Sayf asked.

"Patience. The Ottomans were patient, as was one of your heroes, Saladin. Though Tamburlaine the historical conqueror was not patient but bold. And that reminds me—how's your Kurash?" The king referred to one of the martial arts Sayf trained in.

"I have the balance of a tiger and the bite of a lion," Sayf said. A young man knocked and entered. "My king?" he said in a whisper.

"Yes?"

"A few of the Amirs, sheiks and Kuwaitis are here."

"Then I shall see them."

"I must go." Sayf hugged his father in the formal way, kissed both cheeks and left through the long hall. He didn't like his father's answers, the way things had gone in the past or the way they were headed now. Nor did he like his father's plans for the future. He realized that his own plans could no longer wait; to complete them, he must seize his own destiny.

His secure encrypted cell buzzed. He opened it and decrypted the text. The message said that Sa'id had died in the police raid, and that Umar had been killed in his apartment. Sayf closed the phone. He smiled, made a fist, and paused.

Sayf refused to see his own life pass by, like every other king's son. He wanted much more. Not to be comfortable, but to transform himself and everything else. To put The Kingdom on the right path, so it could be glorious once more. He was at a turning point. This was the middle game of a great chess match. The endgame was in sight. It was all about combinations and interpolations. By setting his plans into motion, he was about to move the pieces on the chessboard of life. The Arabs and the Saudis would no longer be the little people, greedy and barbarous and cruel—but like a colossus who shook the foundations of the world. A world that would soon quake beneath Sayf's feet.

CHAPTER 9

DEAD GHOSTS

My hour is almost come,
When I to sulphurous and tormenting flames
Must render up myself.

—*HAMLET* BY WILLIAM SHAKESPEARE

MIKE STEPPED FROM THE unmarked police car at the morgue. It was a small, blue, brick building at Thirtieth and First Avenues, with all kinds of graffiti on the front, barred windows, and piles of red medical waste bags stacked out front. He went inside. He hated coming to the morgue; it just reminded him about what he could see or might see, the future and his own past all in one place—and the pain of what he'd lost as well. The reality was, this was where it all ended—here, or at a funeral home. The memory of one's existence would be forgotten over time. Regardless of how they lived, everyone wound up a statistic under a tombstone. What could anyone hope for, but to have love in what time there was.

The investigation was moving along, but he couldn't yet gauge when or where it would end. It wasn't about deductive logic, but a trail from the past that, once discovered, would reveal a possible future. What people did in the past brought them into the present, and what they did in the present created the future.

He stared absently toward the TV in the lobby, which showed a report about riots in the Middle East. "It looks like Saudi Arabia and Iran are building up troops in the region," the CNN reporter said. Nations once more preparing for a feast of blood cloaked in some popular–ism, when in reality it was all about the ambitions of men who lusted for political power or financial gain. He flashed his tarnished gold detective's shield to the morgue doctor, who walked up to greet him. "I'm Detective Maclaymore."

"I'm Doctor Patterson," the doctor replied. She was cute, thin and blonde. "Just give me a minute," she said, and walked off again.

Turning to his left, Mike saw a beautiful and exotic-looking woman. She radiated a quiet dignity, but seemed stoic and distant. He realized a few seconds afterward that he'd failed to see the two men standing beside her. They looked like bodyguards: paramilitary haircuts, hidden sidearms, electronic devices in their ears. He offered his hand to the woman. "I'm detective Mike Maclaymore," he said. "Just call me Mac."

"I'm Šahrāzād," the woman replied, smiling. She was physically fit, with raven black hair, deep olive-brown eyes, and honey-colored skin. The words "bronze sun goddess" came to mind. She had a pleasant scent, perfect posture, and intelligent eyes. He noticed she used some kind of makeup to cover a small scar on the left side of her face. Her expression was serene. Mike thought of what his Russian grandmother would have said upon seeing her, *Ohy, kahk kruk-see vuh;* Wow beautiful!

"Where are you from?" Mike asked.

"The Kingdom of Saudi Arabia."

"And you're here because . . ."

"I'm here to ID the body of the diplomat," she told him.

"May I ask for your ID? It's just procedure."

One of the bodyguards handed her a folder. She removed a passport and offered it to Mike. Opening it, Mike saw her photo and full name: *Ḥawwā Šahrāzād bin Aziz Al Saud.* The passport was diplomatic and identified her as a princess. He handed it back and wrote her name on his cell phone's note pad. Her facial muscles appeared taut for a moment, but after a few seconds she seemed to become more relaxed. Why would a princess ID a body? It didn't make sense.

Dr. Patterson returned and led them all down a flight of stairs. The rancid smell of death assaulted Mike's nostrils, overlaid with the musty-salty scent of formaldehyde. The walls of the basement morgue were off-white, the floor covered with blue and white tiles. Brushed stainless steel gurneys awaited new arrivals, as did metal trays filled with sharp steel knives and scissors designed to slice up body parts. A janitor in a green jumpsuit mopped the floor nearby.

"How did he die?" Šahrāzād said to Dr. Patterson.

"Cut at the neck, but first he was tortured, and then strangled, and then . . ."

"Beheaded," Mike said. He noticed that Šahrāzād didn't react; she was stoic, with a perfect poker face.

"May I have copies of these reports? And also a copy of the death certificate?" Šahrāzād asked, her tone implying the question was a formality.

"Yes," Patterson said simply. The women seemed distant from one another; further confirmation of Mike's theory that attractive women always consider each other rivals.

Patterson led them to a steel table at the long room's far end. The table had green drainage holes near the top and bottom. She pulled the blue sheet from the body's torso and folded it back. The head was present, positioned in its normal place. The dead man was now pale white, with hints of spider-like blue veins.

The dead always looked different, Mike thought, *What had he looked like when he was alive?* The dead seemed eternal, somehow, as if their spirits made peace or war on earth and then departed, leaving the body at rest.

Then Dr. Patterson pulled the sheet back up.

"That's Umar al-Husayni," said the princess. "I have another question I must ask. Do you have another body related to this case?"

Mike paused for a second, but held his cards close and decided to see how things unfolded.

He was taken aback for a second, but he'd expected this from her. "How do you know that?" he asked.

"A man died the other day in a shootout in Manhattan. Is he here?"

Mike nodded to Patterson, who led them to another room and another body. This time she pulled the sheet back just enough to reveal the face. The princess looked but said nothing, and they went back upstairs. When Dr. Patterson left them, the princess nodded to her bodyguards, who went to stand on the far side of the room.

"I'm going to have to know soon." Which was a bit of a bluff on his part, as diplomats were under no obligation to answer police questions.

"I'll tell you soon," she said. "But not now."

Mike handed her his card. "How do I get in touch with you?" he said.

"Meet me at Central Park tomorrow, near the castle. Quarter after twelve." She signaled one of her bodyguards, who stood about twenty feet away. He came over and gave Mike her business card. Then she donned a pair of Gucci designer sunglasses, lifted them up, gave Mike a look and walked away.

A short time later, Šahrāzād received an encrypted message on her tablet computer, containing a brief synopsis of Mike's life. He'd grown up in the U.S. and West Germany; his father had worked for the CIA. Detective Michael Charles Maclaymore served in the U.S. Army Special Operations; Green Berets. He'd left for unknown reasons and joined the NYC police. His uncle Aleister was a chief in the department, and had helped Mike's mother to raise him. Mike had traveled a lot as a child, and while in the military. He spoke German, French, Japanese, Russian, Arabic, Persian and Chinese with varying levels of aptitude.

C H A P T E R   1 0

TREASURE CHEST

*For thirty years," he said, "I've sailed the seas and
seen good and bad, better and worse, fair weather
and foul, provisions running out, knives going, and
whatnot. Well, now I tell you, I never seen good come
o' goodness yet. Him as strikes first is my fancy; dead
men don't bite; them's my views—amen, so be it.*

—ROBERT LOUIS STEVENSON, *TREASURE ISLAND*

MIKE HAD GOTTEN A TEXT EARLIER, asking him to
meet an old friend regarding a body found on a beach.
He parked his car in a lot near the beach in Suffolk County.
Sand blew across the black asphalt as he stepped from the car.
In the distance, he saw a father and son with fishing poles,
walking toward the beach. It was striped bass season again.
The child was a bit too small for the nine-foot surf casting rod
he struggled to carry.

Mike had never fished with his son, as he had with his uncle. It was Aleister who'd looked after Mike at that age. His uncle had taken him to Kamchatka, Russia, Alaska and the Northwest Territories for pike, trout and salmon. Mike had wanted to do the same with Chris, but never got the chance. He took out a photo depicting his son Chris on a red sled. Mike remembered that the snow had been hurting Chris's face, so he'd turned away from the sled to face Mike instead. Chris's cheeks were red as they went down the slope. Mike couldn't win; when he thought of Chris he felt pangs of guilt. He didn't want to forget, but suppress the memories just to function. He put the photo away. He hated himself for being so busy at working toward retirement. It was a memory he wanted to have with his own son but never would. He bit his tongue and got to work.

He saw the police about fifty yards away, near the water. Already he could smell that same rotting-flesh death scent he'd encountered too many times before. He made his way to Detective Rogers, who'd left the NYPD for greener pastures. Rogers was African American, six feet and solid, with a round gentle face. "Good to see you again," Mike greeted him. "Thanks for the text about the headless body. Even though it was four a.m."

Rogers wiped gray Long Island sand from his palm and shook Mike's hand. "Well it isn't every day you see a beheaded DOA. And you're not the only one missing sleep."

"I have to find the thread that links them," Mike said. "I think I'm getting used to it. I'm not shocked by anything anymore. Haven't heard from you in a while. How's the big change to Suffolk County PD?"

They both looked up as a sprinkle of water from the sky touched their arms. It looked like rain, but could be just an early morning drizzle. The waves were getting bigger, with more foam as the tide rose, invading the land and pulling it back into the sea. The clouds were red in the sky as the sun started its ascent.

"Better quality of life," Rogers told him. "More pay and less politics. I heard about what happened to you, and I supported you all the way."

"Thanks man. So what do you have?"

"Fisherman found a car. His sonar detector went off and he hauled it up with this pickup truck, thinking the car was filled with silver."

"Why did he think that?" Mike asked.

"Remember a few years ago, that burglary in the Hamptons—millions in jewelry and silverware stolen?"

"Yes. Something over fifty pounds in silverware alone."

"Yep," said Rogers. "The case was never solved and the burglar was never found. But some scuba gear was discovered a month later, about a half mile from this beach."

"Well the fisherman's greed did us a favor," Mike told him. "Time of death?" he asked.

"A week or so."

A few yards away, a large chest sat on the beach beside a rusty car that looked like a Ford. The trunk resembled an old pirate treasure chest, with rusty iron rivets and straps holding the dark lacquered wood together. A few newly arrived surfcasting fishermen looked at the crime scene from afar. One of them took pictures with the zoom on his cell phone. Mike lifted the blue plastic sheet covering the body in the chest. The corpse was wrapped in chains and a red and gold Middle Eastern carpet. It wasn't bloated, but smelled like a horrible mix of salt, shit and rotten meat. The body had no head or hands, so there was no way to reconstruct the face, match dental records or get prints. If they were going to ID the body, it would have to be a DNA match.

The corpse was as blue as dried ink in some places, and pale white in others. The muscles where the head had been cut off were a deep, dark red; almost deep purple. The bones were yellow and black from dirt and metal rust. Large blue veins looked like thick electrical wires.

The cuts were clean, as if done by a surgical saw in the steady hands of a killer with ice for blood. Mike lowered the tarp, took out some antibacterial Purell gel and cleaned his hands.

Every dead body had a story to tell, Mike thought. Some were novels, others poems. We all die, and it happens in a million different ways. Some reach horrific endings, others die in peace; some die cowards and others heroes—but everyone dies. "Any ID?" he asked, already knowing the answer.

"No. We did a whole missing persons database check of different police departments in the tri-state area. And since we got no hands, we got no prints."

Rogers walked over to the car and knelt down. He took out a few cotton swabs and touched dried bloodstains on the car seat. He put the swabs in a bag and zipped it up. "DNA results should come back soon," he said.

"What do you think?" Mike asked.

"I can't say too much right now," Rogers told him.

"I hear you."

"So what kind of car is this rust bucket?" Mike looked at the car. The plates were gone and the VIN number on the door had been partially filed down. Mike used his cell to photograph the partial VIN on the hood, and ran an app to do a search. "Ford Hybrid," he announced. "The partial VIN comes back as registered to Enterprise Rent-a-Car. It does look like a rental, all equipment standardized with nothing personal in the car."

"What's the killer up to?" Rogers asked.

"We have a few possibilities," Mike said. He shook his head in disgust.

Rogers said, "I have to figure all of this out."

Mike took out a piece of gum to chew on. Part of him wanted this to be over, and another part wanted to see this picture that someone else had painted. They were doing these things to create a new image, one that would become the future they imagined.

"You're in over your head," Rogers told him.

"That's the way I like it," Mike said.

"I did some research. This case, the way the body was found, was almost the same exact way a murder happened in *One Thousand and One Arabian Nights*. The story was called *The Three Apples*."

"Tell me more," Mike said, ears perking up.

"It's one of the first murder mysteries, about a man found in a trunk by a fisherman, with chains and a rug," Rogers told him.

"What was the end result?"

"The guilty man was found. After all the movie-thriller twists and turns."

"Why was the person killed in the story?"

"The murderer thought he'd been betrayed. Turned out he was wrong, but by then he'd killed his lover and it was too late."

"What you're saying is, the killers may be looking for a traitor?"

"I don't know," Rogers admitted. "But it's a great way to get rid of a body."

Mike squatted down and looked around the crime scene, pen in his mouth. He popped the gum in his mouth. The truth is in front of us, he thought; it's just fractured by the violence of time. And time rusts truth. It also rusted relationships; his own was more than on the rocks, and he wanted to fix that. After this was over. He did a Yelp search and found an Enterprise Rent-a-Car on the north shore.

A short time later, he walked in the door and made his way to the counter. "I'm the detective you spoke to over the phone." He took out his shield and ID and showed them to the manager.

"I made you copies of his rental agreement and also his driver's license," the manager said. She was smiling as she handed him the papers, but it was a fake smile. Mike looked at the name: Reza Amir. The body in the trunk might now have a face and a name—assuming the body belonged to the guy who'd rented the car, and that the ID was legit. "So what you said to me over the phone is that he renewed via Internet?" Mike asked.

"Yes, that's more common than one would think," the manager said. "What is this all about?"

"An investigation, it's really nothing," Mike told her.

"Really?" she said in a low, fearful tone of voice.

"Yes," he replied, mirroring her tone.

"Does this have to do with what was on TV an hour ago?" she said. "The body found with the car?"

"No, well, I can't say," Mike said. "Excuse me; I have to make a call." He stepped outside and dialed Jack.

"Yes?"

"Run this guy's name: Reza Amir. I have no connection out here to the PD's intranet for name searches. Find out if he's missing."

"Hold on," Jack said. Then, a few moments later: "No one reported him missing."

"Any record of him at all?"

"Hang on a sec . . . He may be a geophysicist with a visa from Germany. The name on the license may not be a full name. Hmm, he might be this guy here, an Iranian national: Reza Amir Rafsanjani, that's all the phonetic search came up with. He may have used a truncated name for the license. He likely used his real name to enter the U.S., now that it's so strict."

"Why would anyone want to kill him or make him disappear if he's just a geophysicist?"

"He's Iranian and involved in the oil and gas business," Jack told him.

"And what does he know?"

"That's the 64,000-dollar question. I really should say the trillion dollar question," Jack corrected himself, "since energy is one of the biggest national security issues."

"Enterprise told me he extended the rental agreement after the estimated time of death," Mike told him. "So police wouldn't be looking for the car or the driver."

"Clever way to delay a report," Jack noted.

CHAPTER 11

THE FALCON AND THE PRINCESS

Shahrazad had perused the books, annals and legends of
preceding Kings, and the stories, examples and instances
of bygone men and things. Indeed it was said that she had
collected a thousand books of histories relating to antique
races and departed rulers. She had perused the works of the
poets and knew them by heart; she had studied philosophy
and the sciences, arts and accomplishments; and she was
pleasant and polite, wise and witty, well read and well bred.
—RICHARD FRANCIS BURTON,
THE BOOK OF THE THOUSAND NIGHTS AND A NIGHT

AT THE FALCONRY EXHIBITION in Central Park, Šahrāzād
stood next to a magnificent hooded falcon that clutched
its perch with razor claws. The event took place by the gray
stone Castle Belvedere. Šahrāzād's bodyguards stood nearby

as Mike walked up the steps. She gave him a smile. She found him handsome with his square jaw, Romanesque nose, dark brown hair and deep-ice eyes. He had a straight posture, an intelligent gaze and a gentle face. He walked over to her as she tended her falcon. He took a bite from a green apple as he came, and when he spoke his voice tasted like her father's: liquid gold. He cleaned his hands with a hand wipe, which made her think he knew something of her culture. He offered his right hand, and they shook.

"*Sabah El-Khair,*" Mike said. Good Morning. His voice was the same as she remembered, like *dhahab* and *asal*: gold and honey. Pure, sweet, honest, good with nothing evil.

"*Arabee?*" said Šahrāzād. Arabic, and he speaks very well. Some hints of Gulf Arabic and Iraqi, as if that were how he'd learned the language. She noticed he was attracted to her but tried to hide it. Also that he hid it very well. He seemed a good man, more subtle and restrained than most. He looked at the scar on her face again, and she saw that he wondered how it had come to be there.

"*Baa'ref Arabee Showayya,*" Mike told her. I speak Arabic, a little.

"*Nicht schlecht,*" she replied in German. Not bad. "*Wo hast du Deutsch lernen?*" Where did you learn German?

"*Meine Mutter ist Deutsch und Russisch.*" My mother is German and Russian.

His German was also good; clean and crisp with not much of an American accent. Very Berlin-ish, she thought. The sounds tasted crisp, burnt—like a good hot meal on a cold day.

"*Und Sie?*" And you? Mike asked.

"*Schweiz.*" Switzerland, she said.

"I have many questions."

"Go ahead," she said.

"It makes no sense for you to burn your time on this, so—why?"

The princess was taken aback by this, but didn't consider it an insult. More like a direct question. His voice still tasted like gold, but a hot gold. He had no ill intentions. She sensed by his voice that he didn't quite trust her, which was understandable. "There is a falconry exhibition starting at two. A few more are going to show up and do some demonstrations for the general public. But to your question: this is part of who I am, and the history of my country. I understand you're saying it's a hobby, but it's an art and also a science. We need to do more things that don't make sense, to make greater sense of the world.

"Ask yourself, what is it that the falcon does? I trained him to hunt, but it's also part of his instinct; I just made some minor adjustments in regards to conditioning. That's what all of us do every day. We are what we are, as Lord Tennyson would say, but with adjustments we become better, more focused with the details."

"Well said," Mike replied. "Why were you the one to identify Umar, the diplomat? You're a royal."

"He was my friend and my cousin, and he was murdered."

"How did you know about the other man in the morgue?" Mike asked.

"It's my job to know these things. We are investigating a few people in our government. I can't say too much about it. Can you tell me what time it is?" She glanced at the black paramilitary watch on Mike's left wrist, with its glowing green numbers.

"Just after noon. What does your name mean?" Šahrāzād noticed him watching her as she ran her hands through her long flowing black hair. She sneaked a second look at him, and saw that he'd caught her in the act. "It is an Arabized name of Persian origin, from my father's favorite book, *Arabian Nights*.

"As the story goes, King Shahryar believed all women to be unfaithful, and had executed all of his past wives after one night of marriage. But each night, the Persian Queen Scheherazade would tell the king a story without an ending. To hear the rest, he had to keep her alive for another day."

"How does the story end?" Mike asked. His voice now a cooler gold. He seemed to become more trusting. "The stories of *One Thousand and One Arabian Nights* are metaphors and lessons on human nature."

Mike smiled. "Falconry. Beautiful bird," Mike said.

"This is a really interesting sport. It's thousands of years old. Do you want to hold him?"

"Depends. Will he tear out my eyes?" Mike regarded the bird's razor-like claws and sharp beak as it sat on its perch.

"No, he's very well trained. Birds of prey are intelligent, with large brains. In fact, the brain-to-body-size ratio of some birds is huge. Parrots are the smartest; some can form short basic sentences. Ravens can solve puzzles. These saker falcons are trained with operant conditioning, using a food reward as positive reinforcement."

"What's its name?" Mike asked. The tan and gold Saker falcon turned its head toward him and opened its menacing gray beak.

The princess carefully removed the hood from the falcon's head, and the bird's large black eyes blinked. Šahrāzād smiled. "Muninn, which means memory." He was still hiding his attraction; he wasn't the type of man who would fall for a woman right away. Still, she sensed that he was lonely, secretly in crushing pain of some kind. His voice, the various flavors of gold, brought out so much. He looked at her, aware that she was reading him, but not in a hostile way.

"Is that Arabic?" Mike asked.

"Norse. Muninn is one of Odin's ravens."

"It's perfectly designed," Mike said, looking at the falcon.

"By nature," Šahrāzād added. "You should put a gauntlet on."

"You mean a glove?" Mike said, reaching for the glove under the falcon's perch.

"We call it a gauntlet. We use it so our hands don't get sliced up by the talons. Let me hold your apple." Šahrāzād took it from him with her right hand, and took a quick bite.

"I didn't say you could taste it!" Mike said. He grabbed the soft black leather gauntlet and put it on his left hand.

"I didn't think you would mind." Šahrāzād flashed a mischievous grin as she chewed the sweet fruit.

"I don't," Mike told her.

"Put your hand near his perch," Šahrāzād instructed. The bird climbed onto his hand and sank its powerful talons into the gauntlet.

"Whatever you do, move slowly." She touched Mike's arm, and he caught her sneaking a glance at the bicep bulging beneath his sleeve.

"What are those things on its legs?" Mike asked.

"Those are grommeted leather straps called jesses or kangaroos; the one on the right leg is a mini-GPS, the other one is its tether." She saw a bright, fluorescent orange hornet land on the falcon perch. It made a figure eight, and just as quickly buzzed away.

"Does it mind being tethered?" Mike asked.

"No, but does anyone like being caught?"

"I guess it depends on who does the catching," Mike replied. "So why am I here?"

"Umar was a good friend. In fact, he was a great friend and the son of the man my father trusts most. I'm also best friends with Umar's sister Aaliyah. Umar may have been killed looking into something. My father, the king, will be here in New York City in a few days. I would prefer to tell him the news in person, but I'm sure he already knows . . . How many have you killed?" she asked, seemingly out of the blue.

"Seventy-seven confirmed kills," Mike replied. "Have you killed?"

Her gaze was steady, and she paused for a full second before answering. "Yes."

"Wolves eat dogs in this world," Mike told her. "I'm sure you had to."

"I wish it wasn't necessary, but it is."

"It's what we are and always will be."

"It shouldn't have to be, but it is," she said.

"We both have the scars to prove it," Mike noted.

"Do we change the world or does the world change us?" the princess asked.

"Both, I think . . . So you want me to catch this guy who killed your friend."

"Yes. Take this." She gave him a red apple from her bag.

"I prefer Granny Smiths," he said.

"You'll like this one. I had my people get information on the man you killed. It's on a mini flash drive inside the apple. You should go now."

He held the apple in his hand for a full second, then put it in a pocket and nodded his thanks. "If you have anything else, call me," he said, and shook her hand before leaving.

To Šahrāzād, his hands were electric, wired with emotions pulsing in his veins. He had so much going in his mind. She saw so much; he lived so many lives in this one life.

Later, riding in the back of her limousine, she decided she wanted to know more about him. He was suppressing some part of himself, and that made him a mystery. She had to know more.

She turned around to look at her hooded falcon in its cage. She typed Detective Michael Charles Maclaymore's name into her encrypted cell phone, surfing the secure Internet. She found articles with titles like *Cop's son killed by mysterious unknown assassin called the Ghost of Rahman, Cop's Mother Killed by Russian Mobster Vronsky,* and another article: *Cop's Family Had Ties to Russian Gangster During Cold War. Father of Cop was CIA.* She skimmed through one, reading "Vronsky, who died this year, was a former Russian military intelligence officer turned mobster stationed in East Berlin, who allegedly purchased secrets relating to the 'Star Wars' and 'Project Thor' programs during the Cold War. He was allegedly one of the biggest heroin dealers in the world, along with Tamerlaine of Central Asia."

Both figures had purportedly made hundreds of millions trading diamonds for heroin, which was then traded for human sex slaves they trafficked from Saint Petersburg to the Middle East. Vronsky owned many of the biggest diamond mines in the world. Owing to his political connections, he was never prosecuted for his alleged crimes. His son was a high-ranking member of the Spetsnaz. Šahrāzād thought for a moment. She disliked spying on others and using her gifts, but now she had to, because she didn't know who to trust. One of her bodyguards gave her a folder. "You may want to look at this," he said. "A few phone calls were made to get this." She opened the folder and gazed at all of the redacted words on the files inside. She skimmed the pages. The upshot was that Michael Charles Maclaymore had been part of a CIA team in Afghanistan, over 15 years ago . . .

CHAPTER 12

OCEANS OF OIL AND THE SILK ROAD

I did not write half of what I saw,
for I knew I would not be believed.

—MARCO POLO

MIKE'S SQUAD ROOM DESK was covered in clear plastic, the floor around it hidden by sheets and towels. Painters applied coats of eggshell white on one wall and powder blue on another. The room's small desk fans hummed back and forth, drying the latex paint. The smell was faint, but still there even with the windows open. "Two more days, detective," one of the painters told him, wrapping up for the day.

"Thanks."

"See you tomorrow." The painters left.

Mike surfed the Internet with his iPad. He wanted to learn more about Middle Eastern history. We're guided by our pasts, he thought. To see the future clearly, one must look at the past with an unfiltered lens. He read about the history of Persia, Saudi Arabia, the Wahhabis, the Assassins, Saladin and the Crusades, Amarco, Hubbert's Peak Oil Theory, Triffin's dilemma, the Iranian revolution, the failed Siege of Mecca by the Mahdist revolutionaries in 1979 and the Soviet Invasion of Afghanistan. He also read about Nixon taking the U.S. off the gold standard, and his deal with Saudi Arabia: the U.S. would always be the first buyer, and the Saudis would accept payment from all parties only in U.S. dollars.

"How long is this office mess going to last?" Wellerin said, coming into the room. He seemed more tense than usual, but Mike didn't say anything about it. Department morale was horrible and always had been, and the city was as thankless as ever. Mike set the iPad down and massaged his eyes to give them a break from the fatigue of research. Wellerin got a cup of coffee and stared at the plastic.

Eva came into the squad room seconds later, handing Mike a small square piece of paper. Mike looked it over. "So I got the detail for dignitary security on Madison Avenue?" he asked. "Two people mentioned that *soiree* to me this week."

"I had that last year," Wellerin told him. "It's on East Side Avenue. We shouldn't have to do these, we're so short-handed. I got thirty cases building up."

"Security is just a reason to get in the door," Eva said. "It's part of the investigation; see what you can get." She looked to

Mike. "The detail is an easy gig. A bunch of bigwig hotshots show up: Iranians, Saudis, Libyans, Egyptians, Turks. Plenty of oil and gas industry folks. Even the King of Saudi Arabia."

"Is Jack going to this?" Mike asked.

"Not his time. He's still busy updating the Ring of Steel. Not a lot of cops with engineering degrees. I'll be back in a sec." Eva disappeared into her office.

"So," Wellerin said, "you're going to a party but minus the alcohol. You can hang out with royalty while we plebeians man the fort." He brushed the lint from his red tie.

"There's truth to that, comrade," Mike told him. "We cops are pawns of politicians."

Wellerin looked at him. "Did you like that magazine subscription I sent you, *Modern Drunkard?* Badda bing! And may I ask if you've ever considered penis enlargement surgery?"

"Your soon-to-be ex-wife told me you needed it." Mike said.

Wellerin's cell rang. "I got to go and do some real police work, AKA an investigation. You know, the place you forgot about—that we, I mean I, am staking out for you? AKA the lost art of this job that no one cares about?" Wellerin left the squad room.

Eva came out of her office a few moments later. She sat down next to Mike while he was reading an intelligence report. He poured a cup of coffee for himself, then offered it to her. She took a sip and set the cup down next to him.

"Is this gig official?" Mike asked.

She paused, and didn't answer right away. "Yes and no."

"I trust you, but when the committees come and subpoena us for answers . . ."

"I know," Eva said. "Anyway, in a few days I'll get you access to a new data mining computer program at 26 Federal Plaza." She put her hand in his pocket, took out a pack of gum and popped a piece in her mouth.

"You could have asked," Mike said.

"Ask if I have bad breath? You would have said no." Eva smiled. "Anyway, from what I hear, this new computer program can take small pieces of information and build trees of information around them. Did you get anything new?"

"We just got results back, and we did get one print off the front door of the raid apartment. The print belongs to a man tried for check fraud about 15 years ago. It doesn't match any of the dead bodies. Must be an unknown person still at large . . . You've always sensed my impatience."

"I know. Anything else?"

"Nothing so far. This case is going to take too long, and a plot is still in play. I just don't like the fact that the DOAs at the raid were professionals, ghosts, off-the-map, invisible people with no concrete identities, even fake ones."

Eva noted. "Probably the identities of dead people."

"We might not have much time," Mike said, "The only good news is that the ghosts are leads."

"We should assume the worst," Eva told him.

"Agreed."

Eva looked around and leaned close to whisper. He liked the closeness. "What about Detective Wellerin? Doesn't he have a Persian girlfriend?"

"This is McCarthyism," Mike said. "He's been staking out that address he found longer than Jack and me combined and squared. He's doing me a big favor."

"You didn't address my point. I just need to make sure we don't get burned."

"I know," Mike said. "We never answered that question."

"Which one?"

"Where do we go from here?" Mike said.

"I don't know what to think," Eva said. "You need to move forward."

"I want to, but . . ."

"I understand."

"After all of this is done, I'll put in my papers," Mike told her.

"Just because I'm civil with you doesn't mean I'm not—"

"It was a bad time for both of us," he said, cutting her off. "By the way I saw that princess. She's really pretty. Stunning, in fact. You met her in Central Park?"

"Business," Mike said. His tone was low, almost a grumble.

"Okay."

"So anyway, what's the new password to the intranet?" he asked.

Eva looked at him. She was going to say something, but then he changed the subject. She handed him a slip of paper with the password written on it. She came closer and sipped his coffee. Then her cell rang. She checked the screen. "I have to take this call," she said. "I'll see you later."

Mike looked again at his iPad, and then looked up. He checked her out as she left, watching the sway of her hips, her hair, her walk, body, personality—everything. She turned around and glanced back to catch him looking at her, then tossed her hair as she walked away.

Mike refocused on the task at hand. He put down his iPad and looked at the upper-right corner of his computer monitor, which showed the most recent counter-terrorism news: a group of Al Qaeda had left Pakistan after the government was toppled, and were wanted by Interpol. Millions of dollars in gold bullion had disappeared from the Pakistani central bank after the overthrow of the government. Nuclear materials were said to be missing, though the Pakistanis denied this and were in fact the chief suspects.

He looked at the screen, which told him Umar had been part of a group seeking to reform The Kingdom. He put the princess's flash drive into the USB port on the computer. He opened up a .docx file with the filename "Felani Yaroo and Khalid Zahrani Khorasani." Mike then logged into a police database on the department intranet and searched "Felani Yaroo."

"Felani Yaroo," he said to himself. The name was linked to Iran, from years ago. The data before him said Yaroo worked for a bank in Kish, Iran.

Only one link came up. When he clicked on it, it told him that Felani Yaroo was the Persian equivalent of John Doe. He then checked for Khalid Zahrani: nothing. Finally, he looked at another name on the disk and punched in the name Sa'id al-Dussari—but again he found nothing. Had the princess lied to him? Or maybe the names weren't in this database, and he'd have to check another. If this was a real lead, he'd have to figure out the puzzle.

For the moment, he was back to square one. He ran another search on a secure intranet and found that a Khalid Khorasani was connected to an extremist group in Iran. The name itself didn't make sense, because Zahrani was Arabic and Khorasani was Persian. A photo came up, but the face was different. Maybe he was switching IDs?

Mike typed in the dead diplomat's name: "Umar al-Husayni." It took a few seconds for the results to pop up. Umar might have been a member of the Liberal Princes, an organization that favored radically reforming Saudi Arabia into a secular modern state.

Next he typed in "Šahrāzād." He saw a photo of her in a traditional black *Abaya* cloak that left only her face exposed. There was a scar on her cheek. In the photograph, the sky was a perfect blue, and the dunes behind her were reddened by a colorful sunset. There was an article about a car bomb years back; the queen had been killed by fundamentalists, and her daughter—Šahrāzād—had been injured. That explained the scar. The attackers were part of a group that sought to over-throw The Kingdom and set up a orthodox theocracy, just like the Mahdists in Mecca in 1979.

Šahrāzād was now the CFO of Amarco, Arabia's state-owned oil drilling and processing enterprise. Another article said she'd given money to pro-secular human rights and pro-democracy groups around the world, and that she was an amateur photographer who'd taken photos for National Geographic around the world. She held degrees in finance and evolutionary psychology.

Clicking on the latter term, he found it was an approach to psychology that included natural sciences, and viewed traits and perceptions, language and social aspects of human natural as traits that are evolutionary adaptations. He thought for a moment. The princess was secular.

He then clicked on the link for her brother Sayf; he had a degree in history, was an avid martial artist, had served in the Saudi Arabian military for over a decade and donated millions to various charities around the world. He clicked on another link to another website containing the name of the princess's brother Sayf. He'd been a Special Forces soldier for The Kingdom, with extensive training. He had a B.A. in history from Harvard and Ph.D. from Cambridge. He'd given money to the Red Crescent and supported various other charities. He currently served as one of Amarco's board members.

He did another search and clicked on the word Amarco. The company was the richest corporation in the world, worth more than a trillion dollars. It was essentially a state within a state.

A few minutes later, another headline on a different website showed a small digital video clip of an oil operation in Arabia. The website said that Amarco was about to purchase controlling shares in Exxon and several other oil and gas companies. One of the financial websites alleged that Iran was lowering their oil output, and to counteract that The Kingdom of Saudi Arabia—referred to as KSA—would raise their own output over the coming year.

He saw the word "bourse" and clicked on it. Apparently, the *bourse* program was Iranian, and traded oil in gold and non-U.S. currencies. Since the government of Saudi Arabia still had billions in U.S. government bonds, it did not view this favorably.

"What's up, Mike?" Jack said, coming in behind him.

"'Sup, Jack?" Mike replied. The veins on the sides of Jack's forehead popped out as he chewed tobacco.

"What are ya workin' on?" Jack asked, then spit some nicotine-laced tobacco juice into a plastic bottle.

Mike showed him a photo of Šahrāzād. Jack looked at the monitor. "Wow, I'd hit it."

"She's even more gorgeous in person," Mike told him. "You just can't not be dickish, can you?"

"Nope."

Mike got up to stretch his legs.

A detective opened a door and called in. "Jack! ADA Swanson is calling."

"Tell him I'll be there in a sec." Jack walked off into another room.

Mike looked over the photos above Jack's desk: pictures of Egypt's pyramids and Luxor, Hagia Sofia in Turkey, Red Square in Russia, The Wailing Wall in Israel, Christ the Redeemer in Brazil, and dozens of Irish castles. There was also a photo of Jack's soon-to-be wife. She looked exotic.

A few minutes later Mike saw Jack in the hallway, and walked with him to the elevator. They didn't say anything to each other; both were preoccupied with their own swirling thoughts. The doors swished open, then snapped shut behind them. The lights in the elevator dimmed as they descended. The doors opened, and they walked into another hallway.

Mike's cell rang. He picked up. "We got a hit!" Wellerin said on the phone. "Two male suspects at the address from the raid site brochure. One of them is leaving right now. And by the way it's an Iranian front."

Mike tapped Jack on the shoulder. "Activity at the stakeout. And an Iranian front!"

"Huh?" Jack said.

"The address on the brochure?"

"Yes, now I remember."

"You there?" Wellerin asked.

"Yes," Mike responded.

"Two suspects drove up a few minutes ago. One of them just left. Someone's sitting on the other."

"Follow the guy who left," Mike told him.

"Doing it now, boss." He gave Mike the details.

Mike turned to Jack. "He just crossed the Queensboro bridge, going into Manhattan."

Jack nodded. "I'll have the car in front of the precinct in a minute."

"Ten-four," Mike said to both Wellerin and Jack, and hung up.

Mike ran back to the squad room and put on his jacket. He took a small bag with an extra hat and sunglasses, grabbed his radio and ran out the door.

"Be safe," Eva said as they passed in the hall.

"I will!" He was out the door a moment later. Jack pulled up, and he slipped into the car.

CHAPTER 13

THE WORLD IS A BEAUTIFUL VASE FILLED WITH SCORPIONS

Homo homini lupus est.
Man is a wolf to his fellow man.

S AYF SAT AT AN OUTDOOR TABLE in front of a smoke-filled café and hookah lounge in Strasbourg, sipping Turkish coffee. The French city was beautiful, its intricate medieval architecture a cultural fusion of Germany and France. The two nations had almost merged during the days of Charlemagne, but geography, weak decentralized government, time and the catalyst of history had kept them separate. Still, the beauty remained: the proud statue of General Kléber, the gothic sandstone Cathedrals, the black and white timber-framed buildings and medieval cobblestone streets. Each building seemed designed as a work of art, its purpose to keep the identity of Europe alive.

Sayf held three gold coins in his hand, each from various rulers of the Middle Ages. One was from the Mughal dynasty, Akbar; another from Saladin, the Kurdish warrior who defeated the Crusaders; the third from Suliyman, the greatest of the sultans of the Ottoman Empire.

Coins were the first means of mass political propaganda, with their slogans, art and faces of men who'd lived and died—most of whom had now been forgotten by all but a few well-learned individuals like Sayf himself. When it was all over, would that be all he left behind? Was that the most he could hope for—to reach the pinnacle of success, only to be frozen in time and the pages of history? He put the coins in his pocket and looked at a map of the Middle East. It showed the entire area, including Iran, in green and black—all under his own flag. Arrows pointed toward Europe, Asia and Africa.

Sayf looked up at the gray stone building beside the café, and the vines clinging to its walls. A centuries-old gargoyle perched on a corner, smirking down at him. What are we, Sayf thought, but a collection, a patchwork, a magnificent loom of our memories, all sewn together in the thread of our own narrative? That is what all men were; stories woven of lies and truths. The statues, languages, arts, these were just mere signposts, symbols of our history—a written testament to the collective memory of a society, a narrative of political identity.

These people would soon be conquered; they had declining demographics and no pride in their past, and were ashamed of their identity and history. They didn't remember the Opium Wars, and now I'll do it to them. Drugs are weapons, ideas are weapons, history is a weapon, money is a weapon, words are weapons and I use these as tools in The New Opium Wars and The New Great Game. The world is a chess board, and people are pawns in the game of life. It helps that with every generation, the West grows weaker. Their patriotism, morality and spiritual life are all broken, and soon enough they will be destroyed from within.

To change history, one must change memory itself. But it was the will of God that made men great or insignificant, rich or poor. He looked around and saw young men watching a flat screen television: a soccer match between Iran and The Kingdom of Saudi Arabia. Old men sat in a group along the walls of the lounge, patiently smoking from blue-colored hookah pipes—octopi of tubes and water-filled glass bowls that filtered burning fruits and herbs.

Sayf's phone rang, "How did the meetings go?" the king asked him.

"We secured a few good oil deals," Sayf told his father, "and my sister is going to have Amarco buy a few companies in the U.S. This will help us get cheaper oil and increase our margins."

"Good."

"How's New York?" Sayf inquired.

"Not as hot, and a much needed break."

"Now I must return to The Kingdom and settle a few accounts and contracts," Sayf told him.

"Fill me in on the good news then," his father said. "You are three steps ahead of everyone."

"I see things as they are" Sayf said, and hung up. He'd seen the same car drive past twice in the last 10 minutes, almost if someone was trying to ensure a positive ID. This made him uneasy. Sayf took a drink from his Turkish coffee, then turned and looked across the street. One of his bodyguards—Mustafa—was nearby, wearing dark sunglasses that covered his eye patch. He'd lost that eye in Afghanistan. Mustafa was dressed like an older tourist, in jeans and a collared shirt, with an American baseball cap covering his salt and pepper hair.

Mustafa looked at him and nodded slightly, his lips moving to say "two." In between the parked cars, two clean-shaven men in black suits with dark sunglasses were reaching into their jackets. Very military or ex-military. A third and fourth man were already on the sidewalk across the street, behind a black SUV.

Sayf felt his face flush with blood. His eyes were hot and his skin tingled with fear. He touched his side; his compact .40 caliber HK was still there in its holster. He pulled it out. He heard the distinct whizzing sound of an RPG from above as Mustafa led him into the coffee shop.

"I'll be back!" Mustafa said, leaving him inside.

Two more bodyguards jumped from the back of the SUV to defend him. Shots rang out, and bullets whizzed by Sayf's head.

An explosion rumbled. Concrete and rock dust clouded the air like morning fog. Burnt and bloody arms and legs littered the area. The people in the café screamed and ran in all directions, emptying the shop. The two clean-shaven men were now on the sidewalk, their bodies twisted and contorted in pools of their own blood: would-be assassins who'd met their own ends instead.

The other men from across the street had taken cover behind the engine blocks of parked cars. They started firing. Sayf looked to his right and saw that another bodyguard lay next to him, his pink brains leaking onto the floor.

A fusillade of bullets came his way. Sayf took cover and fired a few return rounds, downing two of the gunmen with perfect headshots. Another man fired in his direction. Sayf fired back, killing the attacker. Mustafa came back and led him out through the rear of the café, into a waiting SUV. The car surged forward. Thirty feet ahead, a black van drove in front of them and stopped. Its driver jumped out and ran away.

"It's a trap!" one of the bodyguards yelled. Sayf put his hands in front of him to stop his head from smashing into the seat as the SUV braked hard. The driver put the car in reverse and floored the gas, spinning the car around. Shifting into drive, he accelerated in the opposite direction.

Another van stopped fifty feet ahead, its driver bailing. A bodyguard gave Sayf a Kevlar vest. Fearing another rocket attack, they left the SUV. Sayf stayed low to the ground as bullets hissed past him. He heard police sirens in the distance, getting closer. The attackers disappeared as fast as they'd come.

Sayf felt his neck; a bullet had gouged a bloody trough in the skin. "*Neik,*" he cursed. It felt like a hot iron had branded him. He looked at the blood on his hand. He was so close to success, he couldn't die now. He'd done too much, waited too long. Decades. He needed to create his empire. And he needed to find out who wanted him dead.

"*Salaam alikam,* you shall live through this," he said to himself.

"An ambulance is here with a police car right behind," a bodyguard told him.

"Where's he hit?" the EMS worker said before he got close enough to see. Two policemen ran up right behind him. The head bodyguard flashed his diplomatic ID. "We are diplomats from Saudi Arabia; the king's son just survived an attempted assassination."

One of the officers got on the radio and called it in.

"Anyone get a good look at them or their vehicle?" the other Strasbourg cop asked in French.

A bodyguard answered. "Black SUV Benz, I do not remember the plate. Several men in suits, some European-looking, a few Middle Eastern, maybe Turkish or Israeli. Two of them are dead across the street." He didn't mention that some of Sayf's bodyguards were already searching for the attackers.

"You're lucky, just a nick," an EMS worker said, treating Sayf's neck. "Are you a gambling man?"

Sayf watched as his own blood stained the medieval street. "It is the will of Fate," Sayf said. "There is no such thing as luck."

The medic ran back to his ambulance to get something. Sayf answered his vibrating cell.

"Four of them are dead," Mustafa told him from thirty feet away; too far for the medic to hear either of them on the phone.

"Good."

"And I caught another. He's in the back of one of our SUVs right now, bound and sedated." Mustafa gazed at his own hands, which had specks of blood on them.

Sayf smiled. "Even better. Whoever did this has their ledger red with their own blood."

"I will find out who is behind this and kill them," Mustafa said, and threw a disinfecting cloth on the ground. It was brown with the blood from his hands.

"I have faith that our success will come to pass," Sayf told him. He looked at the silver coin of Tamerlaine in his hand. It was covered in blood.

CHAPTER 14

KNIGHTS AND CASTLES OF CENTRAL PARK

In hoc signo vinces, "In this sign you will conquer."
—CONSTANTINE I

MIKE AND JACK RACED ACROSS Central Park on Eighty-Fifth, turning south on Fifth Avenue to follow Wellerin's suspect. Adrenaline and anxiety dripped into Mike's stomach, giving him a small electrical jolt; that feeling of what might happen, what could happen, what should happen if . . .

"Where's this all going to lead?" Jack asked.

"I don't know. But we may have someone alive who's linked to the raid site." This was a race through a maze, where each turning point of information brought them closer to the end point—if the clock didn't run out before they got there.

"We can't arrest him for material support too soon, or it could fuck everything up," Jack said.

Mike answered his cell; it was Wellerin. "He's in Upper East Side Manhattan, going West," Wellerin told him.

"Fucker is on the move," Mike said to Jack.

Wellerin gave him the play-by-play on the phone. "Suspect near Hunter College and the 19th Precinct right now, going north."

Jack raced across Manhattan like an Indy 500 driver, weaving in and out of traffic like a driver on hell's wheels. Mike put the phone on speaker.

"He's driving a hybrid Toyota," Wellerin told them. "Black four-door sedan, New York plate Charlie Victor Adam 7,3,3,1. Comes back to Hertz rentals from Pennsylvania. He's slowing down; I'm three car lengths away from him. He turned, now going westbound on East 79th street."

"This is fucking great," Mike said.

"Now going North on Third Avenue," Wellerin said a minute later. "Now going toward the Metropolitan Museum of Art. Slowing down. Looks like he's parking."

"Thanks, I'm going on foot," Mike said. "More in a minute." He hung up.

"What the fuck!" Jack spotted the suspect stepping from a car across the street. "This guy shops at Banana Republic?"

"Everyone around here is a tourist; he fits in," Mike said.

Jack found a quick parking spot. "Be my backup," Mike told him. "I'm going to shadow him. We'll switch it up later."

He put on a NY Yankees cap and a pair of Ray-Ban sunglasses, and got out of the car. He stuffed a second pair of sunglasses and a FDNY baseball cap in his fanny pack.

"I got your back," Jack said, and rolled up the window.

Mike called Wellerin back. "I'm very close, in sight," he said. "I have a visual. He's near the Met and going into Central Park."

"He's wearing a black baseball cap," Wellerin told him, "and a traveler's vest. Camera and a small backpack, he's 5'11"and looks like a solid 180."

"I see him, got a lock on our guy," Mike said, nodding as Wellerin drove past. Mike caught a glimpse of the suspect's face as he turned: lean and military-looking. Mike was now scanning behind him every few seconds, just to make sure no one was shadowing him or the suspect.

The suspect walked along the north side of the Metropolitan Museum of Art and entered Central Park. Mike kept his distance, staying thirty feet back, keeping his footsteps in sync. He saw the man put something on the grass, near the sixty-eight-foot-tall Egyptian obelisk called "Cleopatra's Needle." The suspect walked away, took a piece of tape or something similar, and put it on a black iron lamppost in a way that would hide it from the casual observer. He then walked westbound on the winding trail to a field of grass, the Great Lawn in Central Park.

Mike hung back, avoiding the suspect's field of vision as best he could; endeavoring not to be a repeat pedestrian to his mark. He passed the twenty-foot-tall black metal statue of King Jagiello of Poland, crossing his righteous swords in celebration of his victory over the Teutonic Knights. Mike saw a small scratch near the base of the black iron lamppost nearby.

He watched as the suspect sat on a bench and pulled out a cell phone. He played with the phone as if surfing the Internet. After a moment, he got up and walked around. His path seemed absent-minded, but after a moment Mike realized it was a search pattern. The man was looking at his cell the whole time. It occurred to Mike that he was looking for a short-range wireless connection—some type of electronic dead drop.

Mike brought up his own phone, using his hacker apps to scan the area and find the suspect's cell. He saw it accessing a secure encrypted network and downloading encrypted data from the wireless dead drop. The man's cell was both a sophisticated secure cell and a regular cell phone, each with wireless networking. Mike scanned the other man's phone; it did have a firewall, but a weak one. Mike's app shielded his own cell, so the suspect couldn't see it. Mike's hack confirmed that the man's phone was unable to see his own cell.

Why go out in public instead of emailing? Mike wondered. No possible interception, for one thing, which could happen on a computer network. Wireless connections died within 100–150 feet, and the wireless computer was usually set to turn off once accessed—which was an excellent way to avoid detection. Unless of course the user was being shadowed by someone like Mike. Everything carried a risk.

The man walked west toward a small round building: the Delacorte Theater. He entered the bathroom on the far side of the path. Mike stayed back and bought a drink from the hot dog vendor about thirty feet away, then sat down on a bench. He wasn't sure if the suspect was going to take off, or go to another spot. He checked his watch and waited, while the suspect stayed in the bathroom for ten minutes. A text came in from Jack: "We lost sight of you."

"I'm near the theater," Mike texted back.

"I see you now," Jack texted.

The man exited the bathroom and looked around. He now wore a new shirt—and a mustache. He was attempting to dry clean any follows, Mike saw. He trailed the man to Eighty-First Street and Central Park West, and texted his location to Jack.

The suspect crossed the street. Mike watched carefully from a distance, making sure he wouldn't be seen and checking to make sure he wasn't being followed himself. So far, the suspect had good dry cleaning, trying to make sure he wasn't trailed. Mike kept a greater distance than normal.

A black limo pulled up in front of the Museum of Natural History, and the suspect got in. A few seconds later, Jack pulled up with the unmarked car and picked Mike up. Another unmarked police car followed them, two cars back. "Where the hell is this guy going?" Jack said. "We have another car, right?"

Mike nodded. "Do we know who he is?"

"Not yet," Jack told him.

Mike kept his eyes on the road as the limo went southbound, toward Midtown Manhattan. They went around Columbus Circle. The massive towers at Ten Columbus Circle were graffiti'd and run-down. Hundreds of windows were broken, and hadn't been fixed for years. The silver metal globe on the north side of the street was rusting away. The Circle itself was filled with pedicabs, street gangs, low-level drug dealers and skelly prostitutes. "The bad old days of New York City are back, it's like that movie *The Warriors*," Mike said, shaking his head. "Switch it up, everyone," he said into the radio.

Mike and Jack slowed down and disengaged the follow, letting the car behind them take over while they stayed back. The idea was to keep anyone in the suspect vehicle from seeing the same car in the mirror for too long.

The limo stopped at Park Avenue and East 42nd Street: Grand Central Station. "He's going to meet someone," Mike said.

The suspect stepped from the car in new clothes, wearing a backpack. The guy was a professional, assuming surveillance even when he didn't see it. He'd lost the camera and mustache, added a hat and business suit, and silver mirror-shades. Mike put on a thin fleece pullover, changed his hat and sunglasses, and left his fanny pack in the car. He was still a guy in a baseball cap and shades, but it helped just enough as he set out on foot. He saw Jack home in on a parking spot across the street, while the unmarked car with Wellerin followed the limo. He wished they had more manpower to position units ahead of possible locations where suspect might stop, but he had to go with what they had.

Mike kept back at all times, following at an angle. The suspect appeared calm, a real pro. But what was he doing? He stopped at the coffee shop outside Grand Central. He lingered but didn't reconnoiter; he was all confidence now.

Mike thought about how much the city had changed through the years. Grand Central used to be like a Galleria mall; now it was turning into skid row. He watched the suspect bring a cell phone to his ear.

The suspect took a few pictures with his cell—like any other tourist—and walked away. Mike didn't like it, as he might show up in the background. The suspect looked around to see if he was being followed. Mike kept some extra distance for a few minutes, took a picture of his own and with encrypted email on his cell sent it out to the facial recognition database. He saw Jack on his phone, walking by across the street. He blended in well, looking more like a stockbroker than a cop. Mike ducked into a coffee shop and put on a wig from his small backpack, along with a baseball cap. He added a press-on mustache from his jacket pocket.

The man went into the station, then downstairs, through the food courtyard and into the bathroom. Mike followed, pretending to take a leak as the man went into a stall at the end and locked the door. Jack came in, wearing a hat and fake latex nose. He washed his hands and left.

Mike saw another man in a suit exit the stall beside the suspect's, with the same exact backpack the suspect had been wearing. Mike pretended to drop a pen, checking beneath the stall door as he bent to pick it up. It was a hand-off he hadn't seen. Mike took a picture of the mirror in the bathroom as the second man—shorter and stockier that the first—walked by, and texted it to Wellerin. This made the investigation deeper and more complex; more actors in play, their plot steaming forward like a machine while all Mike could do was watch and wonder what the hell was happening. He texted Jack about the hand-off, and told him to follow the second suspect. Jack confirmed.

Mike saw the first suspect leave the stall and wash his hands. Mike kept his distance. It helped that the bathroom was large, with lots of people coming and going. It was easier to blend in here than it would have been in the smaller Central Park restroom. Mike noticed the backpack was gone from the stall, confirming the hand-off. He washed his hands and followed at a distance as the suspect walked back up the ramp to the main concourse. Mike strode past the spherical, brass-and-steel Grand Central clock. Businessmen and women walked to and fro on their rat race treadmills, chasing mirages called dreams.

Mike kept twenty to thirty feet away, matching the suspect's brisk pace as they left the station. The crowds on the sidewalks grew thicker as they moved into Times Square. The sea of people ranged from a homeless man with a shopping cart full of bottles and cans, to filthy drug addicts, small packs of the endangered wholesome American family, and of course the tourists from Europe and Asia with their ever-present digital cameras, taking photos of the Square and the locals. He saw a veteran of one of America's many wars, holding up a sign. He seemed legit.

Mike reflected on the absurdity of it all—this case, the war, the society he lived in, these strange pockets of extreme wealth, tall buildings amid the poverty of homelessness. Yet in the war he now fought, it was not about survival of the fittest, but survival of the luckiest—as if life was a lottery ticket, and time the big payday. Yet in the midst of this Kafkaesque city, everyone was struggling and clawing their way in the true Darwinian fashion, seeking their piece of a fading American dream. What was he really defending? He pushed aside those thoughts and refocused.

The sides of many buildings bore massive flat screen billboards, an endless array of vivid pulsing scenes and magical marketing directed at the sea of people below. The crowds no longer looked to where they were going, but up at displays of unreachable dreams.

Mike's quarry reached the Times Square subway station. The way he went down the steps made Mike think he suspected a tail. Mike took off the wig, baseball cap and mustache and threw them away. He dialed Jack on his cell. "I'm going in the hole," he told him, and put the phone on speaker.

"Ten-four," Jack replied.

The subway station was filled with thousands of people, all coming and going. A homeless man jangled a tin cup, while another played a fiddle next to him. Mike caught a look at the suspect, fifty feet away, going down a staircase to get the uptown 1 train. Mike heard the train's brakes echo as it rumbled closer.

Mike leaned to where the train and the platform met, trying to see if the suspect was boarding. He saw what he thought was the suspect, getting on as the doors began to close. The more Mike looked at him, the more he seemed to be a professional, a spook. Mike had a feeling he was no longer "black" but had been made by the suspect. Mike grabbed the closing doors and held them until they reopened. The conductor on the train yelled out on the intercom. "Do not hold the doors on the train!" He shut the doors as Mike jumped inside.

Mike moved between train cars. "I'm on the 1 train uptown," he texted Jack. "He's here."

"Okay," Jack replied.

The subway cars' metal doors were grimy. Moving between cars, Mike saw how close the tracks were as the ground blurred past beneath him. Looking through the windows of the next car, he saw that the suspect was also moving from car to car. He felt the train begin to slow down. People sitting on the train started to get up. Mike entered the next car and dodged between passengers, trying to get closer. Then the train stopped.

A tsunami of people exited the subway cars as more poured into the metal coffins from outside. Mike pushed his way into the crowd at the 50th Street station in Midtown Manhattan's west side. He knew the suspect had exited, but he lost him in the crowd. He zigzagged through the people, cutting his way through the masses like a barracuda hunting its prey. He went this way and that, searching for his quarry. He had to find him; he was a piece in this puzzle, and Mike needed him to find his way out of the maze this case presented.

Mike hated ignorance. He needed to unravel this plot, whatever it was. He felt like he was reaching for matches in a dark room and lighting one at a time, seeking to illuminate the final truth. Then he could move on from this world of smoke and mirrors, and into the real world. But it was not to be. Not today, anyway. He phoned Jack. "I lost him, I fucking lost him! Where are you? I just can't lose this fucker."

"I'm at 44th Street and coming your way," Jack said, breathing hard.

"Double fuck!" Mike said to himself. "What about your guy?"

"Fucking gone, these guys are pros."

"At least I got a pic of your guy."

"Good."

"Fuck! We couldn't cut him off."

"There's a fire with injuries," Jack told him. "I'm in total gridlock here."

"Double fuck!" Mike yelled.

"You said that already."

"I know and I'm fucking pissed!" Mike said.

"These guys clean their follows well."

"I texted the image to Wellerin as soon as I took it," Mike said.

"He ran it through the facial recognition database and got a hit," Jack told him.

"I got an address on the guy." Mike said, looking at a text from Wellerin. "Let's go!"

"Out of gridlock?" Jack asked.

CHAPTER 15

OPEN SESAME

He uttered these strange words: "Open, Sesame!"
And forthwith appeared a wide doorway in the
face of the rock. The robbers went in, and last of all
their chief, and then the portal shut of itself.
—*The Arabian Nights*, translated by Sir Richard Burton

"WHY ARE THEY IN Manhattan?" Jack said as Mike drove them through downtown to the suspect's apartment. "And why SoHo?"

"Who would imagine it?" Mike answered. "I know I wouldn't. It's off the radar as a base of operations, since everyone thinks it's a target. We'd think Queens or Brooklyn or Florida or Jersey."

"I hear ya."

"I guess the Bronx is too dangerous for terrorists," Mike said.

"Ha, ha! Good one. Mike, we got no warrant for this, we should wait."

"It's not a search or investigation, just light research. We have to know what's up right now. If I find something, we can always get one later."

"You sure you want to do this?" Jack asked.

"I'm not waiting a few weeks for a warrant from a judge who's never been in danger, was born with a fucking silver spoon in his mouth, and eats caviar for lunch. And who, by the way, will come up with some bullshit excuse on why we can't do a warrant. The sad thing is, if we were feds, we wouldn't need warrants in the first place."

"Tell me how you really feel," Jack said.

"I'm going into the guy's apartment, period. My cell is on vibrate; text me if one of these guys shows up."

"In fifteen minutes or so it's going to be night out."

"Gotcha," Mike said. Then, as he stepped from the car, "These aren't the droids you're looking for."

"I'll be across the street."

"Ten-four," Mike told him.

A moment later, Mike was inside the building. He walked the halls near the apartment. Jack might be right; this could be too risky. But at this point he was almost obsessed, and had to learn more. There had been so many twists and turns in this maze of a case, and he felt like he wasn't even halfway to the end. He knew there was likely an active terrorist cell in the city—but what kind of cell? Financial, logistics, networking? Or the worst and, from what he'd seen so far, most likely kind—the ones that killed?

He put his ear to the apartment door and listened for a few seconds, but heard nothing. He knocked, but no one answered. He took out a thin, flat, metal, tension wrench, put it on the bottom of the keyhole, and turned it. Then he used a flat metal pick and slid it in along the top of the brass cylinder, feeling for the pins. He turned the tension wrench all the way, and the door unlocked.

His heart sped up as he slipped inside, shut the door and looked out through the peephole. No one was coming. The apartment had white carpets and walls, and was too neat. It looked like a model unit, the kind that real estate agents show—something temporary rather than lived-in.

Moving into the bedroom, he saw a brand-new, custom-built computer. He touched the keyboard, and the screen asked for a password. The computer was connected to a phone and another electronic device. It was a secure phone line, with 4096-bit encryption. After a few seconds, the computer went back to sleep. Mike checked his watch and pulled out his cell to take pictures. Next to the computer he found a few papers and business cards, one of the latter for an importer and exporter and called Emerald . . .

His cell vibrated and displayed a text message from Jack: "GET OUT NOW!" The text had been sent a minute ago.

He heard the front door lock pop and click open. Heart pounding in his ears, Mike thought about going under the bed, but if found there he couldn't fight or run. He opened the walk-in closet door and hurried inside, closing it. He hid behind outdated clothes on metal hangers.

He couldn't make a run for it, since he was all the way in the back of the apartment. So he listened, closed his eyes and focused. The suspect went into the bathroom, took a long piss and cleared his throat. Mike heard the toilet flush. The suspect went into the living room, then opened the refrigerator in the kitchen. Finally he came into the bedroom and made a call, speaking Arabic—but so low Mike couldn't make out the words. The suspect hung up three minutes later, and made another call in Persian. The second call lasted about a minute. Soon after, the phone rang, and the man spoke in English. "Meet me at the place in SoHo," he said. He stepped to the closet and opened the door, but didn't turn on the light.

Mike held his breath. It was definitely the same guy he'd been tailing. The phone rang again, and the suspect turned away to pick it up. He listened for a few seconds and hung up. Coming back to the closet, he retrieved a round key and opened a safe in the closet floor, near Mike's feet. He removed a pistol, and something small that Mike couldn't quite make out. Locking the safe, he shut the closet door and left the apartment.

Switching on the closet light, Mike saw a black Kevlar safe screwed to the floor. He pulled on the latch, but it was locked. He wiped his prints with his handkerchief, killed the light and left things as he'd found them. He checked the peephole before leaving the apartment, it was the same guy he'd photographed in Grand Central. He texted Jack: "Suspect is armed and just left, may be leaving the building."

Mike walked the long hallway and made a left to the elevator. He heard the suspect talking on his cell, so he back-pedaled and took the stairs, wondering why the ID had led to a legitimate person and address.

CHAPTER 16

SPIES AND ASSASSINS

There will come a time when it isn't "They're spying
on me through my phone" anymore. Eventually,
it will be "My phone is spying on me."
—PHILIP K. DICK

M IKE WALKED DOWN THE STAIRS and left the building, walked a block and turned. He saw Jack parked
in front of a bus stop. It was dusk, and traffic was starting
to build up. Mike saw the suspect across the street. He was
already a block away, walking east on the north side of the
street. A gust of wind blew, and the man pulled up the collar
on his thin brown jacket.

Mike followed. This was gumshoe work, a lost art. He was
one of its last practitioners. The suspect didn't walk like everyone
else, but with a certain purpose to his step. He took out his cell

phone and pretended to be on it while checking his surroundings. Mike saw Jack a good ways back, following in the car.

Mike followed on foot for another block and saw the suspect go into a subway station. Mike turned to look for Jack, who pulled alongside. "No parking spots," Jack said. "If we park we'll get towed."

"I got this, I got this," Mike replied. He didn't like repeating himself. Jack did notice.

"Let me know where you exit," Jack said. "One more thing. Take off your baseball cap." Mike tossed the hat in the car as Jack sped off. The sidewalk rumbled as a train approached beneath the street. Mike ran down the steps to the station. The brakes on the subway cars screeched, metal scraping metal.

As the train stopped, Mike saw the suspect he was tailing to the right. Mike boarded the car in front of the suspect's, donning glasses that hid his eyes. He sat down and kept a keen watch on the suspect. The train stopped and opened its doors, and the man got out. Mike followed at a distance. The suspect walked a few blocks, then used a key to enter a brownstone apartment and headed upstairs.

Mike looked around. The block was strangely desolate. He took out his cell, but there were no bars. Using an app on his phone, he found the area wasn't dead but blocked by a cell phone blocker. A few moments later, he heard voices and loud banging in the same brownstone. He checked his cell again—still no bars, no signal—and ran to the building.

The front door was already open; black electrical tape covered the door latch, preventing it from locking. He heard tires screeching, and saw a black SUV whipping around the corner. Entering the building, he heard male voices on the next floor, speaking in Arabic. He paused for a second, knowing he might be heading into a burglary, robbery or who knew what else—with no backup.

Šahrāzād heard noises in the darkness outside. She hated being alone in the Iranian double agent Reza's apartment in SoHo, but she had to find out more: Why was he here, what had Umar known and when? Why had Umar been watching Reza in the first place? Umar had told her that the active cell was watching him and waiting, but why? Was the terrorist cell planning on using The Kingdom in some way? She had to know—and she had to find out alone, because she didn't know who to trust. Even bodyguards could be compromised.

The lights in the apartment flickered on and off. She heard noises in the hallway and put her ear to the door, but heard nothing. She peered through the peephole, seeing no one. The noises stopped. Her body was covered in a cold sweat. She felt *firri*, evil, *aswad myrrh,* a bitter black taste.

Everything was silent for a few moments. She lifted a phone from a nearby table and dialed 911, just in case, but the phone didn't work. She tried her cell: no bars. Hearing another noise, she looked through the peephole again. A strange man stared back at her. She froze for an instant, then heard a cordless power drill grind into the door lock. The door started vibrating. She knew she hadn't been followed; that was impossible. So whoever was out there must have come for the same reason she had—to find out more about Reza the Iranian. She heard voices whispering in Arabic; they knew she was here.

Mike heard power tools as he moved up the stairs. Reaching the second floor, he saw two Middle Eastern men in the hallway. The one drilling out the lock on an apartment door was the same man he'd followed from Central Park and Grand Central. The other man was the one who'd just left the apartment. He held a small white towel, possibly with chloroform on it; Mike could smell the antiseptic, alcohol-and-acetone scent.

Mike ran up to the muscular man with the towel and pulled out his gun. Quick as lightning, the man whipped out an expandable baton and smashed Mike's hand, knocking the gun to the ground. The attacker attempted to swing. Mike struck back and then tripped his opponent, elbowing him in the jaw as he fell.

The other man was short and stocky, like a weightlifter. He quickly turned and thrust out the drill. Mike sidestepped, twisting the man's wrist in toward his own body. The man dropped the drill, spun out of the wristlock and dropped to the floor. He scissor-swept Mike's feet, dropping Mike beside him.

The muscular suspect pulled out a knife. Mike looked for his gun; it was too far away. The attacker tried to cut him, but Mike pivoted behind him and used his knee to pin the hand holding the knife to the ground. He hit the attacker in the back of the head, knocking him out. Hearing footsteps pounding up the stairs, he jumped to his feet and grabbed his gun.

Šahrāzād heard a fight in the hallway. The sound of voices was like sharp metal: cutting, banging, slicing. She gazed through the peephole. It was the detective, Mike Maclaymore. She opened the door just as another man shoved Mike against the wall.

Mike ducked into the apartment, and they slammed the door shut, securing multiple locks. They heard the attackers rush down the stairs. Šahrāzād wrapped her arms around Mike and gave him a kiss right on his lips: pure impulse. "I could use a friend right now," she said after the kiss. It was more a peck of affection: half-friendly—but also half-something-more.

Mike had her in his arms and that felt right. Her hair was so raven black. He wanted to pull her close again, but didn't. "Me too," he said. "We have to get out of here."

To Šahrāzād, Mike tasted like gold: pure. Everything about him was good, but he had a past: scars that he buried inside of him, parts of himself locked away in different sections, like bars of gold and silver in a vault. She felt so much; he wanted her, but didn't want to proceed. His emotions were a tangled web of wires, wanting to be cut, one by one.

Someone banged on the door a few times, then things went quiet. Mike peered through the eye-hole. "Nothing," he said.

"Let's go." She tried to call 911 on her cell. "My phone doesn't work. Apartment phone is dead, too."

"They're using a cell jammer and must have cut the phone lines," Mike told her. They climbed out the window onto the fire escape and went up to the roof. Mike scanned the surrounding rooftops and pointed. They scaled a few low walls between connected buildings, making their way to the last rooftop. Mike unhooked the shaky iron ladder and lowered it to the street. He and the princess hurried down. Peering around a wall, Mike saw a group of men about a hundred feet away. The men hadn't spotted them.

Mike watched as a second group of men arrived in a black SUV. He saw another man on foot, speaking into a radio, but was too far away to listen in. He turned to the princess. "We can lose them in Chinatown and Little Italy. We're only two blocks away." A short distance off, there was some kind of festival on Canal Street. Mike and the princess raced toward it, and the crowd swallowed them up.

Looking back, Mike could no longer see their pursuers through the crowd. Scoping their surroundings, he saw a man speaking to someone in a black car with dark-tinted windows and no front license plate. He pulled Šahrāzād deeper into the crowd.

The festival had hundreds of vendors, selling spicy Italian sausages piled high with sliced onions and peppers, cannolis, gelato, fried calamari and dozens of other things. The smell of burning meat and the sounds of Frank Sinatra and Luciano Pavarotti mixed with the noise of the city.

"I think we lost them," Šahrāzād said.

"My guess is we didn't," Mike told her. They hurried down the street and turned left, looking back every few seconds. An attacker appeared in front of them, slashing with a knife. Mike grabbed the man's wrist with his right hand and twisted it upward, putting his left forearm into the attacker's inner triceps nerve and rotating the arm to make a circular motion: an arm bar that brought the man straight to the ground and broke his arm. Mike took the knife and threw it across the street. The man let out a yell. Other men raced toward them.

"We have to keep moving," Šahrāzād said, and threw the contents of her small silver foil packet—the nanotransmitters—at the fallen man.

"No shit," Mike agreed. They ran into the crowd, pausing near a restaurant. Mike saw one of their pursuers on a cell phone, looking into different cafés and pizzerias. Mike and Šahrāzād went into the restaurant and through the kitchen. They left through the back, coming out on another street. They saw another black SUV with dark-tinted windows and no front plate, illegally parked. The car started up, and the man from Central Park stepped from the back.

Mike and Šahrāzād ducked into a Chinese restaurant, then went into the building's lobby area and up the stairs. They peered down at the street from a second floor window while Šahrāzād dialed 911 on her cell. This time, she got through. "Men with guns! I need police at Mott and Hester!" she told the dispatcher. Twenty seconds later, police sirens sounded in the distance, growing swiftly nearer. The pursuit evaporated.

"They're spooked and not coming back," Šahrāzād said. "I'm parked a few blocks away."

"Good. Can they track your phone?"

"No, my cell is scrambled."

CHAPTER 17

SECRETS OF THE KINGDOM

Secrets, silent, stony sit in the dark palaces
of both our hearts: secrets weary of their
tyranny: tyrants willing to be dethroned.

—JAMES JOYCE

MIKE FOLLOWED ŠAHRĀZĀD through Chinatown's fish
market with its red snapper, crabs and eels on beds of
crushed ice, and turtles swimming in plastic buckets on the
sidewalk. They passed a Chinese restaurant with oily skewered
ducks roasting in the window, near a glowing green and red
Dragon Tsing Tao beer sign.

"I put a bug on them," Šahrāzād said. She pulled out her
cell phone: location information displayed on a GPS map.
Mike leaned forward to look at the screen.

"They're nanotransmitters," she told him, "microscopic like bacteria. It's a one-time use and doesn't last long, an hour or so. It takes about ten to fifteen minutes to start working."

"New and improved spydust," Mike said approvingly. "Do you have any more?"

"No." She unlocked a sleek black Benz, and they slid into the front. "I like the taste of your voice," she told Mike.

"Huh?"

"I have synesthesia," she explained. "I taste and feel sounds."

"Nabokov had that, right?"

Classical music played when she turned the key. She pressed the pedals, and the engine purred like a black panther in the morning. Mike let out a deep breath as they pulled away; she was peeling out like a teenager fleeing the cops and racing down the street on a Friday night. "You're an honest man in a dishonest world," she told him.

"How do you know?"

"Your voice. I know when someone lies. In my country, they would say you are as rare as a three-humped camel."

"Who were those guys?" Mike asked. He wasn't quite sure what to make of the whole thing.

She was silent for a moment after he asked the question. "I was hoping you might tell me. I know some things, but not as much as you think I know."

Mike smiled. "Where are your bodyguards?"

"I ditched them."

"What was in that apartment?"

"It belonged to a man who used to work for our company, Amarco. The diplomat Umar was killed while investigating him."

"Repeat that?"

"The unidentified dead man in Suffolk County used to live in the apartment you saved me in. That's why you were there, right?"

"I didn't know it was his apartment," Mike told her. "How do you know the body is his?" He tried to be poker-faced. He wasn't entirely sure she was on any side other than her own. But he accepted that; life was a series of gray areas and lines that blurred and blended.

"I have contacts everywhere," she said after a moment.

"You drive very well—and swiftly," Mike told her.

"Why were you there then?" she asked, weaving through traffic like a stunt driver.

"I followed a guy I was investigating; he led me to that apartment. I had no idea where he was going,"

"The apartment belonged to Reza Amir Rafsanjani. He used to work for our company."

"He was Iranian, right?" Mike asked. "He rented a car under a simplified name awhile ago."

"He was an agent," Šahrāzād said. "A mole, sleeper, spy."

"He was missing and no one reported him?" Mike asked.

"He's been ghosted."

"Our database search on your former employee showed no DNA match. And, of course, we have no prints because there are no hands."

"Exactly."

"If he's missing, why is no one looking for him?"

"A ghost," she told him. "You dealt with that all the time when you were on the identity theft squad."

Mike tried to not show his surprise. "What else do you know about me?"

"You were in Afghanistan, Special Forces, and have connections to the CIA and intelligence services. You were recently undercover in Russia, and you speak Russian. Your mother was killed by them, and you wanted justice. You were then betrayed and your family was—"

"You know too much," he said, cutting her off.

"I had to do my homework, as you did on me. This is a dangerous business."

"My mother escaped her KGB father in Berlin many years ago, with the help of my dad. My father died so I could be free. My mother was killed by her own father. I killed him, and then my son died."

The memories flooded back into his mind like a bursting dam. Two years before, he'd had walked down a hotel hallway. He'd seen a man in a suit; an ex-Spetsnaz mercenary. Before the man could spot him, Mike drew his silenced 9mm and double tapped him in the head: once in the eye socket, and one in the forehead for good measure. Mike turned as another merc said something in Russian. Mike shot him in the eye; he dropped instantly. He kicked open the door to the room they'd been guarding.

An old man with a white beard waited inside. His name was Vronsky. "I knew you would come," he said with a heavy Russian accent.

"Where is my son?" Mike shouted. "You took him! Where is he!"

The man was stoic, but he had an aura that was pure evil: a Russian *Shaitan,* Satan. He said nothing. Mike pointed the gun at his face, then grabbed the man's hand and shot off a finger. The man let out a shrill yell. "The ghost of Rahman, the assassin, is the one you want!"

"You killed my mother, your own daughter; you killed my family! *Poslushajtye!* Listen! *Pochemu?* Why?" Was it money, power, revenge?" Mike screamed at him.

"This is what I wanted—to see you die. Not physical death, but your soul. Killing me will never get them back."

"*Spokoynoy nochi, Shaitan!*" Good night, Satan. Three shots rang out, two to the chest and one to forehead: the classic triple tap.

"I'm sorry for what happened to your son," Šahrāzād said, bringing him back.

Mike pulled out his cell and showed her a photo of Chris at the zoo, holding a wolf cub. She scrolled through the images at a stoplight, pausing on one of Chris dressed as a knight with a plastic sword for Halloween, and another of him as an infant wrapped in a bright blue blanket. "He's beautiful."

"Thanks." He put the phone away.

"What was the Russian's name?"

"Vronsky."

"He was trading diamonds for heroin with various Central Asian traffickers."

"I know. I had the DEA seize over a hundred million dollars in diamonds and heroin before I killed him. Now I know who was on the other side of the trade on the drug deal."

"Who killed your son?"

"Someone called the ghost of Rahman, the prince of Kish, Iran."

Mike considered what he had thus far. *It's the same MO. Too much of a coincidence—or is it? How is this all connected?* he thought.

"The ghost we are seeking pretends he is the Iranian, Reza Amir Rafsanjani—who was found in the rental car trunk. He had a Ph.D. in geophysics and engineering. I didn't know he was missing until Umar died. He found out before I did," she asked.

"It's the perfect cover for a murder."

Mike was quiet for a few moments. Who would go through all of this? What was the purpose behind the Iranian sleeper agent's murder and the theft of his identity—and how was that linked to the raid? Why would someone take over another person's life? This was international, as if one group or state was trying to commit fraud or steal information and make someone else look like the bad guy. Or maybe just cover their own tracks to avoid blame, if and when the shit hit the fan. "What else do you know?" he asked.

"The ghost was spying on the man who killed Reza and then took over Reza's life."

"Whoever killed Reza," Mike told her, "also extended the Iranian's rental agreement to buy time." She smiled at him. Mike looked at her, and saw that she knew he understood. "The names you gave me on the flash drive," he said: "Felani Yaroo and Khalid Zahrani. I did a search, but it was the wrong guy and the wrong name, and the other one guy was nothing."

He watched her face for signs of deception but saw none. She was a good poker player, but he could see that she was offended. "That name," she continued, "Felani Yaroo—in Persian it means John Doe. And Khalid Zahrani is also a John Doe, a ghost. Those names are not going to be in the NYC police's Intel and Counter-Terror Division. The name of the man you killed in the raid is Sa'id al-Dussari," she said.

Mike took out his cell and opened a notepad. "Better spell that one for me. The Iranian's name, too." He typed the names as she drove and saved the document.

"Sa'id al-Dussari is former Kingdom of Saudi Arabian Special Forces," she added. "Trained by your government. He has another name, Amir Paria. He may be half Iranian, may have lived in Iran and have family there."

"Former Special Forces?" Mike said, as she was weaving in and out of traffic.

"He resigned his commission."

"Why?"

"Records say disciplinary action, but who knows?"

"Sa'id killed Umar, the diplomat," Mike said. "And Reza?"

"The Iranian, Reza, was a geologist and engineer, and was also Iranian Intel—a mole inside Amarco."

"What was the cell going to do here?"

Šahrāzād looked at him, but didn't answer right away. "They came here to die," she said at last. "Why can't you go to the CIA with this?"

She paused for a moment, after his question, as if she hesitated to speak the truth. "They or someone they know tried to kill me."

Mike leaned back and took a deep breath. Two parts of him were in conflict; one wanted to know everything, while the other didn't want to know the ugly truth.

"Both the FBI and CIA are compromised. That's what led to the attempt on my life."

"What happened?"

"Someone gave me up."

Mike saw her tense as she called up the memory.

"I was meeting my handler in the desert, a CIA agent, but he didn't show up. An assassin came instead. Someone running a cell or cells asked them who the leak was on the Saudi's end; they knew where I would be in the desert to give them information on hundreds of millions of missing money from Amarco."

"Hundreds of millions?" Mike repeated.

"Yes. I'm sure you're wondering why I'm doing this investigation. The Kingdom is on an unsustainable path. Our greatest secret is that we'll soon run out of oil. *Nafadh al-banzeen min al-sayara.* The petrol has run out."

"When I was at the diplomat's apartment," Mike said, "Mr. Abdul from the Saudi Embassy came by. The Saudis wanted to secure the contents of the safe, but it was virtually empty. It looked like it might have been filled with gold coins and hundreds of thousands of dollars in different currencies."

"That just shows me that someone knew Umar was spying on them," Šahrāzād told him, "and wanted to know how much he knew about their plot."

"Why are you leveling with me?" Mike asked.

"The falcon with talent never shows its talons. An Arabian proverb. At any rate, we're going to run out of oil in a few years. That's why my country must be reformed. Over the past hundred years, we've spent billions spreading a poisonous ideology around the world instead of modernizing our society. We have reaped what we have sown."

"Change ain't easy."

"There is a Saudi saying: "My grandfather rode a camel. My father rode in a car. I fly a jet airplane. My grandson will ride a camel."

"Both of our civilizations are destroying themselves," Mike agreed. "Maybe we should let them collapse."

"We are fools. We want to be heroes, though we might die."

"I hope you're wrong," Mike said. "Ask yourself: Why all of this now?"

"Who are you and I to defy the wheels of history, the momentum of the world?" Šahrāzād asked.

"Man makes his own history," Mike observed, "but is also its slave."

"History is the narrative of lies and truths we weave," Šahrāzād opined.

"Narrative should be based on facts and facts alone."

"You are wise beyond your years," she said.

The electronic device buzzed her; the GPS nanotransmitters were active in Midtown Manhattan. She showed the display of the location to Mike and made a fast turn.

CHAPTER 18

FLIGHT OF THE VALKYRIES

Achievements, seldom credited to their source,
are the result of unspeakable drudgery and worries.
—RICHARD WAGNER

SHARP PEAKS PIERCED THE SKY like the white teeth of a carnivore; distant Saudi mountains lined the horizon. The desert peaks were covered with a light dusting of snow, remnant of the predawn chill. Sayf put the binoculars to his eyes; the electronic viewfinder showed the nearest mountain to be six kilometers out.

He looked up and saw eagles in the distance, swooping down on some hapless prey. A moment later they were in the air again, with the bright blue sky behind them. They were so free, and yet forever bound to be what they were—unlike men, who made what they desired with blood and toil, becoming what they wished. Great men, Sayf corrected himself. Commoners were slaves to what they were born to be.

Sayf took the binoculars away from his eyes and looked at all the military equipment. Preparing took so much time, effort, logistics. He wanted success now. He'd already waited for so long, decades—moving his chess pieces one by one, year by year. Finally, the endgame was near—and he longed for the checkmate against those he wished to crush. Would this be it?

To Sayf's left, a group of Air Force soldiers were busy setting up the computers and other hardware needed to test the airship drone fleet. Raising the binoculars, he zoomed in on a small dust cloud some two miles off, in the valley below. The dust had been kicked up by a camouflaged military jeep on its way from the remote-controlled ground-to-air missile systems.

Swinging the binoculars to the right, he saw the other jeep drive off.

He panned to the left just a little, and saw that the anti-aircraft surface-to-air missiles (SAMs) were now ready. Multiple systems had been set up along the valley.

"We will be ready for the drone demonstration in a few minutes," General Amir informed him. Sayf nodded. "If all goes well, you will be one of the architects of my future administration. *"al-Harbaa' laa Yughaadir shajarathuh hattaa yakun mu'akkid 'an shajara 'ukhraa,"* Sayf added. *The chameleon does not leave his tree until he is sure of another.*

"Thank you." General Amir nodded.

Sayf turned. Behind him was one of the jewels of the empire, a game-changing weapon. It looked like a much smaller version of a futuristic stealth fighter, but was semi-translucent and glowed a strange green. It had missiles on its wings, and a machine gun that fired propellant bullets. It was a drone, but not just any drone. This one had artificial intelligence and had been built with exotic materials that made it virtually invisible to radar and satellites.

He'd seen firsthand what drones had done in Pakistan and Afghanistan. They'd crushed entire villages, wiping people from the face of the earth with nothing but burnt ashes left behind. Unlike all of the other jihadis, Sayf saw this not as defeat—but as opportunity. He knew he'd have to learn more of this weapon that annihilated both innocent and guilty in flashes of fire. He'd had his engineers take a few of them apart, and had set up an underground 3D printing and manufacturing facility, so he wouldn't be dependent on the Americans should they become less accommodating in the future. His hope was that this would change everything. Combined with the black flag operation, this would solidify his political success and ensure total victory in completing The Kingdom's hegemonic destiny.

General Amir donned a head-mounted display the size of a pair of large sunglasses, with an attached earpiece. Sayf put it on after the general had adjusted it. Amir had set it up so that Sayf could watch things from the drone's point of view, over an encrypted network. On the right screen was the drone's front-mounted point-of-view camera; on the left, a camera from the valley and the SAM's POV—for a total of three camera feeds.

SAMs now activated!" one of the techs called out. Sayf smiled.

The drone took off. It was surprisingly quiet, and hummed instead of roared. Within a minute the drone was above the SAM in the valley. The drone didn't fire, because its sensors told it the SAM was blind to its presence. Instead, the drone read the network and saw that the SAM's modified AI didn't lock—confirming the drone's invisibility. The drone gained some distance, then fired a ferocious volley of missiles. The other SAM systems awoke, seeing not the flying drone but the attack itself. But by then it was a few seconds too late; after destroying the first group of SAMs, the drone disappeared in the sky. The other SAMs looked around, using their sensors. They saw something coming from the sky high above. The SAMs fired, but the target was not "a" target at all, since the drone was able to use its stealth capabilities to cloak itself. Instead, the SAMs saw dozens of tiny missiles, like metal hornets of war. Hundreds of small explosions rippled through the air with a sound like thunder, ripping the landscape apart. Within seconds, the SAMs had been vaporized. Sayf heard the drone's hum, and turned as it landed quietly behind him. "Impressive," he said.

"Your American friend helped us out, and we made a few adjustments," the tech told him.

"What can stop this?" Sayf asked.

"An EMP: an electromagnetic pulse. But it can be equipped with an EMP weapon."

"When will we be ready to deploy?"

"We are ready now."

Sayf smiled again. He would have his war; his empire was about to be carved out of history. He had his drone air fleet, drone boats, and drone vehicles. No other nation had this: an entire army of drones, with a group of elite Special Forces soldiers, drone hackers, and electromagnetic weapons to back them up.

CHAPTER 19

MAP AND
COMPASS

*Two roads diverged in a wood, and I—I took the one
less traveled by, And that has made all the difference.*

—ROBERT FROST

Š AHRĀZĀD LOOKED AT HER nanotransmitter GPS electronic device, and saw that one of the suspects was close by.

"They are on 30th Street and 8th," Šahrāzād said. "I knew
they would show up there. The place sells Russian diamonds."

Mike nodded, looking at the GPS dot that marked the
location of the "spydust" on the display. He sometimes felt
the princess glimpsed the future.

Šahrāzād parked the car on a broken up and garbage-filled
street. Midtown Manhattan had become run down, its buildings covered with graffiti, its corners host to drug dealers and

hookers. Mike shook his head at how the city had deteriorated over the past decade.

The princess pulled out a set of keys and let them into an abandoned store near the location where the suspects had stopped. She led Mike upstairs. Looking out through the window, Mike saw an adult DVD store / jewelry / pawnshop called Phil Marlowe's.

"Down there," Šahrāzād pointed to two men a full block away, walking toward the place. She pulled her camera out and took rapid photos of one of the men she put spydust on.

Mike watched as the two men came closer, the short muscular guy and another man—someone he remembered well and would never forget: one of Rahman's operatives. He'd escaped from the bust that had stopped the diamond, heroin and human trafficking deal—the same bust that had ultimately led to the deaths of Mike's mother and son. But what was he doing in New York City with one of Tamerlaine's men? Rahman and Tamerlaine—could they be the same person?

The moment jogged Mike's memory, bringing up things that seemed to dwell beneath the surface of his consciousness. He thought of Tamerlaine's catacombs and their thousands of skulls, of the Persian Gur-e Amir—"Tomb of the King," the 14th century Tamerlaine's jade sarcophagus—and the 21st century's ghost warrior and drug lord of Afghanistan. There was the 100-million-dollar Rahman deal with Vronsky . . . Rahman and Tamerlaine were both ghosts; no one saw them, and there were no photographs. It all started to make sense; they were legends, false identities, perfect stories of people who were not real but fronts, shadows, illusions of a master terrorist—someone smart enough to know that one cannot kill an enemy one cannot see.

There was no human intel, no electronic or signals intel, nothing at all on these men—and yet they existed and acted in a similar way, in the same region of the world. He'd almost caught the same man twice, once over fifteen year ago while on a CIA operation in Afghanistan, and once more recently during the Vronsky/Rahman deal. Mike was filled with a hot hate that burned his stomach, but he contained himself. He knew that to get them, to win this, he had to play his moves right. He touched his gold cross and thought of his son and mother and what they meant to him as their images flashed through his mind. Then he put them away like he always did, because he had to be logical or he would fail. He was up against the most intelligent terrorists in the world, and he couldn't afford to lose his cool.

Across the street, the two men disappeared into the jewelry/pawnshop. "Do you have any IDs yet?" he asked the princess.

"The Kingdom's facial recog database has nothing on either of them. Do you think Rahman may be Tamerlaine?" she asked.

"We think or used to think that Tamerlaine was an Iranian-backed warlord in Afghanistan, but we have no photos of him and no name. Just his moniker. But my answer is yes. The more I think about it, the more sense it makes. Both men have same MO."

"We have the same information," the princess noted.

"The man I tried to capture over a decade ago was Tamerlaine, in Afghanistan. The man responsible for my son's death is called Rahman, the Prince of Kish, and his personal assassin called the Ghost. The identities of both men are unknown."

Šahrāzād nodded. "I found out with my own investigation that one of the offices rented by the terrorists is under Reza's name. They're Tamerlaine's men; I have intel linking the little evidence that we have, all the way back to Afghanistan. This place we're in now was rented by Umar, to keep an eye on them from across the street."

She showed him a few papers from the raid. "I found these files in Reza's apartment, a few minutes before you showed up. He was paying for that space via money order from a place nearby. But it wasn't him of course. The money was from a bank in Florida. Before Umar died, he told me about an account number they're using. I tried calling the bank, telling them I was Reza's cousin, but they wouldn't tell me anything."

"Tamerlaine sold heroin in Afghanistan," Mike said. "The deal I stopped was Vronsky buying heroin from Rahman, the prince of Kish, for diamonds and human slaves." Mike thought again, his past haunting him for good and ill. He hoped it wouldn't destroy him. Could he face this again and kill his son's murderer, the ghost assassin of Rahman and kill a man that the CIA had been unable to identify for almost two decades?

Šahrāzād pulled out a second cell phone. "I have this cell I've been carrying around," she said. "I got it off someone who tried to kill me. I need someone to look at it."

"That can be done. Why did he want to kill you?"

"I found out that hundreds of millions of dollars are missing and laundered from Amarco," she said.

"What's the connection?" Mike asked. When hundreds of millions went missing, people would die. He knew that all too well. The sacrifices he'd made were too high, and he regretted them. But now he had no choice; like a shark, he had to move forward or die.

"I don't know yet," Šahrāzād answered. "I'm trying to find one so we can end this story."

"I don't think either of us will like the ending," Mike said. He looked at her as he said it, and saw her nod of agreement. They both knew fairy tales didn't exist in the real world. Sometimes, everyone died.

He thought of himself for one short moment, and how he wanted the future to be like the past. Parts of it, at least. The princess, on the other hand, dreamt of a future different from past and present. He was the past and she the future; together, they formed the present. So many questions swirled in his mind, but there was one he had to ask. The princess was a wealth of knowledge that she herself didn't even know—almost like a magnet, a transmitter or filter; she didn't have the things he needed, but her compass showed the path for him to follow. "You don't want the phone tracked," he said, noting the missing battery.

"My other phone cannot be tracked when turned off. But this one—I removed the battery just in case."

"I know a Russian hacker," Mike said. "Former Intelligence Services—SVR, the new KGB. I can ask him to look at it."

"We should watch these guys," Mike said, looking at the place across the street.

"We should torture them."

"We can't do that," Mike told her. "This isn't the Middle East."

"This is about my country. Your country does it, and you did shadow ops as well."

"One of the many reasons I left," Mike said.

"Who were some of the people you got?"

He paused. Sometimes one had to do a little bit of evil to stop a bigger evil, but that didn't prevent the guilt. "One was a money man, Afghan Arab. He was brought to Poland. He used Tanzanite and laundered hundreds of millions in shell businesses and counterfeit bills, all made with reverse-engineered printers. He was also involved in selling people, human slavery. Sex slaves in Saint Petersburg, India, the Middle East, Thailand, Vietnam, Myanmar, Columbia, Brazil, Japan and Prague. Torture is a line we shouldn't cross. But I crossed it and I had to leave. The quieter life I was looking for didn't seem to work out. I guess gladiators can't retire." It felt good to get that off his chest.

"I'm sorry I put you on the spot. But did that line ever exist?"

"Maybe not. We all have to do what's in our best interests. But I lost my moral compass a long time ago. I lost count of how many I've killed. Their faces are meshed together in my memory."

"You're my compass," Šahrāzād told him. "Without you, I would have nothing. I would be dead."

Mike paused again, thinking on what she'd said. A map and a compass, that's what they were together. Lost without each other.

Šahrāzād looked at her cell again. "My father hasn't answered my texts I just sent. I'm calling him again." She put the phone to her ear. "He's not answering. He always answers me." She looked at her cell and dialed a number. Mike watched her face change. After five rings, she hung up and dialed another number.

"Give me a sec, I'm texting my father again . . . Hmm. Not responding. He's at a party on the Upper East Side. We should go there."

"No," Mike said.

"No?"

"We watch and follow them," he said, indicating the shop across the street.

"I'm leaving, then. My father might be in danger."

The men left the store with heavy bags and climbed into a cab. The short muscular one was on a cell phone. Šahrāzād looked at the electronic device; the spy dust's GPS signal was much weaker now. She looked at the man she'd thrown the foil packet at, and saw that he wore a new shirt.

"Signal's dying," she told Mike.

"Well?" He smiled and moved for the door.

The princess followed him down the stairs and shut the door behind them She checked the GPS signal on her phone again: it was much weaker, but they could see their quarry traveling east, then north. She threw Mike the keys to her car, and they slid inside.

"Where do you think they're going?" Mike asked.

"We'll find out soon enough, but I have a feeling they are going to where my father is . . ."

CHAPTER 20

POLITICS IS WAR

There is a tide in the affairs of men.
Which, taken at the flood, leads on to fortune;
Omitted, all the voyage of their life
Is bound in shallows and in miseries.
On such a full sea are we now afloat,
And we must take the current when it
serves, or lose our ventures.
—*JULIUS CAESAR* BY WILLIAM SHAKESPEARE

S HE WAS RIGHT, they were going to where her father was.
Mike pulled up outside the hotel. After giving the keys
to the valet, he and the princess jogged to the hotel on the
Upper East Side in Manhattan. The night was clear and the
stars sparkled in the sky. Only a few clouds showed above, one
partly covering the moon. The streets were unusually quiet.
Mike had a feeling that would soon pass. The old ivory-white
hotel harkened back to the swanky days of *The Great Gatsby,*

Nick Carraway and Jordan Baker. It was made of white stone and had a regal quality about it, with sturdy black window panels of a kind no longer made.

Mike got a text from Eva: "I'm at 26 Fed Plaza, I should be getting you access to the computer system soon."

He texted her back: "I'm at the party on the Upper East Side. Princess was attacked an hour ago but now okay."

Gravel crunched underfoot as Mike and the princess hurried to the building. Detective Wellerin stood guard outside the hotel entrance, wearing a cheap frumpled suit. A second detective wore an old-school Eddie "Popeye Doyle" Egan porkpie hat and smoked a cigar.

"What's going on?" Wellerin said when they arrived.

"Don't know yet," Mike told him.

The director of security caught sight of them while making his rounds and immediately recognized Šahrāzād. "Your grace, I'm pleased to meet you," he said, and shook hands with the princess.

"Thank you. This man is with me and on the list."

"Okay," the security director said when Mike showed his ID. He gave Mike a white ID badge. Mike put his detective pin on his jacket as the security guard checked the guest list.

"Too much to explain," Mike told Wellerin, and headed inside with the princess.

"I'll look for my father," Šahrāzād told him.

Mike took out his detective's shield as he walked into the giant ballroom. Dozens of glowing crystal chandeliers hung from a vaulted baroque ceiling. There were tables to the sides, and dozens of silver buffet trays along the walls.

Guests milled about the ballroom: presidents and dictators from countries like Abu Dubai, Qatar and Saudi Arabia. Many oil and natural gas executives were already there, and more arrived with each passing moment. Billion-dollar deals would be made here tonight. Mike had read in the papers that Amarco was celebrating its purchase of several offshore oil drillers with stocks and cash.

Tuxedo-clad waiters carried silver trays with champagne flutes. In the middle of the room, a string quartet played Vivaldi's *Four Seasons,* the same song that had played at Mike's wedding. Looking across the room, he saw the king surrounded by a phalanx of bodyguards, and also an outer ring of guards at different posts. He saw Šahrāzād motion to the king's bodyguards. They gave her a bit of space as she walked toward her father. None of the bodyguards seemed tense.

Mike watched Šahrāzād speak with her father, then walk with him toward the rear entrance. It was then that he saw the bodyguard from the morgue.

Šahrāzād approached a bodyguard who seemed to outrank the others. He leaned close and said something private as the bodyguard from the morgue moved closer to them. Then the traitor revealed himself, drew his pistol and pointed it at the king. By the time he fired, another bodyguard had leapt between them. His chest bloomed crimson. The armor-piercing round exited his back and struck the king in the upper chest.

The music stopped and guests fled the room as bodyguards yelled commands. One of the bodyguards tried to whisk Šahrāzād away to protect her and was shot in the head during the chaos by one of the assassins.

"Hold your fire!" the princess yelled. She judo tripped one of the attackers from behind. Mike found himself near one of the many traitors and grabbed his gun hand, performing an aikido wrist lock and stripping the pistol away as he threw the man to the floor. He jumped up and tackled Mike.

Mike tried to counter but fell to the floor, then made the best of it and scissor-swept the traitor—who was immediately swarmed by Saudi bodyguards.

Mike rose to his feet. Šahrāzād pushed away a bodyguard who wanted to escort her from the room. She gestured for Mike to follow her, and said something to one of the bodyguards. She glanced at one of the dead assailants without emotion, then mouthed "Thank you" to Mike.

Bodyguards surrounded the wounded King and rushed him to the courtyard exit in the rear. There was supposed to be a long tent to mask approaching and departing vehicles from sight, but the fabric was gone, leaving only a skeleton of metal bars. Mike paused, thinking the whole area had been screened beforehand—which meant the shooters must have had inside information.

Seeing the missing tent walls, the bodyguards hesitated for an instant, then pressed on. They had no choice at this point, since all of the other exits were worse.

The ballroom was jam packed with people. Mike and the princess followed a few feet behind the men escorting the king.

Three jet-black Mercedes Benz SUVs raced up, screeching to a halt before the king's group with their doors flying open.

The distinctive boom of a rifle shot rang out. Blood spurted from the king's head, and his body went limp. Šahrāzād cried out. She tried to grab onto him, but the bodyguards pulled her away and placed her into one vehicle while the king was placed in another. More bodyguards mimicked placing someone in the third vehicle. The way they crowded around the principals, it was hard to tell who went where. The SUVs sped off in different directions.

Mike took cover behind an Escalade, 40 feet from the entrance. Several bodyguards pointed to a high window in the building across the street. A bright light flashed in the window of a second building across the street, and an anti-personal rocket streaked downward, striking one of the fleeing SUVs. The car exploded in a massive orange fireball, lighting up the night sky. Mike had no idea which car carried Šahrāzād.

A sprinkling of machinegun fire rained down around Mike and the others, coming from above. Bodyguards fired back from behind parked vehicles. One of them took a H&K G36 rifle with a night vision scope from a gun case, using it to scan the roofline and windows.

Under cover fire, two bodyguards rushed the building across the street. Mike went with them, yelling "Police emergency!" at the cowering doorman.

Mike and the bodyguards ran up the stairs, a few detectives trailing behind. Mike's quads were burning for the last three flights. A group of detectives and Saudi security forces broke off to check the lower floors. Ahead, someone kicked open an apartment door, and the bodyguards spilled inside. Mike's leg muscles had turned to jelly. He took a few deep breaths to keep from wheezing, then followed.

The bedroom was pitch-black. One of the bodyguards scanned it with a SureFire flashlight, stopping on a prone figure by the window.

"Don't fucking move!" Mike yelled.

The figure didn't move, because he'd already been shot in the head. His hands clutched a scoped sniper rifle with a suppressor. A submachine gun was beside him. Mounted to the rifle was an aiming aid, one that informed the shooter of the best time to fire after considering recoil, wind speed, and so on.

Mike paused for a moment. Who'd killed the sniper so fast, and from where? Was this some kind of setup? He walked over and touched the assault rifle's ejection port with the back of his hand; it was still warm. That didn't mean it had been used to shoot the king or the sniper himself; only ballistics would show that.

Detectives started yelling "Clear!" as they checked the rest of the room. "The apartments below are clear!" another detective called out.

A bodyguard took a picture of the sniper's face with his cell, then emailed the photo. The dead man looked Middle Eastern, but to Mike's eyes he could have been Iranian, Israeli, Greek or even Turkish. The bodyguard took a few more photos and motioned the other guards away. "Your crime scene," he said to Mike, and stepped back.

"Šahrāzād?" Mike inquired.

"I don't know."

Mike nodded. He couldn't think, not yet at least. He couldn't have prevented the photos if he'd wanted to—which he didn't—because of the diplomatic situation. So he repeated the actions with his own cell phone, then felt the dead man's wrist. He wasn't warm, but he wasn't too cold, either.

"We hope to have a result from these images in a few minutes," the lead bodyguard said in broken English.

Mike sent his own photos to Eva, then called Wellerin. "We need to secure this crime scene. I'm in the apartment across the street. There was also a gunman on a lower floor, and a rocket fired from the building to the west."

Mike stepped to the edge of the room and looked down on the chaos below. Dozens of police officers were in motion. There were EMS and FDNY trucks down the street, and more SUVs lining up by the hotel entrance. The response was one of the fastest he'd seen. He made his way downstairs, legs feeling like rubber.

Eva texted him back: "Negative results on the search, you okay?"

Mike texted: "Just peachy." He met Wellerin on the street. "One assassin's dead. Fuck, this is bad."

"What do ya expect?" Wellerin said, radio to his ear, taking in the endless crackling stream of information. "They're taking the royals to the hospital. I heard one of the paramedics say they were going to York, when they radioed in to tell them to be ready for trauma."

"I'll be there if anyone needs me," Mike said.

He entered the emergency room a short time later. A janitor mopped blood off the floor as nurses in blue and green uniforms raced back and forth. The bodyguards in the emergency care room recognized Mike and let him pass. Doctors labored to save the king. One of the bodyguards lifted blood bags from a wheeled cooler packed with Blue Ice. Mike assumed it was the king's blood, or at least his blood type, kept on hand for situations like this.

Šahrāzād rushed to the king's side, trying to embrace him. "*Father!*" Tears poured from her eyes.

"You're my gift to this world," the king told her. Blood dribbled from his mouth as he spoke.

From what Mike could see, it was a miracle he'd lasted this long. "*Ma'assalama,*" peace, the king said, and closed his eyes.

Mike left the room; there was nothing he could do there. Šahrāzād cried so violently she started to gag. Mike stood just outside the room. Ten minutes later the crying stopped. She seemed to have collected herself, and he heard her speaking on the phone. He wasn't sure he should eavesdrop, but a murder had been committed on his watch. He hated having to make a choice, hated this part of the job—but it had to be done, so he moved a little closer to the doorway.

"Our father has died . . . why do good people have to pay such a price for what is right? Soon things will be different . . . You're coming tomorrow? Good. I have to go. I'll help arrange the funeral."

She stepped from the room a moment later, her face still puffy from tears. She took a moment to compose herself, then said, "I just received a text. Our people say the sniper's prints and face are in our database. He was Iranian. But in light of the ghost, there may be more to this that we need to know . . . I just spoke to my brother."

"Something else is bothering you," Mike said.

"I don't know. I didn't like the sound in his voice. He's holding something from me. When he spoke I tasted fire. Not lies or truth, but something else. My mouth burned . . . I must go. I'll call you later."

"Be safe," Mike told her. She gave him a quick embrace before leaving with her bodyguards.

CHAPTER 21

THRONE OF BLOOD

All men dream: but not equally. Those who dream
by night in the dusty recesses of their minds wake in
the day to find that it was vanity: but the dreamers
of the day are dangerous men, for they may act their
dreams with open eyes, to make it possible.

—T.E. LAWRENCE

GENERAL ABDULLAH AL-HUSAYNI was commander of the Royal Saudi Land Force and kept his office at the military headquarters in King Khalid Military City—which was also known as *Medinat Al Malek Khaled Al Askariyah,* or the Emerald City. The general stood as a dozen paramilitary commandos in full tactical gear poured in through the doorway.

"You're under arrest!" Sayf said, striding in behind his men. He paused to scan the various hunting trophies of exotic animals and the crossed medieval scimitars on the wall.

The general scratched his salt-and-pepper beard. "What is this?" he said. His face was angry, but his eyes showed fear.

"You're under arrest for treason," told him.

"On whose authority?" the general demanded.

"I am the new king." Sayf removed his balaclava mask.

"Well, congratulations!"

The men stared at one another. "You will regret your tone!" King Sayf said.

"Go to hell!"

King Sayf leaped toward the general and grabbed him as the older man tried to draw his vintage Colt 1911 .45 pistol. They thrashed around for a moment before Sayf subdued him with an arm-bar and put plastic flex-cuffs on him. The gold-plated, ivory-handled gun clattered to the floor, and the general's fingers turned blue. "This is outrageous!" he protested.

King Sayf bent down and picked up the general's pistol. "I like this. Where did you get it?"

"From the Americans, during the War with Iraq," the general told him.

"I'll keep it."

"You didn't earn it."

"I'll care for your toys of war."

"I know you killed my son," the general said.

King Sayf turned to the commandos. "Everyone out." The soldiers left the room and shut the door.

Sayf turned to the general. "Your son Umar was telling the West too much, and was about to uncover our plans for America. That's why I had to have him killed," Sayf told him.

"My son had no choice," the general said. "He uncovered your secret, Tamburlaine."

"*as-sirr mithel al-Hamaama: indamaa yughaadir yadii yaTiir,*" the general said. *A secret is like a dove: When it leaves my hand it flies away.*

"But it doesn't matter anymore," Sayf told him. "You almost succeeded in killing me, by the way."

"Almost," the general said. "Your death in Strasbourg would have been perfect. But nothing ever goes according to plan. Now history will be interrupted by you."

"I knew you and your son Umar were about to stab me in the spine with poison daggers."

"You're going to destroy our country," the general said, spitting at him.

"You know too much. You almost found out about my operations. You're a threat to me and my dreams. Do not tread on them."

"Now I know the truth," the general said.

"So you admit it's kill or be killed; I kill you, or you kill me."

"It's the way the world is," the general told him.

"You missed the turning of the tide."

"You will become another tyrant," the general said matter-of-factly, and spit on the king.

"We live in a world in which one must kill a path to the top," Sayf said. "Who doesn't dream of becoming a tyrant and ruling as they wish? Don't you understand? Power is everything. I came to take my country—our country." He wiped the spit from his face with no emotion. "I will be famous, and you will fade from the memory of history. That is the difference between you and me."

"Your father was a great man. He was killed by you for trying to modernize his country, our country."

"We are all our father's dreams and our father's nightmares. You will be denounced as a spy for the Iranians, after you confess to it."

"This is a covert *coup*," the general said.

"The U.S. has plans. If they knew who and what I really am, they would secure our oil fields. An enemy that is invisible cannot be struck."

"You're insane! I hope to see you in hell!" the general said.

"You're already in hell, and I'm in heaven. I don't want to live history but to create it. I am not everyone else; I am a colossus, and you are one of the little people, as Lawrence of Arabia would say. The world shall remember me. You see, politics is war, and blood is what's needed for the engines of history."

"This is just like 1979," the general said. "That failed Mahdist revolt against The Kingdom."

"I will succeed where they failed. I took power without a revolution, and now I shall wield it as a revolutionary. The Americans and the West have corrupted us and used us as a gas station, sucking us dry, paying us in worthless paper while we use their money as petrodollars so that our princes can buy whores and cars and jets. Control oil, control money;

control money, control the world. The Americans don't even know this. They themselves don't know what they stand for. America still thinks we are an ally."

"You are using our religion—"

"All wars are about ideas. Armies mean nothing without belief." He took out a small bag of figs and ate a few.

"You will rule a throne of blood," the general told him.

"A throne of gold," King Sayf replied.

"No, a throne of death. Your ambition is hubris."

"My dreams are my perceptions, and they are what matter. My dreams are poems, and I write them on the pages of history . . ." King Sayf looked around himself. "I really like all of your *shismu*," he said, admiring the heads of lions and tigers on the walls, the red and gold North African 17th-century rug from the time of Ismail the Bloodthirsty, a man with 888 children; and other unique items from around the world which now found their home in the general's office. Also on the wall were two old, crossed Arabian scimitars, their Indian ivory handles etched with war elephants.

On another wall were two crossed, sweeping, sharp-flanged medieval maces. Next to them was another sword that looked much older than the others. Its blade was chiseled with Qu'ranic verses in gold. The sword had flowers etched in its ivory handle. "Where did you get this sword?" King Sayf asked.

"It's one of the many swords of Mohammed the Second, the Ottoman emperor and conqueror of Constantinople."

"Damascus steel." King Sayf took the sword down from the wall and held it in his hand. It was light and beautiful, with hundreds of wavy lines in the steel. The weapon was perfection.

Its owner had conquered the great jewel of Byzantium. Sayf hoped to be remembered as he remembered the owner of that sword. "Do you know who my favorite Syrian is?" he asked.

"Who?"

King Sayf looked up and closed his eyes when he spoke the name: "*Salah al-Dīn.* He was a great man, a real *Wali,* and some would say almost a *Mahdi.*"

General Abdullah al-Husayni said nothing, but looked at the floor and put his head down.

"Where is the sword's sheath?" Sayf sliced the air twice with the sword, and looked at it in his hands. His knuckles turned white.

"In the closet to your right," the general told him.

Sayf opened the door and removed the sheath. It was gilded gold and ivory, etched with beautiful poetry and scenes of ancient battles. "If you don't cooperate," he told the general, "we'll do unimaginable things to your daughter Aaliyah. Do you understand?"

The general stared at the ground with his shoulders slouched.

"By the way," King Sayf added conversationally, "you're going to be beheaded. Sayf motioned to his paramilitary soldiers. He turned to them as they came in. "Take him away!"

King Sayf's paramilitary soldiers dragged the general from the room as Sayf sheathed the sword and placed it on the desk.

The Ottoman fortress Sayf made his home was an ancient relic of one of the most glorious empires in history, now dead and long forgotten. It was King Sayf's fortress now. It was night in the Arabian Desert, and the moon cast a soft blue light on the rustic stone walls of the fort. The castle was a light brown stone, close to the color of the sand dunes on the horizon. Its spires frowned upon the landscape, while minarets called out to heaven five times a day. Voices echoed within the walls, muted by the winds that howled across the desert landscape. Torchlight danced along the outer walls. Inside the fortress, cheers rang out for the sword of King Sayf's brand of ideology.

Sayf sat in a massive medieval chamber with high-vaulted ceilings that were covered with millions of white ivory tiles, painted with sapphire blue geometric patterns of stars and squares. The artistry was perfectly symmetrical. King Sayf took out his sharp, curved, double-edged *Koummya Jambiya* dagger and picked at his fingernails as he sat on the throne. He looked at the old tattered manuscript on the table in front of him, carefully turning the pages and treating each as a goldsmith would treat leaves of gold.

Mustafa was nearby with his encrypted Russian cell phone, talking and nodding. His face was concerned, yet confident. After a few minutes, he hung up. *"Ibn Taymiya!* Original manuscripts!" Mustafa said, approaching and embracing Sayf. "So far everything is going perfectly."

"What about the Iranians?" Sayf said as he walked around the office.

"They are clever," Mustafa said.

"I know. That is why they cannot be trusted. They are undermining Iraq and destroying the buffer state between our countries. We cannot tolerate this." Sayf sat down on a large handmade chair made of crocodile leather and copper.

"I just spoke to one of our agents in America, and I have ill news, my lord," Mustafa said.

"It was going perfectly . . ."

Mustafa paused and took a deep breath. "They are getting closer."

"Who?"

"One of them is named Mike Maclaymore."

"Maclaymore, the detective that almost got me recently, with Vronsky," Sayf said.

Mustafa continued, "He was a Special Forces soldier in Afghanistan when you were there 15 years ago, and part of the CIA's Special Activities Division. He was trying to capture you. He was in the media recently, regarding Vronsky."

"I remember him all too well. They can handle it?" Sayf asked.

"Yes, it will be handled. We will use this man as a weapon against himself."

"This makes the chess game all the more interesting," Sayf told him. He remained poker-faced. He had no sense of humor, nor any sense of grief at the moment. His mind was a calculating machine. His only principle was the score sheet: winning and losing; pure logic, absolute calculus. He'd have to create another identity because of this man, Maclaymore—who was one of the more determined ones. He had to be stopped. "Get me the right answer," Sayf said. His words were like steel, determined and unbreakable.

"Yes, my lord." Mustafa bowed and smiled at Sayf.

"Tell me some good news. What's the price of crude?"

"One hundred fifty dollars per barrel," Mustafa said.

Sayf smiled and nodded.

Mustafa left. Sayf stepped into a stainless steel elevator and went down hundreds of feet below the surface. The elevator opened, and a guard greeted him. Sayf gazed at several sets of large steel doors; at the end of the room was an open vault. There were cameras all over the vault's steel walls. Sayf walked into the vault the size of a basketball court. Stacked on metal pallets on the floor were thousands of 400-Troy-ounce gold bars. This was his new empire's Fort Knox.

He sat down on a chair at the front of the room and looked at a digital photograph of his father and himself together. Sayf sat astride a black Arabian stallion, while his father stood next to the horse. Sayf felt nauseous. Vomit came up from his stomach. He swallowed it, and it burned him. He rose to get a cup of water from a cooler, and felt a razor-sharp pain in his back from too many years of Kurash and Judo.

He washed his mouth out with a cup of water, and went back to sit down. He looked at his reflection in his phone screen, and then looked at the image of his father. His thumb hovered over DELETE for a moment, before selecting CANCEL. He put the phone back in his pocket.

CHAPTER 22

MINING FOR GOLD

We live for an instant, only to be swallowed in complete
forgetfulness and the void of infinite time on this side of us.
Think how many ere now, after passing their life in implacable
enmity, suspicion, hatred . . . are now dead and burnt to ashes.

—MARCUS AURELIUS

MIKE MET EVA IN FRONT OF 26 Federal Plaza, in lower
Manhattan. She was more beautiful than ever, but he
pretended not to notice as she walked toward him. He couldn't
get her out of his mind, unless the princess was around. She
was going to show him the best data-mining computers the
feds had. He'd heard about them and read an article or two,
but he was about to see the real thing. He hoped it would help
with the case, and it gave him a break from filling out all of
the follow-up forms stacked on his desk.

He felt a bit nervous as Eva approached. He found himself attracted to the princess and wanted to explore that, but at the same time he still loved Eva and wanted her back. It was only the wall of civilization around him and his own moral compass that kept him from attempting to pursue both avenues. When a man became involved with two different women, he stood a good chance of losing both of them. He didn't want that, so he'd have to choose—though it was said the woman chose the man.

White Homeland Security trucks were parked at the curb, along with a few black FBI SUVs. Traffic roared past on Broadway as pedestrians moved along the concrete sidewalks in the endless daze of their meaningless consumerist lives.

"I saw the attack on the news," Eva told him.

"It was a warzone," Mike said.

"You survived."

"I seem to have nine lives. I just hope I'm not on number eight."

"You're so grim," she told him. "This is all going to be over soon."

"*Tabula rasa*," Mike said. A blank slate for his life. He knew that after this, they'd have to make big changes, or forever be slaves to a soulless bureaucracy, a prison-city that cursed itself.

"I got you access to the newest database, via the FBI," Eva announced. "I hope it helps. Also, here's a disk I received from Detective Rogers in Suffolk County. It has both the possible suspect's DNA from blood and the DNA from the dead guy on it. You can check this in the database."

"That's some good news at least," Mike said. "This whole case, something about it is much different. It's like I'm in a maze of mirrors, and my perceptions are not reality."

They walked toward the entrance, where two security guards waited in gray and black uniforms. Eva showed their passes, and the guards let them in. Another set of guards waited inside. Eva showed the bar-coded passes again. One of the guards swiped them through. They moved past the turnstiles and into the main lobby.

Eva's heels clip-clopped on the black and white granite floor as she walked. They stepped into an elevator, and she pressed the button for the basement. A moment later, the elevator doors opened and another security guard scanned their IDs. They moved down a hall and entered a room with yet another security guard. "I need two things from you to get you full access," Eva said. "Your DNA and eye print."

"It's like *1984*."

"Not like," Eva said. "Is."

The security guard handed Eva a sterile swab. She swabbed Mike's mouth, bagged the sample, then pointed a computerized light pen at his eye to read the print. When she was finished, the guard took charge of bag and pen.

"All set," Eva said to Mike.

"Thanks."

"No problem. I'm giving you a high level of access regarding this investigation. I had to talk to the Feds in Washington, and I twisted a few arms on this. So make it count."

Mike followed her into another elevator, which let them off several floors lower, in another long hall. They walked tunnel after tunnel of cold cement: a sterile labyrinth—big soulless government at its finest. Mike reflected for a few moments on where the case might lead. He didn't care for any of the likely possibilities; they all pointed toward an abyss that might be impossible to escape.

"Rumor has it," Eva told him, "this place was—maybe still is—a nuclear shelter, with dozens of bunk beds and hundreds of days of supplies hidden away."

Whatever the case, there was much more to the place then one could see from the halls. The room Eva brought him to was dimly lit and the size of a warehouse, with dozens of wall-size 3D monitors displaying data and numbers. People moved about, scurrying back and forth like worker ants. The scene looked like something out of a movie.

They entered a chilly room down the hall from the main data center. Eva sat him down in front of a twenty-foot-wide holographic monitor. The screen was translucent plastic, but had 3D depth and was responsive to touch and voice.

"This is called the Tree of Knowledge," Eva told him. "It's an evolving OS based on artificial life algorithms. The main program is Venom, an animated spider that spins data on the screen. Data mining used to take weeks or months; now everything's done on the fly. All the data is created right in front of you."

"Looks easy enough."

"Want anything to drink?"

"A cold beer would be nice, but no thanks."

Eva left Mike alone. He gazed at the crystal touch screen in front of him; it looked like a flat-screen TV. In the screen's upper-right-hand corner was information on how the bot worked; the middle of the screen showed the data being sorted visually. Text at the bottom announced that "Spider bots are artificially intelligent programs that use both heuristics or experience-based learning, and algorithms or the sorting of patterns, to search internets, intranets and extranets. Teaming with other algorithmic programs, spider bots pare down terabytes of raw information into the organized data points on your screen."

He typed in the real name of the man he'd killed in the alley: Sa'id al-Dussari. The computer's lights started to blink as the red-and-black animated spider named VENOM searched, sorted and data mined, spinning webs of information on the screen. The spider moved back and forth, weaving a web of colored strands. The spider itself looked like a daddy long-legs, creating colorful lines and bubbles on the screen. The colorful bubbles represented information; each one was a digital footprint. He clicked on the bubble labeled "Sa'id al-Dussari," and information expanded to reveal more information: his date and place of birth formed one bubble; companies he'd worked for another; classes he'd taken, prescriptions, subscriptions, bank accounts, stocks, real estate holdings, cars, toll booth usage, sporting event tickets, his family names, possible friends via cross-indexing with other people's data; airline trips, passport files, credit and debit card usage, cell phone and all of the websites he'd visited; his entire digital footprint. Mike saw that the man knew Persian and Arabic, and that he had family in both Saudi Arabia and Iran. He may have spent his time in Iran under the name Amir Paria.

All of the data was then cross-referenced with thousands of other people who who'd visited the same websites, restaurants, countries, etc. Times and dates were noted and compared, as well as homes and workplaces past and present; those that were near one another might make an association more likely.

Mike clicked on the dead man's job history, and found he'd been a covert operative and scalp hunter, talent hunter, and an assassin for Saudi Special Forces. He'd worked for them for over seven years, but what he'd done in the past three years seemed to be unknown. His whole digital footprint vanished at that time—as if his entire life had disappeared. He must have switched to another identity. But why would someone disappear for years?

Mike loaded the flash drive with the Suffolk County handless-and-headless body's DNA. He put in both blood samples—one taken from the body, the other from the car. The DNA results on the possible suspect came back to John Doe, also known as Khalid Al Zahrani, and his info popped up on the computer: the ghost name the princess had given him. He'd been in military intelligence and Special Operations in Saudi Arabia. After that—fifteen years ago—Khalid had been tried for murder in the UK, but had been acquitted. The judge in the trial was later arrested for accepting money from various Pakistani charities run by terrorists, and had died in prison.

He was said to be five-foot-eleven and of medium build, with a square and muscular face. According to the database, Khalid had a master's in computer engineering, and was last seen in the Kingdom of Saudi Arabia, working as a computer security analyst for Silicon Swords. Mike clicked on a purple bubble to the lower right. It showed a redacted name of someone who'd served in the Saudi Arabian Special Forces with both Khalid and Sa'id in covert ops in Afghanistan.

It didn't fit. Mike would have expected to find Khalid listed as dead or missing. Maybe it was his alibi? And why would a *field agent* be working computer security? Mike saw something else on the screen: the other blood sample, from the headless-handless body the princess said was the Iranian Reza Amir Rafsanjani.

Something didn't sit right; the puzzle was just adding pieces to itself, making it harder for Mike to put things together. The man Mike had killed in the alley was off the grid; the other man, the ghost, was a Kingdom of Saudi Arabia (KSA) agent doing black ops while using a dead man's ID from Suffolk County. Umar had been killed because he knew too much about something that Mike was now trying to find out about.

All men were gears in a plot—but to what end, and for whom? When the puzzle was finally assembled, who would be in the picture, and who would not? And who was the puzzle master?

Mike typed in Amarco. The computer created a line, a node bubble. The spider bot drew more lines, building a web for Amarco. Mike clicked on a data bubble, and it expanded.

A veritable encyclopedia of information appeared on the screen. To the right was a massive family tree of the entire royal family; below that, a large bubble with a millennia-long timeline of the Middle East.

On the left was a historical map of the area's tribes, with age and demographics for the past hundred years. Below this was an econometric listing for Saudi Arabia and the entire region, stretching back for centuries. All of this information was arranged in endless bubbles, organized by data type. Amarco had recently acquired two deep-sea oil drilling rigs and dozens of junior cap, oil exploration, gas and oil sands energy companies in massive private equity purchases. Data nodes, links and lines in 3D were created on the screen, a web of information. A data bubble opened up with news clippings about the company's SEC filings on the New York Stock Exchange.

A second window opened up with Šahrāzād's photo. She was listed as Amarco's chief financial officer. Mike also saw a bank named Green Revolution. Another info-bubble popped up, regarding holdings of the Emerald Enterprises company. Mike typed in Emerald Enterprises; a graphic at the bottom of the screen showed hundreds of companies in the Middle East, all linked together in a massive cobweb of past and present transactions. It looked like a massive money laundering scheme with interlinked financial centers.

A few minutes later Mike logged off and left the room. He signed a few legal non-disclosure documents with security, went over to the coffee machine and poured himself a cup, then sipped the scalding black liquid. It warmed his cold bones. Eva opened the door and walked over to him.

"When it's all over, will we still be the good guys?" Mike asked.

"We crossed that line a long time ago. It's all gray now, just different shades."

She looked distressed. "I lied," she said.

"What do you mean?" Mike asked.

"I want to move on."

"Why?"

"You remind me too much of our son."

Tears came out of her eyes. Mike's stomach was burning; the acid was cutting into him, ripping him apart. Each second was like a drop that further eroded him.

"I'm sorry," Eva said.

"I understand."

She wiped the tears from her eyes and checked her ringing cell. "I couldn't wait anymore, and had to tell you this. I have to go. We'll talk about it later."

Mike had to take an entire roll of Tums and a Pepcid. He took a moment to compose himself, then went back upstairs and headed for the restroom. He saw a man in the hallway, looking at him strangely. Later, he saw the same man on a cell in the lobby.

Mike's phone rang. It was Šahrāzād. "Thanks for calling me," he said. "Are you okay?"

"No."

"Sorry to hear that."

"Death is a part of life. My father is trying to modernize The Kingdom, and this is what he gets." She paused. "What else?"

"I would like a bit more information on Khalid."

"Give me a few hours. I should have something tonight."

"I'll hold you to it," Mike told her.

"I'm a princess, I get held to nothing. But for you, I'll make an exception,"

"Thanks."

CHAPTER 23

THE DOORS OF TAMERLAINE

Had I the heavens' embroidered cloths,
Enwrought with golden and silver light,
The blue and the dim and the dark cloths
Of night and light and the half-light,
I would spread the cloths under your feet:
But I, being poor, have only my dreams;
I have spread my dreams under your feet;
Tread softly, because you tread on my dreams.

—WILLIAM BUTLER YEATS

THE GENERAL SAT IN A COLD, dank stone cell, his left hand chained to the wall. The rusty chains colored his skin. The metal flakes cut into his flesh, and he bled the color of the rust. It was black as night, with no windows and no light. His sleep was dreamless as he lay all night on square mortared stones covered with algae and mold. His bones felt like icicles, his muscles old ropes, and his breath smoked from the cold. He shivered; only anger and fear kept him alive, but not for much longer.

He'd played by the rules his entire life, believing what he'd been taught and living the good life. Where had it all gone wrong? Sayf was above the rules, a prince and now a king. Soon to be a tyrant and then what? He sought a global hegemony to rule the world as he saw fit, with his books of philosophy by that 14th-century fool Ibn Taymiyyah, who hated foreigners and who had now poisoned the entire Middle East with his ideology of evil.

The rusty iron door creaked open, and he squinted as the warm light from the hallway cut through the darkness and stung his eyes like sharp knives. He slammed his eyes shut.

Sayf walked in holding a pen-sized LED flashlight. He put the beam on the general's face. "We want you to sign this," he said, and handed the general a piece of paper and a pen.

The general opened his eyes and squinted. "What is it?"

"A confession!" Sayf said with glee.

"To what?"

"Being a traitor."

"Then you should sign it."

"You're brave?" Sayf took the paper back and put it in his pocket.

"I'm a soldier. How many others were arrested?"

"Use your imagination," Sayf said. "If you change your mind so you can sign the papers stating you're a traitor, that's okay; we will have other uses for you. Sayf pulled out a small tablet computer and played a video. It showed the general's daughter Aaliyah with a masked man who held the day's newspaper. Aaliyah was afraid, and asked to be spared.

"If you confess I will spare her."

"I don't believe you."

"Have I ever lied to you?"

"No, but that doesn't mean I can trust you."

"Fair enough."

"If I confess, what will happen to her? Will she live?"

"In my prison. And be released after a few years."

"If I refuse?"

"She will die a horrible death."

"I don't trust you. I will be just one of your thousands of trophy skulls."

"Yes, you will. You'll be in the autobiography I'm writing, sure to be a bestseller."

"All murderers do have excellent prose," the general told him.

"She will die regardless," Sayf said, "and I cannot be trusted."

The general nodded and said nothing.

Sayf left and slammed the metal door shut, turning the small room into a cold black tomb.

A few hours later Sayf strode into a torchlit stone courtyard and sat on a great wooden chair carved with thousands of lines of Arabian poetry. "Bring out the heretic and infidel!" he commanded his guards.

One of his soldiers made a signal, and four guards disappeared down a corridor. Moments later, the general hobbled into the courtyard with rusted chains on his arms and legs. He halted by a large, clean white stone.

A big man with burning eyes and well-muscled arms wielded a broad scimitar. His face and body were covered in a flowing white robe, a stark contrast to the black-clad warriors around him. There was silence. King Sayf stood up and spoke. "Silence! The time is now right. God has opened our path to greatness. There is a turning of the tide, and we shall flood the gates of the enemy. I am the Lord of the Fortunate Conjunction. You are a member of the old regime, and we must let your blood flow. We are starting anew: a clean slate." He picked up the sword he'd taken from the general's wall and strode over to him. "Do you confess?" he asked.

There was a long pause before the general replied. "Yes, I confess. I confess I do not believe you will hold up your end of the bargain, and I confess that I stood up to you, and that you shall lead us all to hell!"

"So I assume I'm not getting your signature," Sayf said. "No."

The watching soldiers laughed.

"Silence!" Sayf paused for a long minute.

"I admire your strength, and for this I will let her live—for now. Perhaps she can be a wife in my harem." Sayf leaned close and whispered in the general's ear. "You just don't understand," he said. "People don't respect anything but fear. They love and admire power. That is all that matters. Where have your silly morals gotten you?"

"You still have some humanity," the general told him. "But it dims with every second you reign. Before I die, I have one question for you."

"What?"

"What did you purchase with the hundreds of millions in laundered money?"

"I bought something very special from Pakistan. You have faith, even though you are on the wrong side of history, and I admire this greatly. But you must die. Hell is being a heretic."

The big man forced the general down on the clean white stone. Sayf drew his stolen sword and raised it above his head.

"You are a living hell!" the general said.

"I am God's punishment," Sayf replied. "And in time I shall be more than a Wali . . . *Bilshifa*," he finished: *Wishing you good health*. The blade whistled through the air and struck bone, vibrating with the impact. "Clean his skull," Sayf said to one of his men.

"What are your orders, sir?" Mustafa said as Sayf wiped the blood off the sword with white Egyptian cloth.

"Congratulations," Sayf told him. "You're promoted to general of all land forces of our future empire. My orders are to go to war with Iran."

The soldiers roared their approval.

Sayf saw a small scorpion crawling where the general's blood stained the ground. He pulled out his knife and put it near the creature. The scorpion walked along the blade and onto his hand.

An hour later, the glowing moonlight touched King Sayf's face as he stepped from his car onto the runway at Riyadh. He looked at the all of the people who'd gathered at the airport:

thousands from all walks of life awaited his arrival: students, soldiers, wives. The security team had secured all cell phones, while at the same time using cell and electronic jammers to keep the king's speech off the Internet. The world's economy had stagflated over the past decade, and the Middle East had been hit hard with high inflation due to government profligacy.

Sayf walked up the steps to the plane with his head held high, having dreamt of this moment for decades. He gazed at the moonlit wisps of cirrus clouds in the black night sky, and at the tarmac awash in the pulsing red rays of the runway lights. He drew his dreams upon reality, making them real. He no longer had to hide who he was, for he had become what he had dreamed; he was now his dream.

Sayf stood like a colossus, a superman. His eyes were searing coals of ambition, his neck like a wrestler's and his arms like powerful writhing snakes. He was a man at the pinnacle of nature's hierarchy. "Our country is at the center of world history," he told the gathered crowd. "And we shall make it the eye of the coming storm! We are no longer the little people, greedy and cruel, but knights under the banner. Now it is time to be great once more."

Hundreds of spectators held burning torches and flags that snapped in wind howling over the runway. The crowd was intoxicated with hate. They were disillusioned by the political realities they lived with each day, and Sayf was the one who gave them hope in their sea of discontent.

"Our enemy Iran will launch a war against Iraq," Sayf continued, "and Kuwait and the Emirates, to steal their oil and gas. But their dream is to sweep into our lands. They will fail, and Iraq will become part of us. We are the rising tide, we shall sweep away our enemies. Our storm is rising! Our ideas are the sword and our believers the wielders of our steel. Too many times and for too long, Arab regimes have been run by the Americans, who are thieves and tyrants.

"The blood of martyrs is the seed of our ideas, and the blood of our enemies enriches the soil in which we sow those seeds. Belief is power, and no weapon or army is more powerful than belief!"

The sands from the desert wind stung his face. He looked up at the sky, at the waning crescent moon. A great peace came upon him; the solitude of the desert. He had always known it would come down to this. The course of human history was before him; he felt its weight. He could change everything, forever. "The Americans and the West wanted democracy in Arabia, and they will soon see that I am—we are—the face of our democracy!"

He waved to the crowd, and stepped into the plane.

Sayf pondered what was happening. It was no longer just a thought or a feeling, but a reality. The memories of what he desired faded when he closed his eyes, but stood there in front of him when he opened them. He turned on the television as he sat down, putting CNN and MSNBC on a split screen. Mustafa came into the room.

For Sayf, the timing of the news was perfect. "Today in Iran," said the newscaster, "a major pipeline was struck in a terrorist attack. Iranian intelligence blames Iraq, and the Iranians have just announced a war with Iraq and Kuwait . . . Just what the hell is going on?"

The newscaster turned to a political analyst Sayf had seen on other newscasts, an older gentleman with moppy hair and dark rings under his eyes. He always wore a gloomy frown when he spoke, which had led some to dub him "Dr. Gloom." Sayf put the TV on mute and relaxed for a full minute, just to absorb the world moving ahead at smashing speed.

Watching the news, he saw thousands of people marching in New York City, protesting high oil prices. Store windows were being smashed by agitators, and the police were in full riot gear. "What can we do?" asked the subtitled text below the images on the screen.

"Every super-state needs its own Emmanuel Goldstein," Sayf said to Mustafa. "I have waited over twenty years for this one moment. Years of creating front companies, years of logistics, putting people in the right spots at the right times—and I have done it. America will cease to be an empire."

"Yes, twenty years," Mustafa said, and sighed with relief.

"We still have so much to do, so much to accomplish," Sayf told him. "We have created more options for ourselves, and fewer for our enemies."

"Yes, the roads are open," Mustafa agreed.

"We dreamers are dangerous men."

CHAPTER 24

FLYING CARPETS

In daylight watch with vigilance of an old
wolf, at night with the eyes of a raven, and in
battle fall upon the enemy like a falcon.
—GENGHIS KHAN

MIKE SENT ALEISTER a text on his phone: "I'll meet you at your office, I'm coming from downtown."

"I'm on my way from One Police Plaza," Aleister replied.

"10-4," he texted back. He got into his car and drove out of the parking garage at 26 Federal Plaza. He felt police fatigue from the long crazy hours. He turned on some mind-numbing techno dance music as he left the parking garage. Soon he was on the FDR Highway, heading home. Every few seconds, the cement lines in the highway would "thump, thump." After a time, it wanted to rock him to sleep.

The highway was free of cars. Mike forced his eyes open as he felt sleep pulling them shut. He squinted and yawned, endeavoring to stay awake. His eyelids felt like a fisherman's lead sinkers. He drifted across the empty lanes. Gazing up at the sky, he saw a glowing moon, and stars that sparkled and glistened. Clouds moved in front of the moon, darkening the world for a moment. But then they passed, and the night sky glowed again. More clouds passing over made the moonlight seem to flicker in slow motion. The wind from the open window felt cold on his face. He could almost taste the air in his mouth. He strained as he yawned, and squinted his eyes again to keep awake.

Things wore on him. He tried to block it all out, but couldn't. Instead he dwelled on it. His mind was stuck on his pending divorce with Eva, and the memories of his son Chris. He put his cell on the dashboard and glanced at a slideshow of pictures: Chris on a red sled.

Mike's neck and upper back ached; his spine felt compressed. He took a caffeine pill to wake up, since it was too unsafe to be sleepy while driving. He felt used and washed out. With the palm of his hand on his chin, he twisted and cracked his neck to relieve the tension.

From all the bank robbery jobs, assaults, criminals resisting arrest, and drunk drivers that didn't want to come to the stationhouse, to the wiretaps, follows, leads, tips, and shootings—could anyone ever really turn it off?

The cool air blew into his face, and he saw the trees on the side of the highway move as the wind touched the branches and leaves. He changed the channel on the digital satellite radio. "*Celebrity drug use and celebrity hookups next!*" one channel stated. "*Drugs in sports: should they be legalized?*" said another. He put on some light Brazilian jazz, and listened to a soothing saxophone and the sultry voice of a lounge singer from another time and place.

Reality brought him back when he looked in his rearview mirror. Flashing red-and-blue lights streaked up the highway, coming closer. It looked like an unmarked police car. Mike turned on his signal and slowed down, moving to the right. As the car drew near, Mike saw the driver's face. It was the same man he'd seen before—the one he'd followed in Central Park and at Grand Central Station. Mike felt anger and fear flush through his body. He glanced at the plate: DXH-something. He picked up his phone and dialed Aleister.

"Come up the highway; someone's following me," Mike said.

"I'll be there with backup, ASAP!"

"Too late," Mike said.

The car rammed him, and the passenger started shooting. Mike saw a second vehicle in the rearview, and then a third: a dark gray van, speeding up and trying to pull alongside. It looked like a van full of angry assholes. Guns fired at Mike from all vehicles. He didn't have his vest on. One of the men in the van opened up with a submachine gun. Bullets hit the car and shattered the windows. Mike only saw part of the plate on the van.

Mike looked in his rearview mirror and saw Aleister, with lights and siren off. The chief had never been one to show his cards.

Aleister rammed one of the attacker's cars and unloaded a clip of 9mm rounds into the vehicle. One of the attackers was hit in the eye. Another pulled out a submachine gun. Aleister smashed the car again, forcing it into the wall beside the highway. He unloaded another clip and struck a second man in the face. Blood splatted like a paint ball as the man went limp. The passenger in the second vehicle popped up through of the sunroof, pulled out an AK and unloaded. Aleister swerved out of the way and shot back, striking the man in the arm, but the second burst from the AK hit Aleister, and his car spun into a cement pillar.

Mike slammed on the brakes, turned around and unloaded into the man with the AK, striking him in the back. The driver of the car changed lanes and sped past Mike. Two men in the vehicles dropped smoke bombs, and all three drove off as sirens sounded behind them. The attackers disappeared faster then they'd come.

"10-13 here on the highway!" Mike yelled into his cell.

"What?" a voice answered.

"Cop shot, partial plate 580 black! I'm on the FDR highway, northbound!"

Mike heard police sirens getting closer, and realized that his attackers might have been listening to police radio calls. "Fuck!" He looked ahead as the smoke dispersed. His pursuers must have taken a construction exit off the highway, another mile up from where he was. Police cars screamed up the FDR. Mike saw an ambulance in the distance, speeding closer.

A highway cop came toward him on the wrong side of the road. "10-85! Cops shot," he said as he saw the wreckage from the shootout.

Mike limped out of his car and ran over to Aleister. He saw the look in Aleister's eyes. He'd seen that look before, in Afghanistan; the gaze of dead eyes. CPR wouldn't help; Aleister's heart was shredded from the rounds. The man who'd raised him after his father was killed, so that he could live a better life and save his mother—was dead. His uncle couldn't have been a better father to him through the years. He saw this too much in the military and on the job; good men dying and bad men living. It wasn't fair.

Mike grabbed the highway cop's radio. "Cop shot!" At least five armed men; three vehicles; two in a car and four in a brown van," he yelled into the radio.

"You okay?" The highway cop asked.

"My arm was grazed." He felt it now, with the adrenaline fading.

The highway cop got on his radio. "Cops shot! Another critical! We're looking for a van and two cars that exited the FDR highway exit ramp ahead no more than a few minutes ago. Both vehicles gray or black; suspects armed." He turned to Mike.

"You're bleeding. Lay down, you're losing blood."

"Huh?"

"You're bleeding from the chest," the officer said.

Mike looked down and saw he'd been hit in the left side. "Fuck! I'm fine; they exited off the construction ramp. Getting them is more important than me right now." He felt weak and lightheaded.

"You hit?" Eva said over the speakerphone as Mike picked up his buzzing cell.

"I'm fine," he said.

"That means you're hit," she said.

"It's just a graze."

"Mike? Mike?"

Mike hit the ground.

"Central, we need EMS; two cops shot!" Mike heard as everything went black.

Mike woke up in the hospital. The heart monitor was beeping beside him. He looked at it; his heart was fine. He touched the bandages on his torso. He felt sore, but not too bad—certainly not as bad as he'd expected. How much of that was painkillers? He pressed the call button. He couldn't relax, and thoughts crept back into his mind. Genuine fear was something he'd not felt since Iraq and Afghanistan. Most of all, though, he thought of his son. He touched the gold cross around his neck. He hoped this was not a harbinger of things to come. He felt that something wasn't right; there was a queasiness inside of him. He felt sick. He squinted and pulled himself together.

"You're okay?" the nurse asked as she came in the room. "Just a graze," she said.

"I'm okay."

Eva came in. Her face was sad. She attempted a poker face, but couldn't hold it. "Aleister is dead."

"I know. I'll get revenge."

"You need to rest." Eva looked at him, and he could see that she wanted to tell him to stop, to leave, to retire and not get killed.

"We have no time," Mike said. "It's just a graze and a bruised rib. I'm full-duty soon right?"

Eva said nothing. She bit her lip. "He was a good man. And yes to your question."

"He was my father's brother. They don't make men like that anymore."

"They made you."

Mike said nothing. He thought about the father he'd never met. What kind of man had he been? He'd died for a son he'd never know. Now Mike had to live up to that, be his father's son and do what was right. Aleister had been a good uncle, a father figure. His wisdom had guided Mike, allowing him to find himself in the wilderness of this world. He was no molder, no tyrant who stamped his image on another's soul—but a man who'd encouraged Mike to explore the world and find his own compass.

CHAPTER 25

UNITED NATIONS

A foolish faith in authority is the worst enemy of truth.
—ALBERT EINSTEIN

FOLLOWING MR. ABDUL'S CALL thirty minutes ago, informing her of an emergency UN meeting, Šahrāzād arrived at the United Nations on East 48th Street. She flashed her diplomatic ID to UN security. She wanted to run, but couldn't.

She started to relax, yet she still had a nagging anxiety about what was about to happen. She knew there was going to be a big speech about her father's assassination. She didn't want to relive it, but knew she'd have to deal with this. She saw Mr. Abdul in the lobby, waiting for her.

"You were fast," he said, giving her a warm hug and a kiss on each cheek.

She returned the actions. "I had to come."

"These times shall pass," he said, and she nodded.

They both walked into the elevator. Šahrāzād stared at the changing floor numbers as they ascended to their floor. The doors opened and they stepped into cooler air. It felt good, calming her hot nerves just a bit, but not enough. Šahrāzād and Abdul walked down the plain carpeted hallways and into their offices. To the right was a large conference room.

Šahrāzād felt like she was in a trance; going through the motions without revealing what she felt. She hid behind a mask, as she'd done so many other times; she was a stoic when she needed to be. She noticed her uncle Mr. Bahar was there in the room. He was bald with a pot belly and a silver goatee. He sat at his large Oakwood table and did not look up.

"Thank you, I know this will go well," she said. She bit her lip. Abdul pretended not to notice.

"War never goes well," Bahar said. He picked up the papers on the desk. Normally, he would have been warm to her, and might have given her a hug, but Bahar was not himself. He pulled on his jacket nodded to Abdul.

"You're ready to give the speech?" Šahrāzād asked her uncle.

"I'm not giving it; he is." He motioned to his left as Sayf entered the room. The king didn't notice his sister, or say anything. He was in deep thought, staring at a paper he had in his hand. He took a folder from a table and motioned for those in the room to follow him.

All three of them were in the elevator with the doors closed. The elevator moved up again, but only one floor. The doors opened. The man left and another man got on with a woman; they were talking. She couldn't even focus on what they were saying; the elevator doors closed again. She wanted to reach out and touch the buttons, to smash them.

Moments later, Šahrāzād watched Sayf stand at the podium, ready to address the UN. He paused for a half-second. She bit her lip as he hesitated. At a nod from the Secretary-General, King Sayf proceeded with his speech.

"Thank you, Mr. President. Mr. President, Mr. Secretary-General, distinguished colleagues, I begin by expressing my thanks that you are here today for this important moment in history." His tone was confident and clear, and he had the charisma of a leader. The words he said sounded like thunder.

Šahrāzād listened closely. Sayf had always been clever, and it was hard for her to know when he lied, though it was rare that he told the truth whenever they talked, which wasn't much for the past few years. Why did her synesthesia not work with him? Was he smarter, or was it because her mind was somehow clouded by their relationship? Her brother had been emotionally distant from her, yet he'd always supported her. He was passive-aggressive, loving his sister because his values demanded loyalty to one's blood. He did not agree with her on every political issue. These thoughts distracted Šahrāzād, and Sayf's speech seemed muffled in the background. But that was normal for her; when she listened to him, she always probed his underlying logic, which impressed her as a troublesome puzzle composed of the labyrinthine words he used to disguise his motives.

"This situation has been festering for over a decade," Sayf continued, "and we need to resolve it now. Preliminary reports of the investigation show that Iran was involved in the assassination of my father, the king of Saudi Arabia—an operation that took place in New York City. We see this as a direct attack on our nation. We do not yet know the results of the investigation into the death of the Saudi diplomat who was recently murdered, also in New York. An investigation is pending in this regard. The Kingdom of Saudi Arabia is hereby officially at war with the Islamic Republic of Iran." Sayf took off his glasses, and wiped the sweat from his head.

Šahrāzād scanned the faces of the various diplomats in the audience, and saw that they were both amazed and concerned. It was a turning point in history. Was this the beginning of World War III?

"We have the right to defend ourselves," Sayf went on, "and we already have the United States on our side to help with this war of justice. I thank all of you for being here, and I hope to one day fulfill our international obligations to the state of Iran, to the benefit of the Iranian people. We should all march forward with this duty. Thank you, Mr. President."

Sayf stepped down from the podium and walked to the back hallway. He took off his glasses, and wiped the sweat off his head.

To Šahrāzād, something didn't jibe; the words and the man who spoke them seemed at odds. To her, it felt and tasted like two different things that had been forced together—like cool mint, *naSnaS,* and spicy hot, *mutabbal.* Her own mind was clouded, and she thought again of her father, the king, and his desires: peace and change throughout The Kingdom, a modernization with the ultimate aim of a real secular democracy. But was it possible to do all that and retain The Kingdom's unique identity? Or had her father been an idealist? Had she and her father dreamed an impossible dream? Many nations were mere avatars of their pasts, and forever doomed. Perhaps she and her father were wrong, and the tyrants of religion and ideology would prevail. Could progress be an illusion? Did the dreams of the Middle Ages beckon the masses to retreat to the safety of the past?

Such doubts crept inside of her. She wanted to believe the best about people, but it was hard sometimes. Her mind clouded with swirling emotions, tastes, sounds and sensations—but she did what she'd disciplined herself to do: remain stoic. "You did well," she said to Sayf.

"al-Hamdu li-llah," he replied. "Praise God, I'm doing well." Sayf nodded to her. He took a few prescription pills and walked over to a water cooler, drawing a cup to wash down the medication Sayf endeavored to be the superman, and to be superior to others—but time and the injuries of war, martial arts and sports had begun to catch up with him.

Abdul nodded to her. She noticed that his eyes scanned her face, as if attempting to read her thoughts. She kept her features emotionless. There were so many things to say, yet no one said anything. Sometimes people said too much, or said things at the wrong time, or didn't say anything. Rarely did they use words with economy and precision, like a surgeon with a patient.

CHAPTER 26

DEEPER INTO THE RABBIT HOLE

If I had a world of my own, everything would be nonsense.
Nothing would be what it is, because everything would be
what it isn't. And contrary wise, what is, it wouldn't be.
And what it wouldn't be, it would. You see?

—M4D H4773R, AKA THE MAD HATTER,
IN *ALICE'S ADVENTURES IN WONDERLAND*, BY LEWIS CARROLL

THE DAY AFTER THE HIGHWAY SHOOTING, Mike stood on a dark street corner. Lightning flashed in the night sky over New York City. Seconds later, a low rumble sounded, and rain started to come down in the mist near Manhattan's Union Square. The streetlights glowed in the haze, creating corona halos in the darkness. Mike picked up his cell and called Šahrāzād. "Meet me in a few at the address I just texted you," he said.

"I just got the text," she told him. Her voice was low over the phone, almost like a whisper. Mike pressed his ear closer to the cell. He liked the sound of her voice and wanted to tell her that, but wouldn't and couldn't. He was a few blocks away from Zed, the Mad Hatter's hive of sin.

There was a pause on the phone; someone must have walked by, or was near her. "We're going there because . . ." she said, voice now a bit weary.

"He's a hacker, and knows about a lot of things. He can help us find the ghost."

"A hacker?"

"His nickname is the Mad Hatter. We have red in each other's ledgers."

"He used to work for Russian Foreign Intelligence Services?" she said.

"You know too much. It's not sporting of me to lead you right to him."

"It was a long time ago," she said.

"And if you'd found him then?" Mike asked.

There was a slight pause in the start of her sentence. "We could blackmail him, watch him, give him up to Interpol, etc. . . ."

"Or other things," Mike added.

She paused. "Or other things. All governments kill to stay alive."

"How ironic that he may help us, and you. You must promise that you won't reveal him."

"No harm will come. What we say in Arabia is that life is a maze in the desert; the dunes always change, but our path is the same." The more she spoke, the more relaxed her voice became.

Moments later, Mike waited under the awning of a small store, keeping out of the rain. It was a few blocks from his destination. He thought for a moment about where all of this was leading. He was going farther down the rabbit hole. This was his Red Queen moment, and he was about to see the Mad Hatter in Wonderland.

He had a feeling this investigation was going to uncover things a part of him didn't want to see. But he knew that was how the world worked; societies rotted, and his job was to expose the rot. But lately he'd begun to see things differently. As he looked around, rot was all he saw.

Nothing was as it used to be, and what had once seemed solid ground was now soft like quicksand. It was interesting to see one's love life and the strange dichotomy of society both falling apart at once; so much to live and hope for, yet the reality was mundane.

He looked at the graffiti on the sidewalks, the streets filled with beggars living in tents, and the open-air drug dealing. All while wealthy elites drove past in limos, as if dwelling in bubbles that shielded their fortress world from reality.

As he waited for the princess, he considered the past twenty years of his life and his career, comparing them to the present. America's economy was now in ruins, the political system and everything around it rotted. He was supposed to shine a light on the darkness, to cure the illness—but he seemed unable to be the medicine anymore, unable to be the light. Either the patient was too far gone, or the doctor himself had become infected. He started to feel as if he was diseased. He was afraid that one day he'd look in the mirror, and see that he'd made so many lesser-of-two-evils decisions that good choices were no longer possible. That maybe it had all been to enforce laws that benefitted the elites and the plutocrats, ensuring that society remained stratified—the top ruling the bottom with the modern-day bread-and-circuses of Internet porn, drugs, celebrity sex scandals, sports, cage matches and virtual reality video games, all used and devoured by the masses to fill the emptiness inside themselves. Had America become a crumbling Roman Empire?

"Behind you," Šahrāzād said, startling him for a second. Her voice was breathless and smooth, like a cold drink on a hot day at the beach. She wiped the rain droplets from her face. They looked like gems. She seemed to be like a wisp of smoke; she came and went, entering and exiting reality so fast it seemed as if the real world were fixed in time, and she was the only thing moving. She was an illusion, but all too real. He hoped she was going to give him a quick impulsive kiss that was moist and delightful, but it didn't happen.

"So where is it?" she asked him. She seemed aloof, and looked at him closely.

Mike looked at her face. "Follow me," he said. "You're good, sneaking up on me like that."

"I try . . . I heard what happened with your uncle. I'm sorry for your loss."

Mike said nothing. His face clinched for a short moment.

"You okay?"

He closed his eyes for second and took a deep breath. She touched his arm.

"I'm okay," he said. "We die. Some of use choose our deaths and some of us don't."

Mike's stride slowed for a moment; he felt more relaxed and confident as the drizzle slowed and turned to mist.

"We were trained by your CIA," the princess told him.

"You have a lot of secrets," Mike noted.

"The most valuable commodity in the world is information." She touched his arm again. He looked at her. They both slowed down as they walked. A moment of silence, both of them looked at each other. He wanted to say so much, but gave her just one of the pieces of the puzzle of himself.

"My father died. I know your own mother died," Mike said. "I have his flag hung up in his memory."

Mike's voice was monotone, as if a part of him had died. He did everything he could to suppress his emotions behind the mask he wore.

The traffic was noisy as they walked to the next corner. "Can we speed it up?" Šahrāzād asked.

"Whatever you wish, my princess."

She looked at him as if to say, *You're a wise ass.* For a moment there was an awkward, almost painful silence. "Any info yet on what we talked about?" Mike asked.

"Here's what I found on our ghost, Khalid." She showed him her cell phone. He watched as an encrypted file decrypted before his eyes. The file icon on the cell depicted a small medieval knight and the numbers 4096 in the upper left-hand corner. "The man was former Saudi intelligence and former Saudi special ops.

"I know this."

"He has extensive training in Insurgency, counter-insurgency, counter-terror, guerrilla warfare, propaganda, electronic warfare, and CBRN," she said, the last being shorthand for Chemical, Biological, Radiological and Nuclear.

"What else is he trained in?" Mike asked.

"He can speak multiple languages, is an expert marksman and, as you Americans would say, an all-purpose badass."

"Damn."

"Well you're up against one of the best black ops intel soldiers in the world."

Mike shook his head. The two of them walked in silence the rest of the way.

Minutes later, Mike turned and looked at Šahrāzād. It started to drizzle again. The air seemed to become more full, a fog encircling the city like something out of a Sherlock Holmes mystery. The princess leaned against a wall and kept her watchful eyes open. She folded her arms as she stood, shivering in the rain when they stopped at their destination.

Mike pointed to a metal door between two large buildings, two blocks away from Union Square.

"That's it?"

"Yes."

Mike knocked on the graffiti-covered metal door, which led to an illegal underground nightclub. "I need to see the Mad Hatter," he said to the doorman on the other side of the rusty steel eyehole.

"Who's asking?" a gruff voice replied. "We're invite-only."

"I'm a friend of the Mad Hatter. Tell him I received the text."

"What's your name?"

"I'm Uncle Mac." Mike felt himself being sized up. "Just tell him that, okay?"

"Sure. Anything else you want me to do Mr. Mac?" The doorman's voice was terse and aggressive.

"Uncle Mac. Look, this is important. Don't be so tense."

"I'm not tense, I'm fucking relaxed man!" the doorman said.

Mike saw the eye move and heard a whisper in the doorman's ear. "I'll be back in a second," the man said.

Mike's cell buzzed a text message: "What does the Vorpal blade cut?"

Mike texted back: "The Jabberwock." He stepped back as the rusty metal eyehole slammed shut. His adrenaline went up. A few moments later, the door opened. Mike motioned to Šahrāzād, and she came over to him.

"Go to the back and then down the stairs," the doorman told them. He was tall, tan and well-muscled, as if his diet consisted of whey protein shakes and designer steroids. He wore a blue Adidas running suit that was a few sizes too tight, to show off his bulging assets. His muscles tensed up as he peered at Mike. "But first I have to frisk you and her for weapons." He stepped toward them.

"No, you don't!" Mike squared off. The doorman mirrored his movements.

"Says who!"

"I say!" Mike showed his gold detective's shield.

The man stepped back. "Are you going to shut us down?"

"I'm not here for that," Mike said.

"Are you here to arrest anyone?"

"Like I said, I'm here to see Zed. If I was here to arrest him, you'd be handcuffed by now." Mike stared at him and didn't blink. "I don't know or care what goes on here."

"Okay, then." The doorman nodded.

Mike and Šahrāzād stepped inside the nightclub. The place was almost pitch-black, with flickering blue and violet neon lights. Fluorescent lasers drew on the walls and ceiling, following the loud pulsing beat of futuristic electronic, house and trance music. The whole place pulsed with radioactive intensity. The beat of the music went right through him and into his organs, vibrating his insides.

The dance floor glowed with energy. The floor was patterned like a chessboard, and the artwork on the walls was pure medieval fantasy. All of the main characters airbrushed on the walls were chess pieces: a queen, a king and a knight, done in a Frank Frazetta fantasy style. Behind the bartender was a large painting of Mos Eisley by McQuarrie.

Women danced on black steel tables, displaying their perfect bodies. Love was for sale here. Wealthy men ate caviar and drank champagne while staring at the beautiful girls and their glistening, taut nude bodies. Mike overheard a man speaking in Russian. He turned to look. The man seemed a bit out of place in his tweed suit, speaking to a blonde at the bar.

"So how did you know about this place?" Šahrāzād asked.

"I know him. He owes me a favor. A big favor. But I owe him one, too."

"How do you know the Mad Hatter?"

"It's a long story. He helped us out with a few investigations. I saved his ass and he owes the debt."

They walked down a spiral, black metal staircase into the basement, where another bouncer guarded the entrance. The place seemed more bunker than basement.

"He's waiting for you," the bouncer said in a thick Long Island accent. He opened a large black door, revealing a room with dozens of large flat-screen monitors. The computer towers all had colorful neon LED lights inside of them. The door slammed behind them as they walked in: a sharp metallic clang.

A large black leather chair spun around. *"Privet Tak chto kartina golovolomk?"* So what is the picture of the puzzle? Zed didn't bother to stand up.

"Koroleva Chervey i Krasnaya Koroleva." The Queen of Hearts and the Red Queen," Mike replied

"Khorosho. Vot chto takoye zhizn': kartochnaya igra, igra v shakhmaty i golovolomka. Zhizn' zavisit ot kart nam dayut i kak my igrayem v igru." Good. That is what life is: a card game, a chess game and a puzzle. Life depends on the cards we are given and how we play the game."

"You always have much to say," Mike replied.

Zed was a small man, yet handsome and lean—but not quite too lean to be athletic. He wore glasses and a navy blue NYPD baseball cap. He had a six-pack of Red Bull next to him.

"Kto russkiy?" Who's the Russian in the club? Mike asked.

"You're paranoid but have every right to be. He's a professor of math at Columbia. He makes a few extra bucks giving me tips on a new encryption algorithm. And he likes the ladies," Zed spoke with a Russian accent.

"So how's the brothel business?" Mike asked.

"Great. Everyone pays for it, one way or another. Even Einstein himself said there was little difference between prostitution and marriage."

"Rumors are you're the new Silk Road part Infiniti," Mike said. "That you're running thousands of drone TOR servers for the dark net."

Zed smiled. "Why, officer, I have no idea what you're talking about."

"I can see you've been busy." Mike looked around, impressed with the small criminal empire Zed was building. Zed's purpose was profit. *My prophet is profit,* read a sticker on one of his custom-made computer towers.

"I'm always busy." Zed took a sip of his Red Bull. He had a stuffed penguin beside his laptop, and a fish tank along the left wall, with a pet Satanic Gecko named Gordon inside. Its eyes were red, and its horned head was sheathed in ferocious evolutionary armor. The wallpaper on Zed's desktop depicted ancient Mayan temples, interspersed with photos of the Himalayas that Mike had sent him while traveling there. "First off, I want to say thanks," Zed announced. "And secondly, I want you to say you're welcome. So, why are you here? Revenge?"

Mike rubbed his eyes. "Vengeance is justice. And I'm here to cash in my rain check."

"Revenge is the ultimate payment."

"That it is."

"Everyone's got a rain check to cash," Zed told him. "By the way, who's your sexy friend? She looks like one of my dancers." He leered at the princess.

"Do not speak that way to me!" Šahrāzād said, sudden fury in her eyes.

"I can't not look at you; you're a magnificent creation of evolution."

"I think Zed has a point," Mike commented.

"First time I've been insulted and complimented in the same sentence," Šahrāzād said. "You Americans sometimes lack subtlety."

Zed cracked open another Red Bull, spiked it with some Saki and took a sip. "Are you one of those crazy Latinas?"

"I'm an Arabian princess!"

"You're also a member of Mensa," Zed told her.

"Why did you ask if I was Latina when you know who I am?"

"Because I'm a *zhopa* and *sutenyor* asshole and pimp, and I like to test people. I, too, am a member." Zed's eyes roved up and down her body.

"I need info," Mike said.

Zed turned to Šahrāzād. "What does Quilty know about the chief of police?" he asked.

"A thing or two that makes him his slave," she answered. "I taste sounds; what am I?"

"A synaesthete," Zed replied. "Are you?"

"I am. Lexical-gustatory synaesthesia. Your voice is plain and has no flavor. You are a chameleon, just like someone I know."

"You're also the daughter of the King of Saudi Arabia," Zed said. "You're a princess of a dying political system, a fossil. That's why the Middle East has so many problems; it's unevolved."

"You're audacious, and you're a Russian," she told him.

"Hey, I'm American now. One cannot taste any success without the heart of a gambler who counts a few cards along the way." Zed had the cool face of a poker player, and the voice of someone who never lacked for confidence.

"Are you always sardonic when you rain insults on others like broken glass?" Šahrāzād asked.

"All of the time, *suka*," Zed replied.

"We're tight on time." Mike touched Šahrāzād's wrist and looked at his watch.

"Are you in a rush? You're not Russian," Zed remarked.

"My mother was half Russian and half German," Mike said.

"We say time is gold in Arabia," Šahrāzād replied.

"I'm guessing you need me for something," Zed opined, taking another sip of Red Bull.

"I need to find a ghost," Mike told him. "We need his photo."

"A ghost is out and about? I take it this is not about the apparition of a lost soul, but someone who took over a dead man's life, and the dead guy is MIA."

"Right," Mike told him. "Except the MIA is now KIA. We found the body."

"He's going to commit an act of terrorism," Šahrāzād announced.

"A man living a double life?" Zed paused as he said this. "Well you can't live a double life forever. One life eventually seeps into the other. Right, Mike?"

"I burned the Russians while I was undercover, and they got to me. I saved you, and then the department stabbed me in the back. People died, but in the end you saved my ass with all the evidence you gave to Interpol and the FBI. Thank you for getting me out of that hole."

"You're welcome. You gave me the USA! Anyway, I'm guessing a black flag or false flag attack. The attacker wants to make it look like someone else did it, like Poland's fake invasion of Germany, or the burning of the Reichstag."

"I was thinking the same thing," Mike said.

"You both guess well," the princess said. "But you have to ask yourselves why."

Everyone was silent for a full minute.

"No one believes in conspiracies except crackpots on the Internet," Zed mused. "And the mainstream media buries that stuff and bullies the people who believe it."

"Even if we're right, we have an uphill battle," Mike agreed.

"My IQ is 172; I am statistically almost always right," Zed announced. "I know these things, and on this we are right."

"Anyway," Mike said, "we need to learn about his past—both the real man and his ghost."

Zed pushed two ergonomic chairs in Mike and Šahrāzād's direction. They sat down.

"I need a name," Zed told them. Taking another swig of Red Bull, he cracked his knuckles and readied his fingers at the keyboard.

"Khalid Al Zahrani may be the ghost who stole the identity of Reza Amir Rafsanjani," Šahrāzād told him.

Zed smiled. "I don't want a get out of jail card for this. I want a stay out of jail card."

"I'll do what I can," Mike told him.

"Good enough. Persian name and a Saudi name, hmm. I have to say whoever is behind this is smart, to have a Saudi ghost an Iranian." He punched the names into one of his programs. The letters flowed across the screen like a digital river.

Šahrāzād pulled out her cell and showed Zed the image of the Iranian she had. He was in his late 20s or 30s, clean-shaven with glasses and a medium build. He didn't look too much like the typical Middle Easterner; more Greek than Iranian.

"And this is?" Zed said.

"The dead man," she told him.

"And you need a picture of the man pretending to be him, right? Shouldn't you be able to get this information with your own databases?"

"I can't. My cousin Umar was killed, and he was a huge contact for me. My other contacts are laying low."

"He may be somewhere in the tri-state area," Mike said.

"When do you think the ghost took over?" Zed asked.

"A few days ago," Mike said.

"He's ghosting; he can't be off the grid. He has to keep the dead guy's identity visible," Zed stated. It's a high-stakes poker game, but how many cards will he show?"

"It's about a theory of mind," Šahrāzād said. "He's guessing how dumb or how smart we are."

"Perception is your reality," Mike said. "And not only that, but we have to prove this. What do we have so far? I need more." Mike saw this whole thing as a puzzle of deception.

He started to see the picture being drawn in front of him, and didn't like the future it showed.

Zed smiled again. "And your perception is your enemy's deception."

"Show too many pieces you want to be seen, which are not true, and you're exposed," Mike agreed. He saw a stack of cards on one of Zed's shelves.

"When was the body found?" Zed asked.

"A few days ago," Mike told him, and watched as Zed hacked the Realtor database, looking for apartments rented by anyone in the tri-state area over the past week and a half. He also checked to see which credit card companies had been notified of an address change.

"The ghost wants a trail, but not too much," Zed explained. "Just enough crumbs. I wouldn't use the same name if I were him, but a variation . . . Ha, I have some hits on our search results."

They looked at dozens of rows of digital photographs, downloaded by Zed from hotel desk cameras. It appeared the ghost was staying in different hotels, spending a few days at each; as if he didn't want to be recognized, yet wanted to leave a small trail.

"Just as I thought," Zed told them. "He's using variations of a shortened version of Reza's name." He scrolled through hundreds of images on the hard drive. "I'm trying to sync the images to the times when a possible ghost logged in or out of a hotel: time stamped."

"Stop on that picture," Šahrāzād said.

"Right here?"

"I think that's him, the ghost. I saw him in Qatar and Kish, a few months ago. My brother was with me. Sayf was with an American whose family is in the oil business; now he's in the drone, security and data mining businesses. He's connected politically."

"That's our ghost, Khalid," Zed stated.

Mike and Šahrāzād took out their cell phones and photographed the image on the screen. It was just clear enough to be a recognizable face. He looked a little bit similar to the man Mike had followed at Central Park and Grand Central. "It has to be him," Mike said.

"Was he wearing a disguise?" Šahrāzād asked.

"Not really," Mike said.

"Plastic surgery?" the princess suggested.

"Yes, I have info saying he had it done," Zed stated.

"Same build as the guy who tried to kill me, but it doesn't look like him," Mike said.

"The data mining program said he was dead?" Zed asked.

"Amazingly, no."

Zed showed him the ears of two men. The computer program looked for a match, scanning the old Khalid's ears from the data mining program's hacked images, and the new one and comparing them with Reza's ears. The tops of the ears matched: old and new Khalid.

"The plastic surgeon didn't get the ears right," Zed announced. "Ears are better than fingerprints, and Khalid, your ghost, is alive and well."

"He was never listed as dead," Mike replied, "which I thought was strange. But he must have had a great plastic surgeon."

Zed zoomed in on the video stills with his mouse, then took a screenshot. Khalid—AKA the ghost—was lean, wiry, and 5'11".

"So you've been to Kish?" Mike said to Šahrāzād. "I've been there too."

"Yes."

"Iran's Revolutionary Guard intelligence division is involved in trafficking, launders money in Kish, and counterfeits U.S. dollars," Mike said. "I could say more, but I signed the nondisclosure agreements."

"Everyone knows they print up U.S. twenty-dollar bills and Ben Franklins," Zed confirmed.

"Was this after you were in The Kingdom?" Šahrāzād asked Mike.

"Yes. I'll tell you about it sometime. You've been to a lot of places?"

"Yes," Šahrāzād said.

Šahrāzād pulled out her phone and took a photo of the screen. Mike did the same.

Zed looked at one of the monitors on his left.

"Yes," the princess said.

"I'm the fucking best. I wrote this program. And they say America has no more good hackers. Look out. Anonymous! Which I'm allegedly the leader of, and I plead the Fifth on that . . ." After a moment of silence, he changed the subject. "Looks like our dead guy has been busy," he said.

"How busy?" Šahrāzād asked.

"Look at all this," Zed replied, pointing to the window on the left side of his center monitor. "He moved lots of money from Kish to Dubai, and made several large all-cash withdrawals. Then, here, he opened up multiple businesses based in Florida and created a corporate checking account, and with that made some purchases at a nautical store. With another account, he bought truck tires and what looks like more boating equipment."

"Looks like there was a boat purchased in Florida," Mike added. "And the address of the registry is in New Jersey."

"He's definitely setting something up," Zed confirmed.

"What would I do if I were him?" Mike thought aloud.

"The corporation bought this stuff months before his death; look at the dates," Zed noted.

"That means they were planning his death months before he was killed," Mike said.

"This date here, April of last year," Šahrāzād pointed out. "That was two months after he came to the U.S."

"I'm inclined to think whoever killed him had been watching this guy for a while," Mike said.

"Whoever's doing this is patient," Šahrāzād agreed.

"I need copies of this," Mike said.

Zed made sure the image was on the screen, enlarged it and paused for a second. Mike took a few pictures of the screen "Can you be traced?" he asked.

"These computers are NSA-proof, and I should know; I was a contractor for them and worked for the SVR, the new KGB."

"Very Sun Tzu," Mike noted.

"I need you to look at something," Šahrāzād said, and handed Zed a cell phone with no battery.

"So you didn't want to be traced with this phone?" Zed asked.

"Correct," she said. "Whatever info is on the phone, I would like to have."

"You're asking for more?" He took the phone apart and examined the circuit board. Then he found a tool and touched the board with it. He tinkered a bit, then put it back together, replaced the battery and used the phone's wireless network to connect to his desktop computer. He typed a few commands at the computer's Linux command prompt shell.

Mike saw the screen light up with a series of numbers.

"This is a list of all phone numbers called and received," Zed told them. The people and businesses listed on the screen took up about fifty lines.

"Wait a sec." Mike recognized a phone number on the cell.

"What?"

"The company at the top of the list, Emerald Enterprises, it might be the same company card I saw in someone's apartment. He's calling them from this secure cell."

"That company is being used for something," Šahrāzād said.

"How do you know?" Mike asked.

She pulled out a USB drive. "This jump drive is the reason someone wanted me dead." She handed it to Zed, and he popped it into his workstation. The data was already decrypted.

"Hmm . . ." Zed looked at the documents on the disk: thousands of financial statements, info on various shell companies, and more. One of the companies was called Emerald Enterprises. Zed ran multiple searches of the company on the Internet. "Emerald Enterprises has electronic footprints," he announced. "And they have boats in Cyprus, Kish, the Bahamas, Ireland, New Jersey and North Carolina."

"What?" Mike asked.

"The company is linked to a few other shells, which have bank accounts at the same banks in Dubai and Kish, Iran. It's all smoke, my friend, but at least you see the smoke. You're Theseus in the Minotaur's maze, and your friend here is Ariadne."

"Why don't you like it?" Mike asked.

"It has to be a government or a group of terrorists with government or corporate experience."

"Now I know that what I thought is true," Mike said.

"This is some type of operation where someone powerful, or some group in the government in the Kingdom of Saudi Arabia or Iraq, wants someone else to be blamed for something," Zed told him.

"This whole thing," said Šahrāzād, "is a game-changer."

"Look at what's on TV." Zed pointed to one of his monitors, where streaming video from CNN showed massing naval forces from Saudi Arabia in the Strait of Hormuz. The text message on the bottom of the screen said that Iranian forces were lining up along the Iraqi border. Another message said the U.S. military was trying to protect shipping lanes and harbors in the region.

Mike focused on that word on the bottom of the screen: harbors. The ghost had bought a boat.

"Let's go back," Zed suggested, "to where they had a boat in New Jersey via the front company."

One of the screens in front of them showed a yacht. Mike thought about the evidence, about what they'd been discussing and what they'd seen in regards to shipping. It jarred his memory just enough; the gates opened up and the idea expanded. He recalled that Einstein had written a letter telling President Roosevelt that a nuclear weapon could be brought into a harbor by boat. Mike knew the bad guys were up to some kind of false flag operation, but now he saw it for what it was. No one would believe the truth.

It made sense. Why would anyone go through all this to do a black flag op? It might be by boat, since that would be the easiest way to get a nuke into Manhattan. The ghost, the raid, the backgrounds of the dead—and now boats linked to one of the dead. "I'll be right back," Mike said. "I have to make a call."

"Go this way for a signal," Zed told him. Zed got up and opened the door, leaving the office open. The princess saw Mike needed a bit of privacy as he pulled out his cell and stepped from the room.

Mike hoped Zed wasn't listening in, but didn't have much choice. He took the wedding band from his wallet and looked at it, then dialed Eva.

"What's going on?" she asked.

"There might be an attack soon, possibly with a boat."

"And you know this how?" Eva asked, her voice becoming louder.

"My investigation shows the ghost started a dummy corporation a few months ago and used it to purchase boating equipment."

"What you're really saying to me is that we may not be able to stop it."

Mike was silent for a moment before replying. "Yes."

"I hope you're wrong," she said. "The city doesn't care about you or me."

"I have to do this," Mike said.

"America doesn't want to be saved," Eva told him. "If you die for them, you won't be their hero. Heroes are celebrities to these people."

"I know what you want to say, so say it," Mike said.

"Your mother died, our son died. But for what?"

"I might be the only one who can stop it."

"Does that mean you have faith, Mike?" she asked.

"I've sacrificed too much. I have to do this."

"Where are you now?" Eva asked.

"Zed's. Why ask me?"

"When I saw you after the raid, I cried, but I couldn't tell you," Eva said. "It's hard to tell the truth, even to someone you love. I would have traded a million lives just for you. To hell with the world. I love you."

"I love you, too."

"We both have to wait, once this is over. Keep your phone on." She hung up.

He paused for a moment to digest the call. So much had been said. Too much, really. Years of closure in a minute of time. Time had become compressed. But what did his love mean? He'd loved her since they'd met. They had a connection like gravity, like two stars in the night sky, pulling each other into a common orbit and dancing until they died.

Mike went back into Zed's office. Šahrāzād seemed more relaxed, and was sitting down. Zed pointed to various computer monitors as he and the princess discovered new facts.

"I have to go," Mike told them.

"The party just started," Zed replied.

"Sorry, but it just ended," Mike announced. "If I were either of you, I'd leave the city. Something's going to happen."

"I'll take your word for it," Zed told him.

"I can't," Šahrāzād said. "I have to find out more. I'll call you when I have something."

"Agreed."

Mike turned to Zed. "Thanks for your help. I want you to know I knew you'd do the right thing."

"I'll give you two a minute," Zed told them, and left the room.

Šahrāzād stood up, and Mike noticed pearls of sweat on her honey-bronze skin. He embraced her, and each slid a tongue into the other's mouth. "Who doesn't love a rebel princess?" Mike said at last.

"Who doesn't love a rogue cop?" Šahrāzād said.

They both smiled, but realized it just wouldn't work in this world.

"I sense you love someone else," Šahrāzād said.

"I had to kiss you," Mike said.

Šahrāzād gave him a hug, gazed sadly into his eyes, and left. He stood there as she ran to her own warrant of hope. Mike had chosen the worst path, and realized he might just die after all. He wanted to run, but something held him back. Was it out of some sort of honor? A quest for justice, or truth? A need to atone for his sins?

He sat down for a moment. Was Šahrāzād a mirage of an oasis in this barren world, in this reality? Was the attraction mere curiosity, or the fact that fate had put them in the same boat? Or was it that she was one the few honest people he'd ever known? She was a princess trying to change her country so it would survive. In a day and age where no one cared, and almost everyone lived only for fame and vanity, she did care. She didn't have to live like this; that was her choice. She could ski in Switzerland and have lunch in Paris on the same day, then party the next day in Manhattan—or do lines of coke and hang with celebrities and American politicians. Instead, the princess chose to be loyal to her own set of morals and ethics, things far more abstract and forward-thinking than any writer of *Foreign Affairs* or *Foreign Policy* magazine could comprehend. She could have written for them, but chose to be written about; she subterfuged not for selfishness, but for a better world.

CHAPTER 27

NEW YORK NOIR

My way of learning is to heave a wild and
unpredictable monkey-wrench into the machinery.
—DASHIELL HAMMETT, *THE MALTESE FALCON*

T HE SKY WAS GIVING OFF a brown and purple haze. The
city was slowing down and speeding up at the same time.
Šahrāzād looked at the large polished stainless steel works of
art in front of the bank on 50th and 6th Avenues in Midtown
Manhattan. She had her trusty mirrorless camera with her,
customized for infrared and low-light photography. The
information she had gotten with it through the years was far
beyond what most would assume, and yet it was just a tool,
like a painter's brush or a writer's pen.

Her best friend, whom she'd met at Harvard, was a
photographer. She was *zajjid,* good, with a voice that tasted
like *khajoor,* Arabian sweet dates. She was the one who'd
showed and taught Šahrāzād how to use cameras as tools

for information. She'd taught her to purchase cameras only with cash, and to use hacked Photoshop programs to scrub the GPS and EXIF quasi-stenographic data that embedded the camera's serial number in every image. Using the camera, Šahrāzād zoomed in from fifty feet away, focusing on the man she was following; he was one of the those from Reza's apartment. She took rapid, sharp shots. He had a generic look; he could pass for anyone with multiple identities, which is what they look for in the field of intelligence: someone who could be anyone. One thing that made him stand out just a bit, though, was that he seemed to be in excellent condition, like a professional fighter.

The man entered the bank, and Šahrāzād thought of Mike for just a moment. His timing was right; in fact, it always seemed right. In this crazy world, he was there for her. He didn't even know if she could be trusted, yet he was there. She put her camera away in her pocketbook and adjusted her wig and sunglasses.

As Šahrāzād entered the bank, she overheard Khalid talking. She recognized his voice, but couldn't place where she'd heard it before; somewhere in her distant past. The bank was cold and ultramodern. Clean glass counters and Lucite walls divided everything: barriers in empty space. The floors of the bank were bright vanilla and off-white, polished marble.

"I would like to access my safety deposit box," Khalid said to a female manager. He was a few feet away from Šahrāzād. She knew being this close to him wasn't going to last, so she focused in on his voice as much as she could. He had a poisonous *murr* voice, a horrible voice of evil.

"Come with me," the feminine manager said to Khalid. The manager's heels echoed a staccato *clippy-clopp* on the white marble floor as he followed her down the narrow hallway.

As they both took the escalator downstairs, Šahrāzād pretended to fumble with her pocketbook. She pulled out her cell as she followed both of them on the escalator. He was ahead of her and just out of earshot. She looked around, so she'd look like she had something to do, then waved one of the bank managers over. *I need to have a reason to be here; I have no accounts in this bank, nor does Amarco.*

Šahrāzād looked again in her purse and saw she that did have information on one of Amarco's subsidiary corporations, and a passport with a false name on it. She paused for a second and then smiled. "I would like to open up a corporate account," Šahrāzād said to the bank employee who approached her.

"I'll be glad to help you," the handsome man said. "Come this way." His voice was like a perfume, the smell. Šahrāzād walked to a desk on the left side, near a long hallway. She saw her target, Khalid, walk down the hall with one of the managers, toward the safe deposit boxes.

"I'll be with you in one moment," he said to her as they walked away.

Moments later Šahrāzād saw Khalid shake the hand of the manager and walk briskly toward the exit.

"I'm Robert," the employee extended her hand to the princess.

"I'm Sarah," Šahrāzād replied. With her other hand, she pressed an app on her phone, which made it buzz. "It's nice meeting you. Oh, sorry, I have to take this call." She put the phone to her ear, turned and saw Khalid leaving. *Dammit,* she thought. "I'm sorry; I have an emergency," she told the employee. "When I come back I'll be sure to deal with you."

"Anytime, I'll be here," he said.

Šahrāzād's eyes locked in on Khalid as he left the bank, slipped into a black limo on 6th Avenue and took off. She moved outside, jumped into her Zip rental car parked a few spots away and followed.

She kept her distance as she followed. They drove through Randall's Island, a contrast to the civilization of Manhattan. Almost all of the homes and apartment buildings were run-down and empty, stripped of their copper pipes and wires, windows smashed, graffiti everywhere, with a few scatterings of homeless people wandering the empty streets. Yet the city was haunted, as if the spirits of the past were disappointed in the present, and frowned upon those still living.

Šahrāzād watched Khalid park his limo at a construction site on Randall's Island. She turned down another street and parked her car near Icahn Stadium. She looked around; the wind howled between the ruined buildings. She caught a chill that burned her skin like sharp ice and then faded. She stepped over a couple of deep puddles of blackened muddy water; after the recent rainstorms, puddles were everywhere. The sidewalks were filled with open garbage bags, Pringles canisters, chicken bones and empty beer cans. Garbage was piled up beside the streets. Mice ran between the garbage. The streets oozed with slime and raw sewage; the smell was horrid. The streets were quiet.

Šahrāzād heard a window slam shut in the distance. A cat hid under a car. The bricks were brown, and green mold was growing on the sides of the nearest building, which was painted with a diversity of colorful graffiti. A large dirty rat darted across the street. A lone homeless man with a heroin-induced shuffle walk pulled his rusty shopping cart nearby. Ambulance sirens echoed in the distance.

She took a deep breath to calm herself. She looked at the stars and wondered if her future was in them or herself. She took out her camera, turned it on and set it to infrared and silent. She looked around to make sure there were no cars or people nearby. The homeless man vanished into an abandoned building. It was a ghost town. She walked off the road toward where she'd seen Khalid go, just a few blocks away.

The building was half-completed, vacant and abandoned. It had no windows and was made of cement and twisted metal. It was an ugly skeleton of cement floors, wavy sheet-steel ceilings, and red-rust steel beams, ten stories high.

Šahrāzād hid behind some garbage cans, using her camera's zoom to scan the area. She saw someone on the building's roof, and moved closer. She ran between the buildings and went in a side entrance. Her skin was drenched with sweat. She paused for a few moments and remained quiet. She heard a faint whisper that made her freeze.

After a few moments she started to hear voices inside the building. The fear made it feel like dozens of baby spiders crawling all over her naked body. She watched where she stepped. She peeked through a hole in the wall and saw Khalid. He was about thirty feet way, with a lean man who wore a very expensive suit and a gold watch. Šahrāzād pulled out her camera and took a few shots in the dark, using the infrared setting, then switched to video mode and silently turned up the recorder volume to listen so that she could hear them.

"We're on schedule," Khalid said, handing over a small envelope. The man in the suit looked at it and put it in an interior jacket pocket. Šahrāzād felt the hatred in the unknown man's voice; it tasted rotten, *natin,* and smelled like death: a corpse, *zuooa.* Her synesthesia sometimes made her wince in pain. "Is he going to be in our way?" Khalid said.

"If he is, I'll handle him," said the man in the suit. "I have something good to put him on ice." His voice tasted metallic, like bitter metal.

"We can't have any setbacks," said Khalid.

"It won't happen."

"This will be the last time we meet." They nodded to each other, hugged briefly and walked from view. The angle prevented Šahrāzād from seeing more, but she heard two cars start up and saw them drive past, thirty seconds apart. The man from the roof was in the second car. She waited a few minutes, biting her lip. After a moment, she breathed out. She looked at what she'd caught on her camera: only a few pictures, but good ones—all in RAW file format.

She peered around the corner—carefully, watching and listening. Hiding behind the wall, she used her camera's IR to scan around the window. Nothing. She then popped her head out and looked around. Chances were, they'd left. She took a deep breath, feeling flush with adrenaline and exhilaration.

She heard a noise from behind, and turned. The man in the suit—the one with the rotten voice that tasted like death—locked eyes with her and grabbed her with one hand.

She dropped her camera. His eyes told her that he knew. He held a gun. She wrist locked it right out of his hands. She saw that he was surprised by how she'd reacted; she didn't freeze in fear but struck hard, her years of training paying off in the crucial moment.

Her attacker lurched forward, trying to drag her to the ground. She grabbed him and put her foot on his hip, using his forward momentum as she dropped her hips and thrust her foot into him, pulling hard. She somersaulted backward with him. He landed right on his back on the hard street, stunning him; a perfect judo throw: *Tomo Nage*.

The man flipped over on his stomach and started to rise. She roundhouse kicked him in the head for good measure. She looked to the gun on the ground, fifteen feet away, but didn't have time to pick it up. Spotting two more men, both coming her way, she ran to the car and drove off.

CHAPTER 28

SAILOR ON THE SEAS OF FATE

I know not which I prefer the look of—those
who attack us, or that which defends us!
—MICHAEL MOORCOCK,
THE SAILOR ON THE SEAS OF FATE

MIKE'S CELL PHONE RANG while he drove West Side Highway toward the PD's Harbor Unit in Battery Park. He slowed down to take the call; it was Eva. He put the phone on speaker and set it on the console. "I just got a call from the Coast Guard," she told him. "They have a strong radiation reading off one of their buoys, coming from a large yacht, but we got no hit on our nearby Ring of Steel detectors."

"Something wrong about that," Mike replied.

"You may be right."

"We don't have enough time for proof," Mike said.

"We have to assume the worst," she told him, "but make sure we're right."

They were both silent for a moment, realizing what was unfolding before them. Ice flooded through Mike's veins. It all made sense. He didn't want to see or think about what Zed had shown him because the reality was too horrible, yet he had to see what all of this evidence might lead to. The puzzle pieces were beginning to form a picture, to the point where Mike began to see a possible future: the dream of his enemies, a nightmare for everyone else. This was what they'd been planning all along.

The thousands of man-hours of planning, from taking over someone's life to getting rid of those who knew too much and so threatened the intricate steps of the labyrinthine plot. Mike broke the silence. "Now we're starting to know what their plan is."

"We should have known, but we as a society don't want to believe it," Eva said.

"I'm guessing some of the detectors don't work," Mike told her. "It could be a false positive from the Coast Guard. Tell ESS to turn off their cell phones when they're near the boat, and only use the high frequency on their radios. Also turn on cell phone blockers, just in case."

"I'm also ordering a test on the Ring," Eva said.

"How close is the yacht right now?" Mike asked.

"A few miles off. There's a tugboat on fire out in the Atlantic, keeping the Coast Guard busy."

"I don't like it," Mike said.

"There's nothing to like."

"I was tracking a possible lead, and boating equipment came up," Mike told her.

"I'll call the commish."

"We need to call up aviation," Mike said. "Verify the source and make sure it's not a false positive." Everything was happening so fast, it seemed as if the past had caught up to the present, and the future was sprinting toward him. He had to move, or be crushed by reality.

"How fast can they be airborne?"

"They're already on the way," Eva said.

Mike heard a chopper buzz past overhead. It reminded him of past wars, and how they always came home.

"One of the aviation choppers will start scanning the East River," Eva told him,

"Have this one land and pick me up," Mike said. "I need to be on that boat."

"You got it."

The sky was a perfect blue, clear and crisp in the early afternoon of downtown Manhattan. The roar of the police helicopter's blades drowned out the sounds of the city as the metal bird touched down on the wide sidewalk near City Hall, opposite the Brooklyn Bridge. The rotor wash bent the trees, and screaming police cars were everywhere, shutting down traffic on the bridge and around City Hall and One Police Plaza.

Mike closed his eyes as a massive cloud of dust and garbage flew past him.

"You Detective Maclaymore?" the silver-haired co-pilot yelled, holding onto his earmuffs and twisting himself in the seat as he yelled beneath the roaring blades. The pilot next to him nodded to Mike.

"Yes!" Mike climbed aboard the chopper. The whole vehicle vibrated on takeoff, and roared. They turned right, to the East River. "We've got hundreds of square miles to cover and only a few choppers," the pilot said. "Captain says you're the boss."

Mike checked the radiation detector's display in the cockpit. It was similar to a GPS device, but portrayed the world below like a Google map: virtual terrain with pins in various locations, spots of radiation lit up in yellow and green. A Ring of Steel detector picked up a radiation hit from the yacht.

"I just got a call," the co-pilot said.

"And?"

"We scanned that yacht again from over a mile up to see if it was a false positive, and it wasn't."

"Where's the burning tugboat?" Mike asked.

"About a mile out in the Atlantic ocean, a bit south of here. The other two choppers headed out a few minutes ago. The yacht is about a mile away." The co-pilot pointed to the computer display and the blips that showed all boats and planes in the area.

"Lynam told me a buoy's radiation detector didn't go off and there's the yacht near it," the co-pilot said. "He's checking on the yacht's registration. What do you think?"

"The detectors were damaged. Something's out there," Mike said. He gazed down at the mile-long Brooklyn Bridge. He saw the police harbor boat and a U.S. Coast Guard boat on the East River, five hundred feet below. He looked at the Brooklyn and Manhattan skylines, the arrayed fortresses of new empires with their barons all dreaming to be the next master of the universe. Just for a second, Mike felt calm as he looked out at the horizon.

To the right, Mike saw the greened copper Statue of Liberty, the Roman goddess Libertas forever holding up her dimming Promethean torch, illuminating Plato's cave. She was a speck in the distance as they flew toward the yacht.

Mike picked up his cell. "What's the registry of the yacht?" he asked.

"A company called Emerald Enterprises," Eva told him, "from Florida and New Jersey. One minute ago we got a positive, and now another unmarked PD Harbor boat just got a positive hit for radiation from the same yacht. Coast Guard is coming with a cutter and the fastest tugboat to pull the yacht out to sea. State Department and FBI are on the way."

"Ten-four."

In the distance, out in the Atlantic, Mike saw a white-and-orange Coast Guard ship, with FDNY fighting a tugboat fire. The chopper flew closer to the suspicious yacht. Two police boats and one new U.S. Coast Guard boat were moving in. Mike saw how fast ESS was, ready to strike at a moment's notice.

As the chopper descended, Mike saw one of the police boats below, where ESS officers were donning their black balaclava masks, Kevlar helmets, and Spectra and Kevlar vests. They carried flash-bangs, smoke grenades, Glock pistols and M4 rifles. Everyone was getting ready to board the yacht.

Two police boats pulled up alongside the massive 300-foot mega yacht. Two heavy military-style helicopters hovered above the yacht as police in full tactical gear fast-rappelled down onto the ship's bow.

One of the Harbor Unit boats moved closer. Police poured onto the luxury yacht like army ants. Machine guns fired at the police. Mike saw an officer go down. Bullets dinged the chopper's metal skin. The pilot took the bird sideways and then down, away from the gunfire, which came from one of the yacht's windows.

On the ship's bridge, muzzle flashes lit up behind dark-tinted glass windows. The sound of multiple flash-bangs reverberated over the distinctive rattle of Kalashnikov rifles.

Mike saw one of the terrorists near the front of the yacht, sliding down the side into a raft. Mike opened up the container next to his seat and took out a bullet-resistant raid jacket. He felt its weight on his neck as he put it on. The jacket was extra-heavy; it must have ceramic plates to help stop rifle rounds. He put his gold detective's shield around his neck, then turned off his cell phone and turned on his VHF radio—which wouldn't interfere with any electronic devices or CBRN materials. He watched as more ESS cops rappelled down onto the ship's deck. Mike opened up the rifle case and took out the M4 rifle and loaded it and slung it around his back.

"I'm going down." Mike said. The co-pilot got out of the seat next to the pilot and stepped into the back. He pulled out a black, webbed Petzl harness and blue alloy friction tube from a duffel bag. Mike stepped into the harness, then tied a figure eight knot in the black-and-green rope on the metallic green screwgate D-ring carabineer.

"Done this before?" The co-pilot said.

"Only once or twice."

"But I heard you were Special Forces."

"I was the typist at Fort Bragg."

The pilot dropped low above the hundred-foot black police harbor boat. Mike was only about twenty feet over the deck, and smoothly lowered himself down. Unclipping, he waved the chopper off, then crossed to the yacht on an aluminum bridge put there by PD Harbor and two ESS cops.

"We got one of the terrorists," a cop said over the radio.

Mike inserted an earpiece with microphone to communicate. ESS Lieutenant Lynam Mike was standing there with a glum expression on his face. "You ready for this war?" Lynam asked.

"I have to be," Mike said. The fear and adrenaline hit him. He felt queasy and lightheaded: half filled with fear, half with anger.

"The yacht's bridge is clear," Mike heard on the hissing radio. He followed a group of ESS cops and helped secure the deck. He saw two twisted bodies with guns in their hands and crimson pools spreading around them. Both of the dead terrorists wore heavy body armor. One of them was shot in the mouth and wore a frightening grimace, his broken teeth scattered over the deck. The second body had been shot in the head and neck. It was almost decapitated. Machine gun fire broke out again, and Mike jumped at the sound. It seemed to come from below. A few seconds later, bullets tore up through the deck. Mike ran down to the yacht's first floor, where the gun fight was.

"Tango down!"

"Tango down!" Another voice said, as they methodically took out terrorist after terrorist during the sweep.

Mike listened to the special radio frequency. "Cop down! Need assistance."

"Where?" another voice said.

"Captain's cabin!" someone yelled into the radio. "Second floor below the bridge."

"You eight! Go!" Lynam said. Then, into the radio: "I got eight going down to you."

"Ten-four."

"It's going to take a while to secure this ship," Lynam said to Mike.

"We got the device! It's in the dining room!" said a voice on the radio. "I'm shot!" the voice yelled as gunshots rang out over the radio, muffling his screams.

"Is the bomb squad here yet?" Lynam said into his radio.

"We're right here, inside already!" said a cop on the radio, who was behind both of them. They were now inside on the first main floor of the yacht, and away from the main deck.

"Cell phone jammers are on board," Lynam said. Several officers entered a room on the first floor of the yacht carrying orange plastic tackle boxes.

"Good job!" Lynam said over the radio.

"Follow me!" one of the cops said. They were in the hallways in groups of four. Mike followed Lynam's group down a spiral staircase. They swept through the galley carefully. Each hallway was lit by dim lights.

"How many decks does this ship have?" Mike said as they jogged through the halls.

Four shots rang out. Bullets whizzed past an ESS cop. Mike turned and saw the terrorist, then aligned the sights of M4 and returned fire, hitting the attacker in the head with a 5.56mm round.

"Man down!" Lynam yelled into the radio. He looked to two ESS cops. "You and you, stay with him!" Lynam pointed to the two cops.

Mike's group walked carefully down the last hallway and into the dining area. Massive crystal chandeliers hung from above. Below these, Mike saw a suspect with his back to him. Beside the man was an olive green tactical warhead; the object was a bit shorter than a small car. The man was furiously doing something with his hands—trying to detonate the warhead? The man turned as Mike pointed his M4 at him. A bullet whizzed past Mike from another direction; he ducked. A second bullet tore through Mike's shirt from another direction. Mike fired once, hitting the suspect in the forehead.

Mike swung to the left, looking for the other shooter just as an ESS cop took two terrorists out. Mike nodded to the cop who'd saved him. The ESS guys cleared the room. Mike approached the warhead, which bore distinctive Persian or Arabic script in yellow, and a timer counting down in red digital diode numbers: two hours, thirty-three minutes and fifty-four seconds remaining. The bomb squad pulled out their radiation detectors and gauged the yield of the weapon.

"How many kilotons?" Mike said to the ESS tech.

"Maybe two kilotons? Not sure. Which would be about a quarter to a half-mile radius."

Mike looked at his watch; it was 1:07 p.m.

"After this is done," Lynam said, "we're going to look at the radiation coming from that warhead to see where exactly the uranium came from. If it's heavy water, we're fucked. But if it's uranium or plutonium, forensics might pin down which country the minerals came from."

"Well that's optimistic," Mike told him.

The bomb squad techs took out more tools, including a laptop with artificial intelligence software that would photo-analyze the weapon's wiring when hooked up to the X-ray camera now being positioned. The program told them the wiring was simple and not booby-trapped.

"Well?" Mike asked the bomb tech.

"Small warhead attached to a timer, pretty straightforward." The man's movements were slow and deliberate, like a Swiss watchmaker, or a madman agonizingly putting together a bomb while plotting revenge for some dark conspiracy with his own horrific plot.

"Does it have a separate switch?" Mike asked.

"Yep," the tech said, and showed them a cell phone he'd disconnected from the device. "Also had a remote detonator via cell." He clipped a few wires and let out a sigh.

"We're safe," he said at last. "Cells can now work."

Mike turned on his cell, took the vessel information and logged into a secure intranet website. He input that info into a vessel-finder app that GPS-located boats and ships. The yacht was not supposed to be where it was, but at Battery Park. Vessel registration data traced back to a Miami company.

Mike took pictures of the writing on the weapon and texted them to Eva.

Lynam said, "The FBI and our Counter-Terror Task Force are coming to look at everything on this yacht."

Eva texted Mike back: "Wellerin says it's Persian writing on the warhead." One Iranian was dead; a Saudi might have ghosted him, and now a weapon with Persian script. It appeared that someone had a plan that would pin the blame on the Iranians.

Mike texted Eva: "I don't feel good about this."

A few seconds later; she texted him: "Hold on, it will all be over soon, and when it blows over, I'll put in my papers to retire. We can both jump off the cliff into the deep unknown: retirement."

"It's a deal," Mike replied.

CHAPTER 29

J'ACCUSE AND DOUBLE-CROSS

*Since they dared, I too will dare. The truth I will say,
because I promised to say it, if justice, regularly seized,
did not do it, full and whole. My duty is to speak, I do not
want to be an accomplice. My nights would be haunted
by the specter of innocence that suffer there, through the
most dreadful of tortures, for a crime it did not commit.*
—J'ACCUSE . . . ! LETTER TO THE PRESIDENT OF THE REPUBLIC
BY ÉMILE ZOLA, FRANCE, 1889

M IKE SAT AT HIS DESK in the office. Everyone was out
in the field. He took a sip of some cold coffee and
stared for a few seconds at all the paperwork piling up on the
case. The endless forms and reports he had to type up from
the nuke on the yacht. His neck was killing him, so he popped
an Aleve. He felt his phone vibrate and picked up.

"It's Šahrāzād."

"What's going on?" he asked.

"Research."

"What kind?"

"The bad kind. His hands are hurt."

"You okay?"

"Let's just say I'll tell you everything when I find out more."

"Be careful," Mike said.

"Will do."

Mike hung up, then received a text from Jack: "Meet me at the Beacon. I got some new information on the cell from the raid. Can't talk over the phone. Stuff I've been working on for a while." Mike texted back: "10-4."

Soon after, Mike was waiting at the Beacon Hotel in Manhattan. Jack was always late. The lobby of the hotel had a reserved look and feel. Not rich like the Waldorf, or cheap like a Motel 6, but with a quiet dignity all its own. Mike looked at his shirt in the mirror; it was full of wrinkles. He turned to his right and noticed the sunken floor and brass railing, where guests sat on brown leather couches.

"Mike, I hope this is all wrong," Jack said, walking up with a grim expression on his face. He wore a clean gray suit, freshly pressed without a single wrinkle.

"I don't know what you mean."

"I'll tell you later." Jack looked away.

Mike turned around and saw ten police cars outside, and dozens of cops getting out of them. "What's this about, Jack?"

"Mike, I'm sorry, but we got a call." Jack coughed a hoarse, raspy cough.

"Call about what?"

"Don't you know?"

"No I don't."

"About you . . ." Jack looked at Mike.

"Meaning what?" Mike didn't blink.

"He's here!" One of the uniformed officers yelled out. His radio crackled.

Mike looked to Jack. A group of five detectives entered the lobby, all with somber faces.

"He's under arrest," Jack told the detectives.

Mike noticed their collective dismay.

"I'm sorry. We have to collar you," Jack said.

"We don't want to do this the hard way," one of the cops told him, pulling out his handcuffs.

"What am I being arrested for?" Adrenaline poured into Mike's veins like ice water. His skin turned cool and clammy. He was both angry and fearful at the same time. He took a deep breath.

"We'll tell you later," Jack said. "It's not my call; the chief of IAB gave me the order, and if I don't comply I'll be shipped to Staten Island."

Mike squeezed his eyes shut, feeling dizzy, then opened them again. One of the detectives took his gun. Another took his shield and ID card and gave him a quick search.

"We have to cuff you, it's just for—" one of the cops started.

"I know the drill." Mike shook his head as the handcuffs crunched and clicked together around his wrists, cold metal cutting into his skin, hurting his wrist bone.

"It's just that we don't want our balls broken by the boss. You know how it is."

"I know," Mike said. "This is just a misunderstanding." The cops stuffed him into the back of a cramped police car and drove him to the station house.

Thirty minutes later, Mike sat in a cold metal chair at an old table in the interrogation room. He was handcuffed loosely to a bar on the table. Internal Affairs Sergeant Evan Smith sat across from him in the small, blue-painted, cement-walled room. He wore glasses with octagonal frames. There were no windows. Sergeant Jack Arnold stood to one side, looking at his cell phone. There was a certain coldness about him.

Mike glanced at the snake-shaped video camera that peered down from above. It all seemed so surreal, like he might wake up at any moment. It was as if the world were a movie, and he couldn't do anything; he was just an actor with no free will, a pawn of the director. He wanted to get away.

Was this how it all ended? The investigation, his career—his life? A false arrest, and then destroyed by the very government he worked for? It was the ultimate betrayal. There had to be some terrible purpose to this, someone behind the madness, crushing him with the wheels of the machine, the system. He was a lab rat in someone else's maze.

Sergeant Smith cleared his throat. "I wish to advise you that you are being questioned as part of an investigation. We will ask you questions related to the issues at hand. You are entitled to certain rights by the State of New York and by the United States, including the right not to incriminate yourself and the right to have legal counsel present.

"I need to inform you that if you refuse to testify or answer questions, you will be subject to departmental charges. Also, that your statements may be used against you in a court of law or in department hearings. You know I have to read this." He took out a piece of gum from a shiny wrapper, smiled and started chewing. "You've been accused of some serious things in the past, Mr. Michael Charles Maclaymore."

"Well how can one go undercover with the Russians and not come out unscathed? I'm innocent. And what am I being accused of now?"

"Did you get off due to your connections?"

"I got off because I'm innocent. One is still innocent until proven guilty in this country, unless closeted fascist assholes like you change that."

"Really? I thought assholes like you got out of trouble with phone calls to Aleister. What you did awhile ago is criminal, and yet you got away with it."

"Fuck you! You would have done the same for your family! And if not, you'd be a coward. Where is Eva? She needs to know about this!"

"We'll get to that."

Jack spoke up. "I hate having to do this Mike, but we have to go by the book on this."

"I want my union lawyer and union rep here ASAP!" Mike said.

"I just called them a few minutes ago and spoke to Swanson," Jack said. "He's coming." Jack showed him his cell phone; Mike recognized the number. "I hope this is all just a misunderstanding."

The blood under Mike's skin was icy. His asthma seemed to come and go, but it was kicking in strong now. It took a moment to get his breath back. "It sucks," he said, "especially when you're innocent. I don't even know what the fuck I'm charged with!"

"How does it feel to have the tables turned, the roles being reversed?" Smith asked.

"How do you think it feels?" Mike replied.

"Let's cut to the chase," Smith said. His phone vibrated, and he turned it off. "Did you hack the police department's computers? And why do you have two million euros and another million in Swiss Francs in bank accounts in Switzerland and Macao?"

"Is that what you arrested me for? Was it for the millions that I don't have?"

Smith smiled at him. "Connections to terrorists."

"How?"

"The money came from Iran. We traced it."

"Why didn't you guys say so?"

"We didn't want to—"

"Want to what?"

"Show our cards," Jack said.

"What the fuck are you talking about?" Mike asked.

"Evidence is what I'm talking about," Smith said.

"What evidence do you have?"

"You'll learn in due time," Smith told him.

"If I can prove you're innocent, I will," Jack assured him.

Mike looked to Smith. "This is a setup, don't you see? Are you blind?"

"No," Smith said. "But apparently phone calls aren't going to get you out of this one, like they did the last time."

"Fuck you!" Mike said. "You think I'm guilty?"

"You're wicked guilty! But I hope you're not."

"Mr. Smith, you're hedging," Mike replied.

"I don't think you're guilty, Mike," Jack said.

"All that matters right now," Mike told them, "is that we find the culprit and not persecute an innocent man—which would be me." Mike's mind was flooded. This didn't make sense. He took a mental step back. This had to be because he was getting close to the plot. They'd been inside the department all along; that's how the Ring of Steel had been sabotaged. It was a viper's nest. He felt like he had a puzzle in his hands, and someone had thrown it on the floor, leaving him to pick up the pieces.

This fucked everything up. Now he was stung, poisoned. He was bleeding, the poison of the lie inside him now, reaching his brain and burning his nerve endings. Everything was a blur in the adrenaline, his perceptions too real: a reality he'd never wanted to see, but was experiencing right now. One of Mike's wrists was cuffed to the table; the other hand was free—for now. Mike looked to Jack, who leaned against the wall.

"I'm sorry," Jack said, his voice almost a whisper.

"How did you learn of this lie?" Mike said to Smith.

"That doesn't concern you, Mr. Maclaymore."

"Go fuck yourself! I don't fuck people over for a living, like you do."

"Is the princess in on it?" Smith asked.

"It doesn't look good with you hanging around this Saudi in the middle of all this," Jack told him.

"I know."

"Answer my question," Smith said.

"No. And fuck you!"

"So where is she?" Smith asked.

"I don't know," Mike said.

"You lie!" Smith said. "I want to hear about this from you." Smith gave a mischievous smile. "You know all of this makes you look more guilty?" Smith said.

"What is it about her you don't approve of?" Mike said to him.

"It doesn't matter what we think," Jack said, "but what a jury thinks."

"We both know that's true," Mike said. "So what you're saying is that truth doesn't matter, but the feelings and opinions of juries do? So I'm your big catch—an innocent cop? Congratulations. What are you going to charge me with?" Mike tried to hold back his raging emotions. He knew couldn't contain his anger much longer.

"I didn't want it to be this way," Smith told him.

"So did you speak to the ADA?"

"Yes."

"Were you always an asshole? What else have you done?"

"Mike," Jack said. "I was the one who spoke to the ADA. So far we have a lot to prove on our end. It's just those millions you have in those accounts and a few other things that look bad. We have to play it safe from our end."

"Gee, thanks, Good Cop!" Mike said to Jack.

"Stop with the bullshit!" Jack told him. "I'm going to get you a fucking lawyer."

"So where is he?"

Jack pulled out his cell phone and left the room.

"We're doing a full investigation on your life," Sergeant Smith informed Mike. "You know: bank accounts, Internet sites, interviewing friends and family. No stone will be left unturned. You know the reason why?"

"Why?"

"You're not a great poker player are you?" Smith said to him.

"Neither are you. I want my lawyer, and I want to make a few calls."

"So tell me what you know." Smith leaned forward across the table. Mike looked at the table; it was covered with ink blotches, carved graffiti and even a bit of dried blood. Mike read Smith's face: he was controlled, yet seemed to be holding something back.

"I know nothing," Mike said.

"What do you know?" Smith said.

"I know nothing," Mike repeated. He tried to slow his racing heart. He couldn't think in a controlled way; his emotions poured thoughts into his head.

Jack opened the door and gave Smith a look. "I need a minute," he said. Smith left the room.

"So are the union rep and lawyer coming, or what?" Mike clenched his fists and felt the muscles in his face tighten up like violin strings.

"So, when was the last time you spoke to her?" Jack said after a long pause.

"What?" Mike looked at Jack's hand, just then noticing some scratches and bruises beside his gold Zodiac watch. "Did you fight with a perp recently? The scratches?"

Jack didn't answer the question. "It's too bad it has to end this way," he said instead. "I liked you." Jack's face changed.

"End how?"

There was a short, deadly moment of silence. Then Jack tried to draw his firearm. Mike jumped up, his right elbow striking Jack across the jaw line and knocking him out. Jack fell forward to Mike. Mike took the cuff key from Jack's belt and uncuffed his left wrist that was locked on the cuff.

Mike listened at the door, then cuffed Jack to the table and made a gag out of Jack's tie to keep him quiet. Out cold, he seemed almost peaceful. Mike took both of Jack's guns, a second set of handcuffs, Jack's and his own shield and police ID cards and car keys. He then used his own cell's wireless network to hack Jack's phones. He saw that one of Jack's phones was a Russian GRU military cell phone, virtually untraceable, even by the NSA. He downloaded all the phone's data, then uploaded software so he could monitor, trace and track both of Jack's cells. When he was done, he replaced the phones where he'd found them.

Mike opened the door and hoped no one was looking. The Detective Bureau had been understaffed lately, and the hall was—empty. He looked around, but saw no one in the main squad room. Then a door opened and Sergeant Smith was in front of him. Smith froze for half a second—long enough for

Mike to punch him square in the jaw, knocking him out. He took Smith's cell phone, put a dirty rag in his mouth, then stuffed him in a storage closet and shut the door on him.

Mike kept his calm and walked out the squad room door. Just as he was about to go down the stairs, he heard someone coming up. He backpedaled, went up the hallway and took the other staircase, exiting through the main lobby and making his way outside.

CHAPTER 30

PASSAGES IN LIMBO

There standeth Minos horribly, and snarls;
Examines the transgressions at the entrance;
Judges, and sends according as he girds him.
—DANTE'S INFERNO CANTO V

THE PRESENT GRABBED MIKE and pushed him like a wave as he ran to escape his past. He squinted in the sudden daylight, scanning the street outside the precinct. His eyes locked onto Jack's BMW, parked at the curb across the street. He ran to the driver's side, using Jack's keys to get inside and start the engine.

Jack staggered out the precinct door, not quite recovered from the fight. Seeing Mike, he reached for his gun—only to find the holster empty. "Stop him!" he yelled. "He just escaped!"

Mike saw an overweight cop waddle from the entrance and move to draw his gun, but he seemed unsure of himself. Jack attempted to resolve the issue by wrestling his gun away and stepping to the curb. He punched the gun out and aimed, but Mike hit the gas as the gun came up, plowing into Jack, who rolled across the hood and up over the roof. A patrol car arrived as Jack hit the pavement and shoulder rolled off the car.

Mike hit the brakes and put the car in reverse. Jack scrambled out of the way. Mike rammed the patrol car, setting off the airbags and immobilizing the officers inside. Then he put the car in drive and fishtailed around the corner.

Mike traveled southbound against traffic, staying on the far right side of the road. An elderly driver came at him head-on. Mike leaned on the horn and swerved around him. "God damn it!"

A short distance away, Mike made a right turn onto a quiet street. He drove halfway down the block, slowed and parked. Hearing a few police cars whiz by in the distance, he pulled into a driveway bordered by a concealing hedge and turned the car off. It was then that he noticed the small Radeye radiation detector on the passenger seat. He put it in his pocket, tossed Jack's keys on the floor and exited the car, locking it. He flagged down a cab and slid in the back. "Columbus Circle," he told the driver. The train station was close, with multiple entrances, exits and subway lines. From there—with luck—he could get to any borough before Jack had time to mobilize a proper search. Mike had a metro card he'd purchased with cash, so he wouldn't be traced.

A few minutes later, the cab dropped him off by the rusty steel globe and the Time Warner mini Twin Towers that glittered in the late afternoon sun. Below, several street-level windows were broken. Columbus Circle was busy, with thousands of people bustling through the concrete canyons.

Many of the store windows were broken or boarded up. Garbage littered the streets, and graffiti was everywhere. Electronic billboards hung from building walls, flashing images of celebrities, gadgets, and travel packages. Below them, on the streets of the real world, the homeless begged and wild kids spray-painted the sidewalks.

Mike spotted two cops, one listening to a radio and pointing in his direction. They started to come at him. He knew more would follow. "Double fuck!"

He started running, driven by adrenaline. Soon his heart was pounding so hard he thought he might have a heart attack and save the cops the chase. He didn't turn to look back, but kept his focus a hundred yards ahead, on the subway entrance. He pumped his legs like an Olympic sprinter, seconds dragging by like hours.

He was determined that nothing would stop him. His head felt like it would explode, his bones jolted with each step, and every cell in his body was screaming with pain from the lactic acid in his muscles. But his mind absorbed it all, became one with it, entering another state of consciousness. Even so, he knew it couldn't last; once he stopped moving, his overtaxed muscles would freeze up. Already he felt dizzy, and the world was beginning to spin around him.

Reaching the subway entrance, he raced down the stairs, pushing people out of the way. A half-dozen cops poured after him, like water gushing down a sewer. Two transit cops saw the chase, but were too late to intercept.

Mike leaped over the turnstiles and raced down a second set of stairs. He broke into a sprint at the bottom, making for a waiting subway car—but the brushed metal doors slammed shut in front of him.

He stuck his hands between the doors and spread them open, like Hercules parting the rocks of Gibraltar. He squeezed into the subway car, and the doors slammed shut behind him. He hid in the crowd, watching his pursuers fall behind as the car started to move.

Mike gasped for air and took a deep breath, feeling dizzy. He was safe—for now. Caught up in their papers, phones and gadgets, the passengers didn't even notice him. He sat beside an overweight kid who didn't move or look up; he was enthralled with his tablet device, playing games with his headphones at full volume.

Mike opened up his cell phone and used it to hack Jack's phone. That was one of the good things the plutocratic mayor had gotten right: cell service in the subways. Checking the phone's GPS in real time, he saw that Jack was headed downtown. He also saw that Jack's phone had encryption turned on.

Why would Jack's cell phone even have encryption, and why was it Russian-made? On Mike's phone, a map of Manhattan appeared on the screen, plotting various points and allowing him to scan Jack's call history. Looking at the cell he saw the phone number for Emerald Enterprises, and found other calls to cell numbers in the Middle East. His phone tipped him off that the cell phones were likely disposable, after looking at the data on the phone and cross-referencing it.

Now it was all starting to make sense. Jack was a mole. But how had he always been one step ahead of Mike—and why try to kill him? He'd put millions into accounts in Mike's name, so that when he died he'd look guilty, making the case easier for detectives to close. But why call Emerald Enterprises and disposable cells in the Middle East using an encrypted phone?

He checked the GPS from Jack's cell phone; he was headed for Freedom Tower, the old World Trade Center site, and Mike knew. It had happened in 1993 and 2001—and it was happening again. That was why Jack had arrested him, and why he was going there now. He was part of it.

Mike called Eva. "Yes?"

"I'm innocent. Jack is a traitor. He had access to the Ring of Steel. His phone has very high military encryption, and he made various calls to a shell company called Emerald Enterprises."

There was a long pause on the line.

"I got a call after the boat shootout at Brooklyn Bridge; a few of the other detectors around the city are down."

"Jack's going to Freedom Tower," Mike said. "That has to be where it is. Call everyone out. I'm going there now."

"I'll put the word out—on that and you."

"I have to end this," Mike told her. Then he hung up, gazing through the windows as the train slowed at the next station. The moment it stopped, he exited. He looked around, saw no one following him, and hopped on another train, this one heading toward Freedom Tower. He got off at the closest station, almost walking into a scraggly homeless man with a large sign reading "THE END IS NEAR!"

CHAPTER 31

ESCHATOLOGY OF THE PROPHETS

I returned, and saw under the sun, that the race is not to the
swift, nor the battle to the strong, neither yet bread to the
wise, nor yet riches to men of understanding, nor yet favor
to men of skill; but time and chance happeneth to them all.
—ECCLESIASTES 9:11

M IKE MADE HIS WAY UP to street level from the subway system. Not everyone would get the word right
away—they never did—and he knew the police would probably
still be looking for him in the subway. He was near downtown
Manhattan, on Fourteenth Street. He felt sure that if he looked
up, he'd see the Sword of Damocles hanging over him.

Cars whirred past on the streets. As the sun descended,
glitzy neon and LED billboards took its place with their endless streams of advertising. The temperature had dropped,

making his legs cramp more after the effort of his earlier sprint. The muscles felt like knives were cutting into his thighs. He massaged them, and after a few moments the pain went away. But his eyes hurt, his mouth felt parched and his nerves were worn. He found a stick of gum in his pocket and put it in his mouth, trying to chew the stress away. It didn't work. He waved a cab to the curb.

The driver, a stout elderly man, looked at him. "Where ya going?" he said with a Brooklyn Jewish accent.

Mike tried the door; it was locked. "This is a police matter. Unlock the doors."

"Lemme see your badge," the cabbie stammered.

"You mean shield," Mike said, holding up Jack's shield. Car horns blared at the cabby, who was blocking the lane.

"Badge, shield, whatever. Is that real?"

"Yes."

Mike tried the door again; it was still locked.

"Does this mean I'm not gonna get paid?"

"I'll pay you myself, now open the door."

"Okay, okay if you're in such a rush." The door unlocked, and Mike jumped in. "I got to be careful these days," the cabbie told him. "I was mugged a few days ago, and they put graffiti on my car. Can you believe that? Five hundred dollars! Gone!"

"I'm sorry they did that."

"Thank you."

"Can you go to Freedom Tower?" Mike said.

"The World Trade Center site? Sure." The cabbie turned around to look at Mike as he pulled into traffic.

"Watch the road!"

The driver swerved to avoid a dump truck. "Re—lax! I got 30 years' experience! So whadda we doing that's so important? Will we be on the news?"

"Saving the city," Mike said.

"Great, I'll be the cabbie that saves New Yawk!" He slowed for a yellow light.

"Go through all the red lights!" Mike told him.

The cabbie hit the gas without hesitation.

"I don't want no tickets. The mayor, he got cameras all over now. It's like *1984* . . . Always wanted to do that," he said as he ran the light, maneuvering through the eddies and currents of Manhattan traffic.

"This is a police emergency, you won't get a ticket," Mike said.

"What if I do?"

"I'll pay it, okay? Me!"

The cabbie turned around in his seat. "Can I get that in writing?"

"Look out!" Mike yelled as a semi-truck nearly T-boned them.

"You said go through red lights."

"Safely! Go through every red light safely! That means looking both ways, Einstein."

"Would you believe I'm related to him?"

"No."

The city pulsed with cars racing to and fro across black asphalt streets as the cab raced toward downtown. Mike's heart sped up as they reached Freedom Tower. He paid the cabbie and gave him his card. "Call me if you get ticketed," he said.

"Can I use this number for all my tickets?"

"Only this trip." Mike shut the door, then leaned down to speak through the window.

"If I were you, I'd get out of here as fast and far as possible."

"No shit?"

"No shit," Mike told him. The cabbie looked at him, saw he was serious, and burned rubber from the curb.

Mike's cell went off. He checked Caller ID; it was Šahrāzād. He picked up.

"Time brings us together once more," she said.

"I see."

"I caught one of them," she said.

"And?" Mike asked.

"They bought the weapon from Pakistan with the money laundered from Amarco, but I may have asked too many questions. He's dead."

"I'm a little pressed for time here."

"Now you tell me," she said.

"How far are you from Freedom Tower?" Mike asked.

"Far enough I think," she told him. "You?"

"Probably ringside, thanks for asking. I have one question, what did his voice taste like?"

"The man I killed? Burning fire." There was a pause, then she continued. "He found his virgins, but he gave me a riddle for a possible date in history. *Who is the hammer and where is the garden of France?* is what he said," Šahrāzād replied.

"What did you taste when you realized the plot?" Mike asked.

"Tasted like morning, chocolate or coffee. I have to go, I'm following another one."

"Tell me more about the riddle?" Mike asked.

The line went dead. "Are you there?" Mike checked the phone. The screen said LOST CONNECTION. He tried calling back, but it went straight to voicemail. Šahrāzād's phone must have died.

The sweat on Mike's body felt icy cold, and his legs were still weak from the earlier exertion. He gazed up at the slick glass towers. They looked like beautiful pieces of sapphire quartz. The main tower was a crystal spire reaching 1,776 feet into the air, and one of the lower towers with its triangular peak looked like carved glass. The other two were reminiscent of the old towers, but with glass that made them look like giant shards of Lucite and steel. The skyscrapers glinted in the darkening sky, reflected the setting sun and scraping the heavens like the Towers of Babel. But these towers were haunted by ghosts from the past. Mike's stomach twisted in a knot at the thought of what had already happened here—and what would happen if he failed today.

Moving to the corner of Vesey and West Side Highway, he checked Jack's location on his cell. According to Jack's GPS, he was on the basement level, in the parking garage. Mike put the phone away and started to run toward Freedom Tower. He passed the 9/11 WTC Memorial, a wall of the dead. If America's enemy succeeded today, there'd be no place left for a memorial.

The air was chilly as the sun descended toward darkness, setting the bottoms of the clouds ablaze and making the whole sky glow red. There were few people on the streets. A dozen police vehicles were parked haphazardly on the sidewalk, their red-and-blue lights cutting through the dusk. Police helicopters hovered overhead. Mike checked Jack's location again: still in the parking garage.

Reaching the garage entrance, Mike noticed the absence of security guards, which was unusual. On the wall above, he saw that the lurking snake-like eyes of the video cameras had unusual electronic devices attached to them. Mike took a few seconds to catch his breath and wipe the sweat from his face. His body felt like a melting ice cube, and his breath smoked in the cool fall air. He reached in a pocket for the cold comfort of Jack's Sig Sauer pistol and entered the black maw of the parking garage. He took out his asthma inhaler, but then realized he didn't need it and put it back in his pocket.

"It's time," Jack said, and laughed. Mike froze for half a second, thinking Jack had the drop on him. But he was too far away. Then he heard another voice say, "America will collapse." Jack was talking to someone else.

"America's center of gravity will be struck once more," Jack replied.

Creeping closer, Mike saw a man he didn't recognize disappearing into a stairwell. The door swung shut behind him. Mike moved forward and took cover behind a pillar. He fished the Radeye from a pocket, killed the sound and switched it on: the radiation reading was off the scale.

Jack stood a few feet away. Mike leaned forward, peering around the pillar. He saw two bodies on the concrete at Jack's feet: overweight men covered in blood. The blood was already drying; it was thick like ketchup.

Jack brought a radio to his lips. "Are we ready?" he asked. "Yes," the radio answered.

Mike took a moment to work up his courage. *I have to do this.* A shiver of fear jolted through him. He swallowed hard, and stepped from behind the pillar, aiming at Jack. "Now it's me and you!" he yelled out.

Almost at the same instant, a stair door opened and a different man stepped out, drawing a gun and aiming it in Mike's direction as the man moved for cover. Mike shot him once in the chest, and realigned his sights to hit him again in the head, just in case he was wearing a Kevlar vest. The corpse fell like a rack of ribs.

Before Mike could pivot back again, Jack closed the distance and grabbed Mike's gun. Jack drew another. Mike twisted Jack's hand and dropped his gun; Jack kicked it away. Mike stayed focused and now aikido wrist-locked Jack's gun-hand. Seconds later, Jack's pistol clattered to the floor beneath a car.

Jack's elbow crashed into Mike's jaw, stunning him. Jack followed up with a low roundhouse kick. Mike managed to sidestep, countering with a sharp left jab that was off by a few inches. The men circled each other, just outside of striking distance.

Mike stepped forward with a solid right cross that squarely connected. Blood spurted from Jack's nose as Mike lashed out with a left. Mike felt blood pooling in his mouth from the elbow strike and spit it out. Mike got behind Jack and spun him into a fetal position. Grapevining and wrapping both of his legs around Jack's legs, he crossed and then locked his legs around Jack's waist from behind, squeezing the air out of his lungs. Mike's body was like an anaconda, wrapped around its prey. He punched Jack multiple times, knocking him out.

Mike disentangled himself and stood up. *I'm surviving.* Thirty seconds later, Jack woke to find himself handcuffed. He tried to sit up but couldn't, then rocked forward and folded his legs, sitting up on the cement floor.

Mike aimed one of Jack's pistols at him. "Where's the bomb?" he said, seeing Jack—for the first time—as he truly was. He couldn't forgive a sin so great. Revenge was required.

"You're smarter than I thought," Jack told him. "You uncovered our plans."

"Where is the fucking bomb?" Mike said again.

Jack didn't answer.

Mike fired the gun to rattle him, missing by inches.

"It's so close you can touch it! So how did you know it was me?" Jack glanced at his watch.

"The one with the gun makes the fucking rules!" Mike's grip on the gun tightened until his knuckles turned white.

"You think I'm going to show my cards?" Jack said.

"I'm asking you. Where is it?"

Jack smiled at the barrel. Things were silent for a few seconds.

"Why are you even doing this?" Mike asked. "How did you fuck up the Ring of Steel detectors to get the weapons in?"

"The department is responsible for my father's suicide. This attack was going to happen eventually, and I was paid tens of millions for doing it. I'm an engineer. I helped design it. You yourself know nothing is perfect; the Ring just makes an attack harder to pull off."

"Is this a false flag operation?" Mike asked. "Who's behind it? Saudis? Iranians? Who's the ghost? I want to hear it from you."

"Then you know." Jack smiled a wicked smile. "It's so much more than that, you have no idea."

Mike looked at him, overcome by a rush of pure hatred burning in his veins.

"So," Jack said, controlling his voice. "Are you going to shoot me? Either way, we're both going to die."

"In fact the more I think about it, the more I want to get it over with," Mike said.

"You know, I hate this fucking city and this country!" Jack told him. His eyes were filled with such hatred, it was as if they glowed red. "They deserve what they get. God damn America, how's that for a slogan?"

"You don't have the right to kill these people," Mike said.

"Do you even believe in our great system? Which you yourself have said is a total failure."

"In your case, street justice will do," Mike told him. "How does it feel, knowing what's coming?"

"You will die." Jack stared at the ground.

"I want answers now!" Mike yelled at him. "Where is the device?"

"Fuck you."

Mike shot out one of Jack's kneecaps.

Jack screamed.

"Let's start this conversation again," Mike said. "Where's the weapon, and how do I stop it?"

"Even I can't stop it now. Too many wheels in motion."

"Where is it? "

"It's so close I can feel it," Jack taunted. "And you can't stop it. No one can."

Mike shot out his other knee.

Jack screamed again. "Where else would it be?"

"How many of you are there?" Mike asked.

"I don't know, we're compartmentalized," Jack replied.

"I can't forgive this," Mike said, wiping the blood from his face. "Why did you set me up?"

"Madness making you deaf? Like I said, you were getting too close."

"Why are you doing this?" Mike screamed at him.

Mike saw fire burning in Jack's eyes. He squeezed off another round, into Jack's shoulder. Jack screamed and convulsed, as if electrocuted. Mike pointed the gun at his face. He didn't have a choice; it was do or die. "What's it like looking down the barrel of your own gun," Mike said, "knowing you're going to die?"

"Just do it," Jack told him. His eyes shifted, looking at something behind Mike.

A gunshot rang out behind Mike. Whizzing past his head, the bullet hit Jack in the eye socket. Mike took cover and turned and looked back.

"He failed me," Sayf called out. "The second weapon wasn't going to go off unless I came here to do it myself. I have to make my dreams possible." He paused and continued. "I almost caught you once Michael Charles. Do you dare to tread on my dreams?"

Mike's heart felt like ice after hearing those words. It couldn't be—or could it? Tamerlaine, Rahman and Sayf all the same man—right here and now. Mike had searched for him over 15 years ago, had nearly been captured by him, and more recently had stopped a massive $100 million dollar drug deal involving him. The man had ordered the death of Mike's son, and now he was right here. Close enough to kill. Mike turned to his left and saw that Šahrāzād had the drop on Sayf.

"Why are you here?" she said to Sayf. "Rahman, the Prince of Kish and Tamerlaine," she ventured.

"You guess well," Sayf told his sister.

"You killed my father," Šahrāzād said. "Our father!"

"I have to do what's right," Sayf said.

"For you?" she asked.

"No, for your people, so that we can become a superpower, become the next empire and replace the West."

"Theocracy doesn't work."

"Neither does the West."

Sayf turned toward Mike, but kept an eye on his sister. He looked like he was closing in for the kill. But which one? Mike heard his voice, he was getting closer and closer.

"You killed my best friend in Afghanistan," Mike said.

"You took my diamonds."

"You killed my son."

"Debts have to be paid in full," Sayf said without missing a beat. "Don't you miss Afghanistan, Mike? The smell of burning flesh? The graveyard of empires?"

"No."

Sayf moved closer to his sister, while keeping his gun aimed at Mike. Šahrāzād moved closer to her brother, keeping him in her sights. Quick as a cobra, she grabbed his pistol and wrist-locked it out of his hand. The gun clattered to the floor. He swung at her, and she countered with block, attempting a judo trip. He sprawled out of it and used his elbow to her jaw to knock her out cold.

Mike jumped up from behind the pillar and disarmed Sayf in a fury of hand-to-hand combat. Sayf then spun around and disarmed Mike with a Spetsnaz hand-to-hand combat move.

They both closed and clinched, then disengaged. It was fast: punch and counterpunch, roundhouse kick and block and strike, takedown and counter-takedown. Mike grabbed Sayf's head with his left hand and struck a right to his temple, then disengaged the clinch. Sayf snapped a left roundhouse kick to the thigh. Mike blocked it by lifting his right shin and bringing his right knee to his right elbow, using it to make a wall of bone and sinew.

Mike closed the space between them and went in for a tackle, but was thrown with a fast Judo *Uchi Mata,* spinning like a corkscrew. Mike somersaulted out of it and then used a Russian Sambo scissor-sweep on Sayf's legs, bringing him down. Sayf spun out of it and got up. Mike then pinned Sayf against the wall and pulled Sayf's leg up, going again for single-leg takedown. Sayf slid down against the cement wall behind him. Mike fell on top of him, and they writhed on the ground like two fighting snakes. Mike was on top, raining sharp elbows down on Sayf's face.

"Police, don't move!" Eva's voice called out.

Mike turned for half a second and saw the ghost, Khalid, with a pistol pointed in his direction, frozen in time by Eva's command.

Eva stood behind a pillar, her pistol aimed at Khalid. Time slowed down as Mike's thoughts sped up.

Eva had the drop on Khalid, and he had the drop on Mike. To Mike's right, Šahrāzād was slowly waking from her brother's punch and reaching for a pistol. A car with black tinted windows pulled up inside the garage to Eva's left, and a man came out. It was one of the men who'd tried to attack the princess at the Iranian's apartment: the short muscular one. Šahrāzād got the drop on him and did a perfect double-tap headshot. Another man burst from the back of the car with an AK-47, firing wildly.

Mike twisted to get out of Khalid's line of fire, somersaulting to grab a pistol on the ground beneath a nearby car. Mike and Eva shot the AK-47-wielding man at the same time, and he slid down the wall, painting it red.

Sayf rolled under a car and took cover between the volleys.

Khalid fired in Mike's direction. Mike scrabbled for cover and fired in Khalid's direction, as did Eva. Khalid took cover behind the parked SUV and slid a pistol across the floor to Sayf.

A shot sounded, and Mike felt the white heat as a bullet grazed his shoulder, burning his skin. He took cover behind a column and caught a glimpse of Khalid near a pickup truck. Mike saw Šahrāzād behind a cement pillar, trying to get a good line of sight on their attackers. Sayf fired off three rounds that just missed Mike's head, then threw a small flash-bang-and-smoke grenade. He then threw a second flash-bang and fired more shots. Šahrāzād nodded to Mike, then pursued her brother through the doorway. "Stay here!" she called out to Mike.

Mike peered around the column; Sayf was gone, but not Khalid. He was against a pillar with his leg bleeding; he couldn't run. Mike had the drop on him. Khalid looked up at Mike and said, "Do it!" Mike pulled the trigger two times, a double tap to the head.

"That was for my son."

Eva scanned the area for anyone else. She then walked up to him and gave him a hug.

"Thank you," she said.

Mike looked in Jack's direction. Blood was everywhere, like a house of horrors.

"You okay?" Eva asked. "We have to finish this." She scanned their surroundings and checked the perimeter over the next minute. "It looks like we're clear," she said.

Mike checked the Radeye again; the radiation reading remained off the scale. He looked around one last time, just in case—but Sayf was gone.

"Thanks," Mike said. He watched Eva as she walked to him, then looked into her eyes. She looked right back at him. "You saved me, and I saved you," he said. "Of course, I'm okay. Chris was the greatest thing that ever happened to me, to us. He's a blessing."

"I know," she said.

She showed him her wedding band, and he showed her his. She wrapped her arms around him, and they kissed. She was his compass in this world, and he hers. After a minute, they both pulled back for air, tears in their eyes.

"Now I know why I married you," Mike said.

They shared a smile.

"Well, where is it?" Eva asked.

"There's too much interference because the weapon's so close," Mike said. "Let's find this bomb. I'm going to check his body." Mike walked over to Jack's body and searched him, finding a pair of keys with no fob.

Mike and Eva began searching the garage. He saw a van. He recognized the coffee-bean logo on the side; it was the same logo he'd seen on the half-burned photo from the dumpster near the raid site. "I got it." He waved her over.

They approached the vehicle. The tires were flat, and the van was chained to a column. Mike kicked something with his foot—a huge link of chain. He bent down and peered under the van. Large U-shaped bolts had been driven into the concrete floor, securing links of chain that had to be three inches thick. The other end of each chain was bolted to the van frame. Each bolt had been welded in place.

"This van isn't going anywhere," Eva said.

Mike tugged on the side door handle; it was locked. He tried Jack's keys, which unlocked the van. They looked inside.

Most of the interior was taken up with a huge concrete block. Iron bars protruded from the corners, and were welded to the van. Sheets of lead covered walls, doors, ceiling and floor—but even that hadn't stopped the big reading. Without Jack's Ring of Steel sabotage, the weapon would never have made it into the city.

Checking the front seat, Mike found a laptop on the passenger seat, with a countdown running on the screen:

13 minutes, 15 seconds. He hoped this wasn't going to be their doom. After all of the deaths he'd escaped over the years . . . He wanted this to be the last, and to one day live a different life, away from the calamities that mankind wreaked upon itself. He didn't want to live and die for society—but for himself and for Eva. He looked at her. She had fear all over her face, but was attempting to hide it.

Putting his cell on airplane mode to kill the wireless connection, Mike took a picture of the Radeye reading. He walked a hundred feet away, so his cell phone's radio frequency wouldn't interfere with the weapon; wireless connections dropped off at that distance. Eva searched the dead men's pockets, but found nothing useful. She joined Mike near the garage entrance—a hundred feet from the van—and they turned their phones back on.

Mike's phone beeped, scaring the hell out of him. He picked up.

"So what's happening?" Lynam said.

"I'm in the garage at Freedom Tower. The bomb is cemented inside a van and we have twelve minutes."

"Jesus. I'm at Church and Liberty Streets, passing FDNY Truck 10 firehouse. ESS Hercules teams and the bomb squad are here."

"There's a laptop hooked up to the bomb," Mike told him.

"I hear you," Lynam said. "Did you find Jack? Maybe we can talk him into disarming it."

"He's dead."

"Do we know where Eva is? I haven't been able to reach her," Lynam said.

"She's here," Mike said.

"Dammit!"

"FYI," Mike told him, "Tamerlaine, AKA Sayf, may be in the area, armed and dangerous: 6'2" male, lean and well dressed, Middle Eastern. He may have left. He killed Jack and tried for me. Eva saved me."

"I'll put it on the radio," Lynam said. "We'll meet you there inside a minute."

"I'm just inside the entrance of the tower with the parking garage," Mike told him, "to the lower right, near the staircase. Tell everyone no cell phones here."

"We'll bring the jammers."

Mike hung up, switched his phone to airplane mode and walked back to the van. He noticed blood seeping from his shoulder, where the bullet had grazed him. The pain stung. Other signals started reaching his brain: throbbing knee, raw-scraped knuckles. He heard sirens approaching.

A moment later, two unmarked vans with police lights raced into the garage, followed by Lynam. Mike held up his shield as heavily-armed tactical ESS officers spilled from the vans, but their weapons were useless here. Mike showed them to the van. "We need to evacuate lower Manhattan at a minimum," he told Lynam.

"I'm on it," Lynam told him, and made a quick call on his cell. He walked away to focus on his call. The bomb squad arrived a minute later.

"Can this thing be remotely detonated?" Eva said when he hung up.

"No," Lynam told her. "The weapon is too deep inside the garage for a remote. I'm thinking it's timer only." Lynam moved back to the van and checked the countdown on the laptop. "Eleven minutes . . . If we can't shut it down, maybe we can drive or tow it."

"Look underneath," Eva told him.

Lynam peered beneath the van. "Motherfucker . . . Okay. I just spoke to the commissioner and the mayor on conference. We're doing a controlled evac of lower Manhattan."

"By the time we have an evac it'll be too late," Mike said. "It's damned if we do and . . ."

"I know," Lynam said, examining the laptop.

"We have no fucking time," Eva said.

"The laptop is interfaced with the weapon," Lyman announced. "But we're locked out of the program."

Mike looked at the countdown: ten minutes and five seconds.

"I might be able to hack it," Mike announced. "But the interface itself may be bogus, to make us waste time. Or trying to hack it might trigger the device. The best I can do is try to guess the password," Mike said.

Several ESS officers approached with a strange-looking device that looked like an electronic snake with a tablet PC attached by a cord: the portable X-ray scanner. They held it up to the cement encasing the bomb. Strange images of the weapon appeared on the tablet's screen.

"It's not remote-activated; no cell connection," Lyman said after looking at its design. "Just timed. Cell phones and radios are safe."

An ESS cop opened the back door, and two others got to work with cement drills. A white cloud of dust sprayed outward.

"It's much smaller than the Hiroshima bomb," Lyman said, studying the image on the scanner. "A suitcase bomb. Far less than a kiloton. We can disarm it, but we need to get through the concrete to do it." The X-ray scanner was removed.

"Is that supposed to make me feel better?" Eva said. Mike glanced at the countdown: nine minutes and forty five seconds. At the back of the van, a cement cutter replaced the drills, spewing more concrete dust.

Mike felt cold. He looked at Eva; her face was white with fear. She said nothing. He held her hand, squeezed and let go. He wanted to throw up. Time slowed to a trickle, and the gears of the world seemed to slow in anticipation of the coming moment that might change everything.

Still, Mike couldn't just stand and watch. Instead, he took a deep breath, grabbed a pointed sledgehammer from the bomb squad truck and swung it like a major league hitter, chipping away at the side of the block encasing the bomb. He smashed at the cement with hyperkinetic intensity.

The ESS officers were now using jackhammers. There seemed to be more concrete dust than oxygen in the air. They all made progress, but not fast enough.

"Nine minutes!" Lynam called out. "You know it'll be painless. Ten million degrees."

"Double fuck!" Mike said. He put the sledgehammer down and stopped for a second to stare at the laptop. "Any luck?" he asked Lynam.

Lynam shook his head.

Mind if I give it a try?" Mike said.

"Be my guest."

Mike stood before the keyboard, punching in the dates of famous battles: 9-11-1683; 4-30-711; 5-29-1453." The laptop screen flickered, and for a moment he thought he'd guessed right. Then a message appeared: LOCKOUT / TOO MANY INCORRECT PASSWORDS / TRY AGAIN IN ONE HOUR. He started an identical countdown on his watch.

Mike looked to the others, reading the hopelessness in each man's face. Then he looked to Eva. "Everyone in your cars!" he yelled. "Get to Battery Tunnel!" The men dropped their equipment and raced for the vehicles. Mike grabbed Eva's hand, and they raced to her unmarked car.

Mike thought as he piloted the unmarked car onto the street. Cops usually drove fast, but he'd never seen anything like this—cars and ESS trucks spread across the street with other traffic, screeching onto Rector Street and then barreling southbound on West Side Highway. Everyone poured into the U-shaped Brooklyn-Battery Tunnel that connected the Battery Park underpass with Brooklyn; they were like rats leaving a sinking ship. Mike checked his watch and spoke into the police radio. "Seven minutes!" he said.

Dozens of police vehicles rushed into the tunnel, racing for the far side. Mike looked north; traffic out of lower Manhattan was gridlocked.

"Are we far enough away?" someone said on the radio.

"We'll know in six minutes and forty-five seconds," Mike answered as they pulled to a stop just short of the tunnel's far exit. He and Eva held hands.

Mike looked at those around them as they got out of their cars. It didn't make sense, but it seemed everyone wanted to huddle together. Fear vibrated through the tunnel. Each second was like a grain of sand, falling through an hourglass in slow motion. Sheer terror permeated every cell in Mike's body. His eyes stung with sweat, and his mouth was parched. And in that moment he realized that he didn't do the job for society. He did it for himself, to make up for all the things he'd done, for his own sense of honor and for Eva. Is nothing else was worth dying for? Without her, the darkness of this world would have devoured him already. He touched the gold cross around his neck, the one his son Chris had given him. Icy fear slithered through his core. *Is this what my life has become?* he thought. *Is this how it ends?*

Mike and Eva kissed. "I love you," Eva said. "You did the best any father could. You lost faith, but now you have it again."

"I now have faith."

There were a million ways to live—and die—in this world. Mike wondered if this would be his. They heard a tremendous burst like the crackling of thunder from inside the tunnel, then the deep rumbling of an earthquake that shook the inside. Dust and rocks rained down on them, then stopped after a few seconds. Mike could only imagine the hellish destruction above.

A flash of white light and then of heat blasted outward from Freedom Tower: burning shadows on concrete walls, reducing people, cars, whole buildings to cinders and spawning a half-mile-wide sphere of desolation. The world roared like a dying dragon. The earth itself trembled with the force of it, the shock ripping through the ground at the speed of sound. A tidal wave of wind and fire screamed across the land, plowing through what was left. Seconds later, the firestorm became a hellish tornado as the vacuum of the blast drew the burning debris back and flung it into the sky, creating a death-cloud above the city. Much of lower Manhattan was vaporized.

Historians might say the city was a victim of its own success: a perfect target that, in time, would inevitably be torn down. A social experiment that lasted hundreds of years, remembered for its glamour, wealth, poverty, decay, decadence, opportunity, love and hate; its streets paved with gold and broken dreams.

The eschatology of the prophets rang true. Others might say the clarion was blown, the mountains and earth moved. *Götterdämmerung* and its end-days filled with smoke. The tongues from the fires of hell licked the sky and brought the lakes of Hades unto the world. The earth became ash and the sky filled with shadows.

When the rumbling earth had grown quiet, Mike looked around. They'd made it; they were still alive: fifty feet underground and half a mile away. They had enough space and shielding to survive, for now. Had the weapon been bigger, it would have killed them all. How many topside had not been so fortunate? His phone didn't work; the electromagnetic pulse from the blast would have destroyed unshielded electronics for miles—which meant that most cars wouldn't work either. He took a deep breath and thought for a moment about what the princess had said to him, that the world was crushing itself as history moved forward toward its inevitable end.

He just wanted to live long enough to see a future in which he would create a new hegemon. He stepped from the car. One of the ESS cops lit up a flare. Another produced a fluorescent green glow stick. The rest of the tunnel was curved and pitch black, but for the dim light cast by dust-choked air at the entrance near the Brooklyn exit, which was farthest from the blast.

Mike saw Lynam looking back at him, face tinted green by a glow stick.

"Everyone in here looks okay, for now at least," Eva said.

Lynam checked his Radeye. Seeing it had been fried in the blast, he tossed it aside. "I think we have some dosimeter badges in the van."

"It's over," Eva announced.

"No," Mike said. "It's begun."

He pulled out the photo of their son Chris: the image of his breath on cold glass and the words *I love you* written there. Mike took the golden cross from his neck and held it in his hand, then looked at another picture of Chris holding a jar of fireflies at night. It made him think of their son's face as he'd run to them while holding the jar. The luminescent light had lit up his eyes and face, while he smiled as only a child could. He'd put the jar down and unscrewed it with his tiny hands, watching as the captives flew out one by one, like souls of light floating back into the night. Chris had looked up as the fireflies drifted up into the night sky, like stars of hope and dreams of light.

CHAPTER 32

BLOOD IS THE GOD OF WAR

And I looked, and behold a pale horse: and his name
that sat on him was Death, and Hell followed with
him. And power was given unto them over the fourth
part of the earth, to kill with sword, and with hunger,
and with death, and with the beasts of the earth.
—REVELATION, CHAPTER 6

THE SARAWAT MOUNTAINS twisted down the western side of the Arabian Peninsula like the spine of an old dragon, running parallel to the coast from Jordan to Yemen. It was morning, and the mountains were dusted with powdery October snow from 6,000 feet to almost 10,000 feet. The trees that had once dotted the area had all vanished eons ago. Below the rocky slopes, valleys twisted where rivers cut and molded the shape of the world over time.

A mile beneath the jagged mountain range, King Sayf and Mustafa rode a stainless steel elevator on their way to oversee the beginnings of a new drone war. They plunged down Dante's inferno toward the ores of the earth, thousands of feet below the surface. The underground fortress had taken over five years to build, using the best German engineering firms money could buy.

The elevator slowed to a stop, and the door opened onto a vast underground military complex. The entire base was both nuclear-weapon-resistant and EMP-proof, and could survive the end of the world many times over. It had thousands of rooms. Dozens of people tended hydroponic plants in the greenhouse. Across the way was something resembling an apartment building.

The facility's ground floor accommodated a movie theater and prayer room. It was almost like a shopping mall with a hotel inside, and featured all of mankind's creature comforts— almost a mile underground, like a great ant colony. At the far end of the place was a manufacturing plant filled with smart 3D manufacturing machines that created parts needed for the general upkeep of the entire underground complex.

Sayf covered his face as they walked around inside a great hall, surveying thousands of soldiers. Some were training, others were off-duty—but all were ready for war. He said nothing as he watched thousands of his elite troops. Some soldiers cleaned their new AK-2020 black polymer assault rifles. Others were engaged in a contest of pull-ups and pushups.

Sayf and Mustafa walked into a large tent. Inside, a 360-degree virtual world of vivid 3D screens gave feedback to soldiers doing simulations. A dozen black-clad commandos practiced assaults and small-building control in a virtual reality, close-quarter, urban warfare scenario. Virtual bullets whizzed past the men. Sayf nodded to one of the captains as they went about their training, then looked around and smiled at his army's inner circle.

He and Mustafa walked down a dark cavernous tunnel, one side of which had small glowing LEDs on the ground to light the way. Toward the end was another massive room, filled with computers and flat-screen plasmas. Dozens of techs operated holographic computers.

King Sayf and Mustafa were on their way to see the general of the Air Force, a man who'd spent years in the United States learning everything he could as a mechanical engineer for Boeing. He was one of the main designers of the new pilotless stealth drones, driven entirely by AI algorithms and guided by GPS and backup navigation systems.

Sayf had made a good choice in promoting Alweed. The man was young for such a position—still in his thirties—but far more competent than anyone else who'd filled the role of general. He knew everything about drones and drone warfare, and had even helped write the drone pilot training manual for the U.S. Air Force. That, along with help from The Kingdom's huge oil revenues and the desire of the U.S. government to help the military-industrial complex remain insanely profitable, played very well into Sayf's plans. He now had a virtual Saudi Air Force of drones. He was already working with The Kingdom's Army, Navy and Air Force to convert them all to drone forces on land, sea and air.

Few people knew that Alweed, Mustafa and Sayf had first met at Harvard decades ago, at Geppetto's Pizza & Subs in Harvard Square. At Mustafa's request, they'd then agreed to meet there each week. Mustafa had been a medical student at the time; later, he'd earned his M.D. and a master's degree at Harvard's Kennedy School of Government. Sayf had met him while studying in the library. They'd had many long discussions in the library about history and politics, which had—decades later—led to their current situation.

Mustafa walked down a few metal stairs into a chamber the size of two high school football stadiums. Along the walls, large flat-screens displayed videos and satellite imagery. All of the soldiers walking by went about their business. King Sayf saluted back and nodded in appreciation.

"How's Khalid?" Mustafa inquired as they both walked down the hallway.

"He's dead. But he died for glory and for the empire," Sayf said.

"We shall have arrangements for him."

"Yes, soon, he was my best soldier by far."

"An army of sheep led by a lion is better than an army of lions led by a sheep," Mustafa said.

"This is true," Sayf agreed. "This complex was finished at the right time."

"Indeed," Mustafa agreed. "My king, I must say one thing?"

"Always speak freely with me, or I'll wind up a madman, a failure or both."

"No matter how well planned, things can go wrong."

"That is what life is," King Sayf replied. "We have to take risks: calculated, but risks nonetheless. We are bold. This is about us; if we succeed, we will become a new global superpower."

"Have you heard yet of your sister?"

"Two reports. One is that she was sighted in France; the other the same day saying she was seen in Dubai."

"I have heard the Americans still don't believe the detective's story," Mustafa said.

"He figured it out, but I added many red herrings. The Americans are easily misled, and their politicians corrupted by money."

"The Iranians may do unpredictable things," Mustafa said, looking at the screens as the war was about to begin.

"I know," Sayf agreed, "and we have to think about this or we will be trapped in a prison of our own making."

Mustafa said nothing.

"I have to take a step back," Sayf said, thinking aloud. "In this war, millions might die, ourselves included. But this is the natural order of things, of how societies and governments exist: they kill or get killed. Maybe I am too abstract to be a humanist, for I see people, myself included, as mere pieces on the chessboard of a zero-sum game of geopolitical power politics. I see things not as they should be, but as they have historically been since the dawn of time."

A tall man walked up to them as they entered the room; it was General Alweed of the Saudi Air Force. He saluted Sayf, then they both hugged and kissed each other's cheeks in Saudi fashion.

"It is always good to see a brother in spirit," Alweed said.

"Yes, we are brothers, and now we must be united as one," King Sayf said.

"We're ready to strike," the general assured him. "The Americans already have one aircraft carrier in the Indian Ocean."

"War with Iran is something the Americans have been planning for a very long time, and now they have it," King Sayf said. "We need to make sure we are the ones who benefit the most."

"A master chess player on the board of nations," Mustafa said.

"If they occupy, they'll further bankrupt themselves, and if they don't, we shall rule," Sayf replied.

"Readiness is always good news," Alweed said.

"What Americans and the West don't understand," Sayf observed, "is that The Great Game isn't just about Central Asia or the Middle East, but about the world. This game hasn't changed, only the players."

"You're the master of the chessboard," Mustafa said. Sayf and Alweed both nodded.

Sayf strode toward the middle of the room and sat down at a desk, gazing at the main screen, watching this war, his war for hegemonic power.

"Do you think they will fall into our trap?" Mustafa said.

"We'll have to see," Sayf told him. "And if not, we have a backup plan in place."

Alweed nodded. "We sent over two hundred drones in various flight formations. They all look virtually the same as Joint Strike fighters and Model 2018 bombers, and all are moving to Tehran. They should be very close to the city by now. Many of them are dummy drones, as a method of subterfuge."

"Which drones did we use?" Mustafa asked.

"The ones in the cave complex 30 kilometers from here. The next set we will send will be from the north."

"How many drones hit so far?" Mustafa said.

"About fifteen have been shot down," Alweed informed him.

"Is this attack on Tehran enough of a distraction?" King Sayf inquired.

"We have three undetectable stealth drones hacking into the Iranians' computer networks right now. So far they remain undetected."

The split screen in front of them showed live satellite videos of the entire Middle Eastern region. The black-and-white images were washed out and glowed in other parts because they were being digitally enhanced in real time. One of the other screens showed live feeds from the drones, looking down on nighttime Tehran. Anti-aircraft fire streaked across the sky, man-made comets lighting up the night and dropping to earth like falling stars.

"Enlarge, please," Alweed said to a computer technician. King Sayf watched as one of the techs zoomed in on a satellite image of Earth, then zoomed down to the Middle East region, then Iran and finally Tehran. The next screen showed a drone's point of view: Tehran at night, with tens of thousands of sparkling lights in dreary green night vision. The drone was above the suburbs of Tehran, still miles from the city's center. Strange flashes burst on the video screen and disappeared.

"It looks like they're going to counter with the EMP weapon," Alweed said. He pointed to a blip on the screen to the right: two Iranian aircraft were moving toward the drones above Tehran. They sped toward the Saudi drone air force. Seconds later, the drone's camera went dead.

"They have it," Alweed said. "Looking at the readings from the other drones a few miles away, and the satellite data, they definitely have an EMP."

"Confirmed. Now we know," Mustafa agreed.

"Must have gotten the technology from North Korea, as we suspected," Sayf said.

One of the computer programmers looked at them, and the general smiled. "Now it's stage two; they can't see our stealth drones."

The general had the tech bring up his own screen on the monitor. There was a vast botnet in place, designed to spread a worm with DNA algorithms, enabling the virus not only self-replicate, but to evolve and counter antiviral software. Millions of cell phones, computers, tablets, PCs, mainframes and even the Iranians' own satellites were about to be destroyed by a foreign power. The digital and electronic grids of the Islamic Republic of Iran were now under a massive electronic siege. The new stealth drones had GPS jammers and scrambled the Iranian radar and computer networks. Twenty new Arabian stealth drones entered the airspace over Tehran.

"It's almost as if we defeated our stealth but had to probe them to see if they had the EMP, now we can use it, so they can't use the EMP," Sayf said.

"They were unprepared for our attack," Mustafa said.

"This is the biggest cyber attack in history," Sayf said. "After this we will launch another wave with stealth drones."

One of the soldiers came up to them and saluted all three. They saluted back. "Sir, we have news," the soldier stuttered to the general.

"And?" Alweed said.

"We cannot contact the Saudi Ghewar oil field's main security."

"What?" Sayf said.

"Yes. Some intelligence just came in," the soldier continued. "It seems that Iranian commandos are there now."

THE END

For more information on future books and more visit
http://www.thekingdomofassassins.com.

Also at the website: the Japanese Manga-styled
comic book *Kingdom of Assassins*.

CAST OF CHARACTERS

Michael Charles Maclaymore
Former U.S. Special Forces Soldier in Afghanistan. Burned out on war, he left for a "quieter life" in New York City, and now works as a detective in the NYC's Counter-Terrorism Division. He speaks multiple languages and is an avid martial artist.

Note: Claymore is Scottish for sword.

Eva Maclaymore
Mike's semi-estranged wife is a captain in NYC's Counter-Terrorism Division. Of Venezuelan ancestry, Eva is an avid hiker and mountaineer.

Chris Maclaymore
Mike and Eva's son.

Vasilisa Vronsky Maclaymore

Mike's mother: She escaped Eastern Berlin and her Russian spymaster father "Vronsky" during the Cold War. Her husband sacrificed himself for her freedom. She raised Mike with the help of her brother Aleister. She taught Mike German, Russian and Russian Sambo, the military martial art of Russia.

Note: Vasilisa is the name of a famous Russian fairytale, similar to Cinderella.

Chief Aleister Maclaymore

Mike's uncle and father figure, he helped raise Mike on a farm in upstate New York. A soldier during the first U.S. Gulf War, Aleister is now chief of NYC's Counter-Terrorism Division (The NYC Police has several chiefs, who serve under the police commissioner). He taught Mike mountaineering, hunting and fishing, as well as Japanese jiu-jitsu, kendo, and kenjutsu (sword fighting).

Šahrāzād

A princess of The Kingdom of Saudi Arabia, her father is the king, and her brother Sayf is next in line for the throne. She has synesthesia: in the novel she can taste sounds; in the comic book she can taste colors. She is also an avid falconer and horseback rider and serves as chief financial officer of Amarco, the Saudi Arabian state-owned oil company. She has degrees in finance and evolutionary psychology from Harvard. She also practices judo. She's named after the princess in the book *One Thousand and One Nights*. She is an avid supporter of democracy and human rights around the globe, but also sees the world as it is.

Note: The real state-owned oil company is called Aramco, Arāmkō s-Saʿūdiyyah.

Sayf

The prince of Saudi Arabia, next in line for the throne, he has a degree in history from Harvard and was in Saudi Arabia's Special Forces, where he took part in many clandestine operations. He is an avid fencer and practices judo.

Note: Sayf means sword in Arabic.

Jack Arnold

A snarky sergeant and sometime-partner and supervisor to Mike.

Reza Amir Rafsanjani

An Iranian mole (embedded spy) who worked for Amarco and then disappeared. The body found in a Suffolk County, Long Island, car trunk may be his.

Umar al-Husayni

A Saudi Arabian diplomat and cousin to Šahrāzād. His father is head of the Saudi Arabian army.

Khalid Zahrani

A former Saudi Arabian Special Forces soldier who now does covert missions and assassinations. His other identities include Felani Yaroo and Khalid Khorasani. He is a ghost assassin who uses the identities of the dead has his own. He recently took over Reza's identity for a black flag operation.

Sa'id al-Dussari
Another former Saudi Arabian Special Forces soldier, he has family—and another identity—in Iran. His Iranian name is Amir Paria.

Tamerlaine/Tamburlane/Timur the Lame:
A distant cousin of Genghis Khan, who was also one of the greatest conquerors in history. In the 14th century, Tamburlaine envisioned a new Mongolian empire and called himself the Sword of Islam. He regarded himself as the Lord of the Fortunate Conjunction. He created one of the largest, yet also short-lived, empires in the world, encompassing all of central Asia. His tomb was called *Gūr-e Amīr,* which is Persian for "Tomb of the King." Timur's tomb is inscribed with the words, "When I rise from the dead, the world shall tremble." The tomb is in Samarkland, Uzbekistan. In the 18th century, the Persian King Nadir Shah stole the jade tomb of Tamerlaine and suffered a run of bad luck which ended when he returned it. He was later assassinated. Edgar Allan Poe wrote an epic poem called *Tamerlaine,* and Christopher Marlowe wrote a play in two parts about the sovereign, *Tamburlaine the Great.* Tamerlaine is also the subject of two separate operas by Handel and Vivaldi. The 21st-century Tamerlaine is a mysterious figure who took this name as his moniker. The CIA has been unable to learn his true identity. He may be an Iranian-backed terrorist and heroin dealer in Afghanistan. Some say he's one of

the many Saudi Princes. It is known that he collects human skulls as trophies.

Rahman, the Prince of Kish
Another shadow figure who acts as middleman in heroin, arms, diamond and human-trafficking deals in the Middle East.

The Ghost of Rahman
An unknown mysterious man, the assassin who works for Rahman. This is also Khalid's alternate identity. Khalid also ghosts Reza.

Note: Ghosts can be stolen identities of the dead and also created identities, or a mixture of both.

Mustafa
An Afghan Arab who fought for years in Afghanistan, where he lost an eye to shrapnel. He is a loyal soldier to Sayf.

Vronsky
A Russian military intelligence officer in the "Main Intelligence Directorate" (GRU), and diamond-mining billionaire. During the Cold War, he stole U.S. "Star Wars" (weaponized satellite) with the help of an unknown mole inside the CIA. His daughter Vasilisa is Mike's mother, who escaped to the West. Her husband (Mike's father), CIA agent John Maclaymore, died aiding her escape. Vronsky was a member of the Spetsnaz in Afghanistan during the 1980s. His son is also a Russian Special Forces soldier.

Note: An unknown mole in the CIA may have killed Mike's father.

Zed, AKA 7h3 m4d h4773r (The Mad Hatter)
A former Russian Foreign Intelligence Services (SVR) agent turned hacker specializing in information, networking security and data collection. He helped Mike during a massive investigation regarding heroin, diamonds and human trafficking. Zed defected and has a false identity for his own safety. He's now a U.S. citizen who brokers information, performs contract hacks and runs a high-end brothel in Manhattan.

Shadow Ops

Black flag and false flag
Methods of warfare or attack in which the attack appears to come from someone other than the actual aggressor.

Buffer state
A state or country situated between countries hostile to one other.

Cell phone blocker
A device used to block specific frequencies used by cell phones. Such devices are banned by the FCC.

CIA
The Central Intelligence Agency, America's main intelligence-gathering entity. Created during World War II, it was originally called the Office of Strategic Services.

Dry cleaning
Actions meant to lose those "tailing" the person doing the cleaning.

Dead drop
A location used by a spy, who leaves an object or message to be retrieved by someone else at a later time.

Drones
AI- or remote-controlled, planes, boats or other vehicles used for warfare.

Data mining
The act of collecting massive data and filtering it with special algorithms designed to map probabilities and patterns by using quantitative mathematics.

EMP
An electromagnetic pulse, or burst of electromagnetic energy, that shorts out and disables unshielded electronic devices.

ESS/ESU
Emergency Service Squad/Unit. New York City's SWAT team.

Facial recognition & ear recognition
The use of data mining points on faces or ears, to identify specific individuals.

FSB
The Foreign Security Service (the new KGB) of the Russian Federation, tasked with domestic security—much like the

FBI or MI5. In Russian it's called the *Federal'naya Sluzhba Bezopasnosti Rossiyskoy Federatsii*.

FIS (SVR)

The Foreign Intelligence Service (the new KGB), is tasked with external (international) intelligence and espionage. It's a separate agency, similar to the CIA and MI6. FIS is also called SVR, *Sluzhba Vneshney Razvedki*.

The Great Game and the New Great Game

The concept of geopolitics in the Middle East and central Asia for influence, power and hegemony.

Ghost

Someone who steals the identity of a dead person. In the story, Khalid ghosts Reza, taking over his life to make him and his government look guilty in an act of terror.

Gold

A stateless currency with no counter-party risk, used by central banks because government notes, bonds and bills are only of value if the government backing them is still in existence and doesn't have massive domestic or trade debts (which, in time, lead to currency devaluation and interest rate hikes).

Ibn Taymiyyah

A radical fundamentalist Sunni philosopher who lived during the Mongol invasion of the Middle East. He may have helped end the Golden Age of the Middle East with his far-right-wing political reactionarism.

Main Intelligence Directorate (GRU)
Glavnoye Razvedyvatel'noye Upravleniye, the Foreign Military Intelligence unit of the Russian Armed Forces.

Mole
An embedded spy working for one organization while remaining loyal to another.

Opium Wars
Two wars were fought in 1839–1842 and 1856–1860, by the British against the Qing dynasty. Great Britain paid China in silver for Chinese goods, thus creating a large trade deficit. Silver flowed into China from Britain, which slowly started to bankrupt the British government. Thus, the British East India company used opium as payments instead, to reverse the flow of silver. The emperor of China refused to replace silver with opium as payments. **The New Opium Wars** are being fought today with the massive global growth in the heroin trade and hashish trade, much of it coming out of Afghanistan. Opium today, like in the past, is used as a weapon of war.

Petrodollar
Richard Nixon eliminated the gold standard in 1971, massively devaluing the U.S. dollar and creating high inflation. A subsequent deal with Saudi Arabia ensured that they would accept only U.S. dollars for oil, regardless of the buyer's nationality.

Rendition
The kidnapping, detention and sometimes torture of suspected terrorists by the U.S. government and/or its allies.

Rabbit
A target of surveillance who is being followed or "tailed."

Redacted
Blacked out; typically refers to government documents with vital information covered up.

Spydust
A chemical or a nanotransmitter used to track a rabbit/target.

SAM
Surface-to-air missile.

Spetsnaz
Russian Special Forces. The Spetsnaz has two main branches— Alpha Group and Vympel—and a third, smaller branch called Zaslon. The FSB has control over Vympel and Alpha Group. Zaslon is controlled by the FIS (SVR).

Special Activities Division
A part of the CIA's National Clandestine Service, which some-times employs Green Berets, SEALs, Delta Force or Marine Force Recon units to carry out secret missions.

Such operations are considered blacker than "black ops," and are referred to as "Shadow Ops."

Salting
The positioning of units ahead of someone who's being followed.

U.S. Special Forces, Green Berets
The Green Berets are one of the U.S. Army's specialized military groups. They are trained in unconventional warfare, reconnaissance, counter-terrorism, psy-ops, humanitarian assistance and other activities.

ACKNOWLEDGEMENTS

I WANT TO THANK ALL of the people that read various rough drafts of my novel. My writing teachers at NYU (Josh Barkan, Meredith Sue Willis, Michael Zam and Mark Degasperi) and New School University (Kate Morgenroth and Nick Fowler), Dave King of Dave King Edits, Peter Gelfan, Erik Bork of UCLA, R.J. Cavender of Cutting Block Press and Dark Regions Press, and most of all John Robert Marlow of the Editorial Department (for your insightful comments and suggestions). Rewriting, rewriting and more rewriting!

In addition, my gratitude goes to Samuel Huntington for *The Clash of Civilizations and the Remaking of World Order,* and to Francis Fukuyama for *The End of History and the Last Man.* Finally, my thanks to two "ancient" writers for the inspiration they provided: Ibn Khaldoun (born 27 May 1332 AD / 732 AH in Tunis; died 19 March 1406 AD / 808 AH in Cairo) for the *Muqaddimah,* and Oswald Spengler (29 May 1880–8 May 1936) for *Decline of the West.*

Side note: 9,125+ cups of coffee were consumed while writing this novel.